NO SIMPLE DEATH

VALERIE KEOGH

BLOODHOUND
— BOOKS —

Print ISBN 978-1-913419-20-2

In memory of Edel
'a purely good person'

22.4.1959 – 9.10.2019

An Garda Síochána: the police service of the Republic of Ireland.

Garda, or gardaí in the plural.

Commonly referred to as *the guards* or *the gardaí*.

Direct translation: "the Guardian of the Peace."

1

They had bought the bed linen together, 400-thread Egyptian cotton sheets that cost, Simon had jokingly groaned, more money than he made in a month. Crisp, yet soft to touch, they had slept, laughed, and loved between them, and when he vanished, Edel Johnson swaddled herself in them, burying her head in the pillows, smelling him, his body, his hair, the essence of him.

She refused to wash them, and they became lank and grubby. Lifeless. Just like me, she decided, before her need for the first coffee of the day forced her to throw back the sheets and head downstairs. Feeling groggy, she held onto the oak handrail. Perhaps she should eat something? She had a vague memory of eating beans on toast a couple of days before, and definitely remembered having a pizza. She just wasn't sure when that was.

It didn't matter. She just needed coffee. Switching on the kettle, she reached for the coffee jar, her eyes closing on a groan. She had emptied it yesterday. Picking it up, she peered in just in case a few granules remained. Nothing. She threw it across the room where it landed on an untidy pile of letters and papers before rolling onto the floor with a soft clunk.

Taking a deep breath, she let it out on a shudder that sent a greasy strand of hair falling across her face. She brushed it back, wondering when she had washed it last. Or herself. Bending her head, she sniffed. Not too bad, she decided, ignoring the sour, unwashed smell. She needed coffee, anything else could wait.

Back in her bedroom, she pulled a baggy blue sweatshirt over her pyjamas and finished off the ensemble with a pair of trainers. Looking down, she reckoned she was as well dressed as half the youngsters she saw around Foxrock. Moments later, keys and wallet in hand, she opened the front door cautiously, alert to movement from the nosy neighbour's house across the road; she didn't want sympathy or insincere concern, she just wanted coffee.

Her house was the last on a road that ended in large ornate gates, a back entrance to the church grounds that was open during services, but at other times was locked with a heavy padlock and chain. A key to the gate came with the house, a right of way through the church grounds written, to her fascination, into the deeds. It was another quirk to a house she had fallen in love with on sight. Separating the key as she walked, she inserted it smoothly into the padlock, turning to close the gate behind her, looping the chain around the bars and fixing the lock back in place.

She followed the path as it wound through the graveyard, before exiting the main church gate. Within minutes, she was in the centre of the small village. She kept her head down, did her shopping and, a short while later, was heading home with her shopping dangling in an ugly, plastic carrier bag which she'd had to pay for the privilege of using since she had forgotten, once again, to bring one with her. The gate was as she had left it. More clumsy than usual, she dropped the padlock on the ground where it landed heavily between her feet, forcing her to turn awkwardly to scoop it up, managing at the same time to drop her keys.

Reaching for them, something caught her eye. A bag of rubbish? It wouldn't be the first time someone had dumped rubbish in the church grounds. Curious, and almost unaware of doing so, she moved slowly from the path, her mind registering and processing what she was seeing on the buff-coloured stone of a box grave, not fifteen yards from the path.

She wished it were rubbish even as her brain was registering the truth. It was a body. Head and trunk lying on top of the grave, legs bent, feet on the ground, arms dangling over the sides like a stringless puppet. It appeared to glisten in the morning sun, and, as she slowly approached, she understood why. Blood, saturating the body, had trickled to the surface of the grave before overflowing in thick, congealed tears down the sides.

'It *is* blood,' she whispered, admitting aloud what she refused to believe, and it was as if her voice, soft as it was, unfroze the action, because suddenly she heard the awful buzzing of insect life and caught, on the slight breeze, the metallic smell of congealed blood, the acrid smell of urine, and another stomach churning smell she didn't want to identify. She saw, as if at a great distance, the face of the man, eyes open, as if in disbelief at this end; mouth open, as if in one final question, or maybe, one final plea. With a shudder, she watched a huge bluebottle land on his lip, and crawl inside.

A stalactite of blood, thick with flies, suddenly broke away, landing with an obscene squelch to send droplets of congealed blood in a ricochet, one landing with a soft plop on the front of her shoe, causing her to recoil in horror. Backing away, she stumbled, falling heavily to the ground where she lay breathless for a moment, then picking herself up and brushing herself down almost hysterically. She took a few more steps, eyes fixed on the awful scene, afraid to turn her back on it until, with a steadying breath, she turned and ran back through the gate, leaving her carrier bag lying, forgotten, on the ground behind her. Reaching her front door, she groped frantically for her keys, realising with dawning horror that she had dropped them at the church gate. With a short cry of despair, she ran back and grabbed them, returning to the door, breathless, hands sticky. She fumbled to open it and fell inside, slamming the door behind her. In the kitchen, she grabbed the phone, and hit 999.

'Police,' she breathed out when she connected. Seconds later, a voice was asking for information that her tongue couldn't seem to provide. 'There's a dead man,' was all she could say. The voice on the phone persevered, speaking in such a calm, quiet tone that her breathing slowed.

'My name... yes, Edel. Edel Johnson. Address... it's... Dublin... number six...' What was the name of her road? Looking around frantically, panic bubbling rapidly to the surface, she saw the pile of unopened post, and grabbed a letter with a sigh of relief. 'Wilton Road, Foxrock.' The voice on the phone, remaining calm, told her someone would be with her as soon as possible.

Edel's knowledge of police procedure was derived from crime novels and television programmes, so when she opened the door, she expected to see a full team of police and crime scene investigators led by some tall, dark, tortured sleuth. What she got was a ruddy-faced, balding, middle-aged, uniformed officer who introduced himself, haltingly, as Morgan, and who viewed her with an air of weary scepticism.

Seeing her surprise, he checked his notebook for confirmation and asked, doubt edging his voice, 'Are you Edel Johnson?'

She nodded, showing him into the kitchen with a wave of her hand. Unsure how to proceed, she decided on the conventional. 'Would you like some coffee?' She turned as she asked, reaching for the kettle before remembering the coffee sitting in her bag at the gate. Squeezing her eyes shut, she opened them to find him looking sharply at her. 'I'm sorry...' she mumbled, 'tea, I have tea. But, I've no milk. That's what I was doing when I found the... the...'

Feeling suddenly weak, she sat heavily at the kitchen table, clasping her hands to her face, fingers pressing her eyes as if to prevent the image of the dead man reappearing.

'Can you tell me what you saw?' Morgan asked gently, moving a pile of old newspapers to the floor, and sitting opposite her. Taking a pen from his pocket, he waited.

She was about to argue that it would surely be simpler to show him, but she didn't have the energy. Hesitantly, she told him what she'd seen, stopping to answer a question or to clarify a point. It didn't take long and the garda, a frown now wrinkling his forehead, pocketed his notebook and pen, and stood.

'Do you think you could show me?' he asked.

Grabbing her keys, she led the way. The old wrought iron gate hung open as she had left it, her purple shopping bag slouching in its portal. It was quiet in the graveyard, the soft growl of traffic carried on the air from the distant motorway providing a low background noise, but Edel, her hearing attuned to another low hum, paled visibly and stopped at the gateway, unable to step through. She could hear it, that insect orchestra playing their deathly tune; she didn't want to see it again, she knew what they were doing.

'Can't you hear?' she whispered, so softly that the garda was forced to bend down and ask her to repeat what she had said. 'The noise, can't you hear the noise?' she repeated.

The big man regarded her with suspicion, then sighed and gave a shrug. 'I don't hear anything, Mrs Johnson,' he reassured her, keeping his voice calm and quiet. 'If you can just show me where you think you saw the body, I can clear this all up and we can get home.'

His tone of voice, and slightly condescending manner, said he didn't believe her; she wasn't sure she blamed him. But he'd soon find out the truth for himself. Keeping her face averted, she raised her hand and pointed. 'It's over there.'

'Wait here,' he said, his tone less friendly and then, with a soft sigh of exasperation, he trundled slowly over to see if there was anything to see.

Within seconds, she heard the heavy footsteps returning, this time moving in haste. She turned to see him, paler now, speaking rapidly to the station. She took a shaky breath. It was true then, there really was a dead body. At least she wasn't going mad. Garda Morgan bustled her back to her house and, moments later, she was sitting in the kitchen on her own, with instructions to wait. There was no difficulty with that instruction. She was an expert at waiting.

She'd had the presence of mind to pick up her bag of shopping as she'd left the church grounds, so she put the kettle on the boil again. Sipping a cup of coffee at last, she tried to think calmly. She needed to talk to someone, but realised, with a shocking moment of clarity, that there was nobody she was close to anymore. Her relationship with her husband, Simon, had been intense and exclusive from their first meeting over a year ago, and she had lost contact with everybody. Their registry office wedding three months later had been attended by an old friend, Joan, whom she hadn't seen since.

They used to share everything, she remembered now wistfully; clothes, gossip, support. She recalled with a sense of shame that Joan had rung a few times after the wedding and then again when they had moved from the north city suburb of Drumcondra to the south county village of Foxrock. Edel had promised to invite her down to see their house, and had, in fact, discussed the idea with Simon. 'Let's not, darling,' he had said when she'd broached the idea, arguing that he didn't want to share her with anyone and, flattered, she had agreed. Soon the phone calls had stopped.

Reaching into a cupboard, she took out a bottle of whiskey, added a shot to her coffee, sat and took a long drink. The alcohol, within minutes, softened the edges of the panic that simmered and she was beginning to relax when the sudden shrill echo of the doorbell made her jump. Coffee sloshed from the mug to trickle down her sweatshirt and onto the already dirty table.

Grabbing a less-than-clean dishcloth, she made an ineffectual swipe at the spilt coffee on the table, causing it to drip to the floor, using the same cloth to dab the stain on her sweatshirt. The doorbell rang again. Stinking of whiskey, and swearing audibly, she hurried to answer it, wrenching open the door and glaring at the two men standing there.

Garda Morgan's call to the police station had been transferred automatically to the detective unit where Detective Garda Sergeant Mike West had been enjoying his own, much deserved, mug of coffee. Like most of his colleagues, he hated paperwork and, like most, he let it build up until he got an earful from higher up. He was determined, to get it all, or at least most of it, out of the way today. Sipping his coffee, he was mentally calculating how much more time he would have to spend to clear the remainder, when his partner popped his head round the door.

'Report of a body at All Saint's Church.'

'Suspicious?' West queried, swallowing the last of his coffee, grey eyes expectant.

Detective Garda Andrews came into the room. 'Garda Morgan rang it in. The body is lying on a box grave.'

'A what grave?' West said, stretching his long legs out with a groan and leaning his chair back so that it balanced, creaking, on its back legs.

'Box. It's what they call those graves that are like... well, boxes,' Andrews explained. 'The churchyard is famous for them.

They date back to the 1800s or maybe the 1700s... I don't know... old anyway. More importantly, Morgan said there was a lot of blood. I told him we'd be there in ten.'

Sergeant West ran a hand through his almost-too-short blond hair with a sigh of relief, and gathering the remaining paperwork, dumped it back into his pending tray. 'That can pend a little longer then, can't it,' he said with a relieved grin. Reaching for his desk phone, he dialled a two-number extension.

'Good morning, Inspector Duffy,' he said politely, 'we've been alerted to a suspicious death in the graveyard at All Saint's Church. Andrews and I are heading out there now. The first on the scene, Garda Morgan, reported seeing a considerable amount of blood so it looks as though we'll need the Garda Technical Bureau and the state pathologist.' He listened for a moment and then, 'Thank you, sir.' He hung up and gave Andrews a satisfied smile. 'Duffy will organise everything and we can concentrate on what we do best.'

Standing, he grabbed his jacket from the back of the door, slipping it on as they walked out, side by side, his six-foot frame easily matching that of Andrews.

Foxrock Garda station was situated in an industrial area, about two miles from the centre of the village. Andrews drove steadily, giving Sergeant West the facts as Garda Morgan had told him, and they soon turned into Wilton Road. It was a short road of only several houses and ended in the full stop of the church gate. Andrews pulled into the driveway of number six, and parked. Turning off the ignition, he pointed at the house.

'That's where the woman who reported the body lives. You want to talk to her first?'

West shook his head. 'Let's get to the crime scene.'

Andrews opened the boot of the car, revealing a well-stocked crime-scene kit. They pulled on disposable jump suits, shoe covers and mop caps and walked together toward the church gate where Garda Morgan stood waiting.

'Morning Joe,' West said, 'not a great start to it.' He gazed through the ornate gate to the old church, its spire reaching into the blue sky. 'Seems too tranquil to be a crime scene,' he said.

Morgan pointed to a corner of the graveyard out of their line of vision. 'Doesn't look tranquil where the body is,' he said.

Following the stubby finger, West saw the outline of the body on the raised gravestone. 'Okay,' he said to Morgan, 'we'll go and have a closer look; hang on here until reinforcements arrive.'

The sun was warm for early May, and there was an audible buzz as they carefully made their way to the body along a strip of grass between neighbouring graves. They stopped a few feet away, silently taking in the scene before them as the dead man's eyes stared relentlessly back. West and Andrews circled the area, stepping carefully over nearby graves. Narrowed, experienced eyes took in what details they could. A combination of odours rose from the warming body, causing West's insides to do a gentle flip-flop.

The box grave was roughly three feet high, three feet wide and about five feet long and was covered with the bulk of the dead man. Looking at the position of the body, West surmised the man had been sitting on the end of the grave and was either pushed or had fallen back. His right arm extended out at an acute angle from the body, the hand drooping downward, purple with congested blood. A dark red puddle had congealed on the cold stone surface of the grave around the body and stalactites of red hung from the edges.

The man's face was turned towards him, eyes open, turning milky in death. West looked closely at the face, trying to ignore the flies that were crawling over it, but it didn't appear to be one of the many that were known to Foxrock station. Turning to look at Andrews, he watched him shake his head at the unasked question, he didn't know him either.

With a final look at the man and the surrounding area, they headed back to join Morgan at the gate. 'You didn't recognise him, did you?' He wasn't surprised at the quick *no*. Life was never that easy.

West looked at the house just visible through the trees. 'I'll go and have a word with the woman who phoned in. See if she has anything to add. What's her name?'

'Edel Johnson,' Morgan said.

'Johnson, Edel Johnson,' West repeated, puzzlement creasing his brow. He knew that name from somewhere. He turned to Andrews, who he knew remembered every detail, every name, making him a godsend as a partner. 'That name rings a bell but I can't remember why?' He could almost see the wheels of the other man's mind spin.

'Married to Simon Johnson, the man who went missing three months ago,' Andrews replied, almost without hesitation. 'Sergeant Clark was handling the case. If I remember correctly, the bloke got on a train in Belfast with his missus, went to get a coffee and never came back. As far as I know, there have been no sightings of him since but no suspicion of foul play either.'

West looked at the house and then back towards the body. 'Her husband vanished three months ago and now she just happens to find a dead body, she's not having much luck, is she? What's your impression of her, Joe?'

'A very thin, unhealthy-looking woman. Greasy, uncombed hair, dark shadows under dull, lifeless eyes. Dirty clothes, smells like she hasn't washed in a while,' Garda Morgan quickly offered, then added, 'I suppose it could be grief and stress, if what you say is true. Can't be easy, her husband disappearing like that.'

'Since you've already met her, it's best if you come along with me, Joe. Pete, I'll leave you to fill in the Garda Technical Bureau when they arrive. Duffy should have sent some uniformed gardaí too, if they don't turn up...'

'I'll give Blunt a shout,' Andrews said, referring to the Foxrock station's very efficient desk sergeant, 'he'll organise things faster.'

West took a final look back at the crime scene. Something told him this wasn't going to be a simple case. He stripped off his paper suit and dumped it and his gloves in a bag in the boot of the car for disposal, and with a nod at Morgan they headed to the house.

The woman who opened the door was certainly unkempt, greasy hair hiding her face as she dabbed ineffectually at fresh stains on an already grubby sweatshirt. West knew enough about women's fashion to know she was wearing pyjama bottoms and not a new trend in trousers, the pattern of ducks and rabbits a definite giveaway. She was muttering under her breath as she opened the door and West's first thought was that Garda Morgan had missed telling them that she was mentally unstable.

He addressed her gently by name and she lifted her face. There were tears in her eyes but just as he was about to apologise for interrupting her, she snapped, 'Did you have to ring the bell so hard? Once would have been enough. Look what you made me do.' She continued rubbing her sweatshirt with what looked like a more than disreputable towel, and made no effort to invite them in.

He quickly regained his stride and, showing his identification said, less gently, 'My name is Sergeant West. May we come in, Mrs Johnson?'

She neither looked at the identification nor acknowledged his introduction but turned abruptly and headed back into the house. The two men, after a glance at each other and a shrug from Morgan, followed her into the kitchen.

West looked around. Despite the dirt and general untidiness, it was a nice room and would be a cosy place to sit. A large oak table of many years sat in the centre of the room surrounded by four unmatched chairs. Opposite the doorway, a large sash window allowed light to stream in, catching the dust motes in the air and on every surface in the room. A number of cups, mugs and other containers sat on every surface, holding liquid in various stages of fungal growth.

He watched the woman as she picked up the kettle and filled it.

'Would you like some coffee?' she asked, switching the kettle on. A flush of colour flooded her cheeks as she looked for mugs. She removed two from the table, emptying the contents into the sink with an audible glug. A sour smell briefly wafted toward the two men, their noses crinkling automatically in response. She seemed oblivious but both men were glad to see she washed the mugs thoroughly before shaking them dry and spooning in some instant coffee. 'Please' – she turned her head and looked at the men properly for the first time – 'sit down. I'll just be a sec.'

Neither man sat, all the chairs, apart from the one she had been using, were piled high with papers and clothes, some clean and some, West noticed with a critical eye, not.

She turned with the mugs in her hand, blushing slightly to see them standing. She put the mugs down, quickly scooped the clothes up and pushed them, willy-nilly, into a cupboard. The papers she shoved onto the floor without ceremony. 'There you go,' she said, sitting and pushing the coffees toward them, and nodding to the milk. 'It's fresh. I got it this morning. I brought the bag back with me when I went out with you.' She looked at Morgan who stared blankly back at her before glancing at West in some embarrassment.

Edel, aware at the same time that perhaps it wasn't the thing to have done, addressed the sergeant herself. 'That was okay, wasn't it? Perhaps I should have left it there, I'm afraid I didn't think...'

'Don't worry, Mrs Johnson. It's not a problem,' West assured her. He added his milk and watched her for a moment while he slowly stirred his coffee. She was a mess, but why? Grief, he knew, could quickly transform people into ghosts of the person they had been. He had seen it all too often, that inability to overcome the sadness and despair of loss, the way it consumed relentlessly.

He had believed that the not knowing involved in missing persons must be the most difficult part, but the mother of a missing child he had sat with earlier in his career had argued otherwise. She had said, that however bad the not knowing was, the certainty of death was far worse. The not knowing, she had explained as he had waited with her while gardaí had combed the area for her blond, curly-haired, four-year-old son, meant there was always an element of hope. The discovery of her dead child in a neighbour's ornamental fishpond had wiped out all hope, all belief in a happy ending, plunging her into the cold, hopeless certainty of death.

But her ordeal had lasted only two days. West examined Edel's worn, pale face. Simon Johnson was missing for three months – that's a lot of stressful days and nights. He felt a flash of sympathy for her.

Sipping his coffee, he waited, watching as she added sugar to her own and stirred slowly. She put her mug down with steady hands and sat back looking directly at him and, for the first time, he could see elements of the beautiful woman she must have been, before grief had done its worst, painting grey shadows, etching lines, removing light and vitality. He put his mug on the table. 'I know you told Garda Morgan earlier,' he started quietly, his voice low and gentle, 'but can you tell me again, from the beginning, what happened this morning.' He watched her closely as she hesitated, started, stopped, hesitated again and then told her tale. She took her time with the telling, he noted, closing her eyes now and then, as if to confirm that what she was telling them, was what had happened.

She finished on a sigh and then, after an audible intake of breath, she added, 'There was so much blood. And the noise. I think I'll hear the noise for a long time.' She lifted her mug and, this time her hands shook, and the mug clinked against her teeth as she took a long drink of the cooling coffee.

'It's not something you ever get used to, I'm afraid,' West admitted. 'People think they know what it's like from television but the reality, as you have discovered, is much different. Perhaps you should talk to someone,' he suggested, 'there are a number of very good counsellors who do work for us when needed.' He ignored the emphatic shake of her head and reached for his wallet, quickly removing a card and placing it on the table in front of her. 'In case you do need to talk to someone, give them a call.'

Edel ignored the card and stared at him coldly, arms now crossed tightly, defensive.

West could never understand why people refused to avail themselves of professional help when necessary. Why was there such a resistance to seeing a counsellor? His mother insisted it was still regarded as self-indulgent nonsense that only Americans resorted to. He never argued with his mother. He didn't have enough time to win. Nevertheless, he had made use of a counsellor when he had needed to, and knew the benefit.

He regarded the tight, cold face before him. He didn't think this woman would take the opportunity. 'I just have a couple of questions and then we'll be on our way,' he said, getting back on track. He hesitated a moment, thinking about the morning's chain of events, trying to get them arranged neatly in his head, looking for a sense of order in the chaos. 'You went through the church gate on your way to the supermarket. Are you certain the gate was locked?'

'Yes, absolutely,' she said clearly without hesitation, her voice firm again.

'And you locked it again after you had gone through?'

'Yes,' she said. 'I always do.'

West paused, thinking about the gate and the position of the body. 'And you didn't notice anything unusual on your way to the shop?'

She echoed his pause, and then stumbled over her reply as she wondered how she'd not seen the body on the way through, when it lay not fifteen yards from the path. 'N... no, I'd... didn't notice anything. I wasn't really awake, I suppose. I've had a lot on my mind and was in a bit of a daze, just looking straight ahead.'

'And on your way back, you happened to look over that direction?' he queried, watching her face intently, seeing myriad expressions flitting across, confusion turning on a spin to indignation.

'No, that's not what happened,' she answered, annoyance flashing in her eyes. She stood abruptly, looking down on him in obvious frustration. 'I didn't *happen to look over*. I dropped the padlock and the chain. It's an awkward system and I was being particularly clumsy this morning. I don't normally drop them. When I bent to pick them up, I turned that way. I didn't know what I was seeing, really.' She turned and walked to the window and stood looking out. When she spoke again, her voice was thick with unshed tears. 'Sometimes people leave rubbish in the graveyard, plastic bags and things. I remember being cross that people would dump such a big bag of rubbish. I don't think I wanted to believe what I was seeing, really.'

She looked over her shoulder at the two men, her eyes shimmering with tears. 'I don't know why I walked over. I don't even remember doing so; it was all a bit of a daze really. Then when I got a little closer...' She shut her eyes as she struggled with the memory. 'I knew it wasn't rubbish. A body... I knew he was dead; there was so much blood and that awful...' she gulped, 'that awful smell. I still couldn't believe what I was seeing, you know, it seemed so bizarre. Then I saw a fly crawl into his open mouth.' She shuddered. 'It's not the kind of thing that's supposed to happen in real life, is it?'

'Did you recognise him?' West continued, ignoring her obvious distress at the memory.

Her eyes opening wide, she gasped. 'Recognise him? No, of course I didn't,' she began, and then stopped and frowned. 'Actually,' she admitted, 'I don't know; I was so stunned by the whole scene. Once I saw he was dead, I backed away, and then, when I returned with Garda Morgan, I didn't go near him at all.'

But his face was turned toward her, and she got close enough to see a fly crawl into his mouth. Even without seeing a full face most people would recognise someone they knew. He let it go for the moment.

He changed tack. 'You have a key to the gate. How does that work?'

'Oh, there are lots of them, I'm afraid. Everyone on this road has one; it comes with the house, something to do with the right of way. Then...' she counted on her fingers, '... the council have one so they can get their machinery in to cut the grass and hedges; the church has one or two; the volunteers who clean the church have one that they share, and the bell ringers have one. And, of course,' she shrugged, 'there may be others that I don't know about. We've only lived here about eight months.'

West nodded and glanced at Morgan. 'I think that's about it,

Mrs Johnson. You have been very helpful.' He stood, and taking a business card from his inside pocket, gave it to her.

'Sometimes people think of things later that they wished they had told us. Please ring me if you think of anything.'

She looked at it for a moment then, looking at him, said sharply, 'I have told you everything, Sergeant West.'

'Keep it anyway. Just in case.'

He made his departure, feeling her eyes following him. Back outside, he was pleased to see a hive of industry. In the fifteen minutes he'd been in the quiet of the house, the Garda Technical Bureau had arrived and were already at work; he also recognised the state pathologist's car. Things could move along.

He pulled on a fresh crime scene outfit, ignored the breathless reporter who had rushed up from the office of the small local newspaper when he had been tipped off about strange goings-on in the graveyard, and left Morgan with the two gardaí who were posted at the church gate.

There was now a taped pathway to the crime scene and on either side of it, he noted with satisfaction, technical bureau officers were already searching.

He joined Andrews, who was dispatching the last of the reinforcements. 'All sorted?' he asked, knowing the answer would be a yes, Andrews being the type of methodical organised person who made lists in his head and ticked things off as they were done.

'That's the whole area covered, Mike,' Andrews announced with satisfaction. 'I borrowed some staff from Stillorgan and Blackrock for the morning. The lads were only too happy to avoid what had been planned for the day.' He raised an eyebrow. 'Inspector O'Neill had wanted a garda checkpoint in both places to check tax and insurance. You know how boring that gets. He wasn't too happy at having his plans scuppered but when I played the murder card, he couldn't really argue.'

West looked around at the white-suited officers who were moving slowly and methodically around the graveyard, heads bowed, eyes focused. If there were anything to find, they'd find it. 'Let's go and see what Dr Kennedy can tell us,' he said, jerking his head toward the group of people around the dead body.

They stepped carefully down the narrow, well-worn pathway, stopping a couple of feet from the victim when a short, handsome man stepped forward to greet them. 'Mike, Pete, long time no crime.'

West smiled in response. 'Niall, it has been a while, hasn't it?'

'Thirty-five days, to be exact. Not that I'm counting, you understand.'

'What can you tell us?' West asked the pathologist, swatting flies away with his hand as he spoke.

Dr Niall Kennedy took a step backwards, shaking off a particularly aggressive bluebottle. 'Rigor is almost complete, I'd estimate he's been dead at least ten hours, give or take an hour. There's a heavy blood pool on the upper abdomen and what looks like a single incision; I was just about to have a closer look if you care to watch.'

West and Andrews followed and stood silently, observing as the pathologist moved in and, with latex-covered hands, carefully peeled back the blood-sodden shirt to reveal a gash in the upper abdomen. 'Just as I expected, a single stab wound to the stomach.' A flash of light made them all blink, the photographer moving in to get a closer shot.

Kennedy used a disposable ruler to measure the wound. 'A three-inch entry wound, Mike. Looks like a smooth blade and...' he examined the wound intently, '...a sharp one. No hesitation either.' He stood back from the body and frowned. 'I'll be able to give you more details after the autopsy, obviously, but from the amount of blood around the body I'd say our perp hit the aorta sooo...' He weighed up the bulk of the body, years of experience allowing a quick, and the detectives knew from previous cases, uncannily accurate estimate. 'I'd say you are looking for a knife four to six inches long and three inches wide at its widest point. Probably a smooth blade but, again, I'll have more details after autopsy.' Anticipating the next question, he continued in a rush. 'This afternoon, okay?'

West nodded and the pathologist, with a careless wave of blood-stained latex to the rest of the team, turned and headed back to his car.

The Garda Technical Bureau, eager to move the body now that the pathologist was finished, were waved back by Andrews. 'We'll need a few minutes.'

Both men circled the body again. 'Well-dressed bloke,' commented Andrews, eyeing the well-cut, charcoal-grey suit. West agreed. Donning a pair of latex gloves, he opened the jacket, ignoring the sucking noise as the congealed blood tried to hold on. Both men's eyebrows raised in surprise as they saw the label. Armani.

West carefully searched the jacket pockets and then, with difficulty, the trouser pockets. He was about to give up when his finger found a screwed-up scrap of paper. Carefully, he undid the folds, smoothing out the creases to read what was written.

'"Come to good,"' he read aloud, raising an eyebrow at Andrews. 'Mean anything to you?'

Andrews took the scrap of paper in his gloved hand and read it for himself, shaking his head. 'Could mean anything.'

'Or nothing,' West muttered, taking the scrap of paper back and putting it into an evidence bag. He handed it to a technical officer for processing, with a request for a copy as soon as possible. Their examination over, they stepped back to allow the body be taken away, stripping off their gloves as they moved.

'Organise a house-to-house on all the residences around the graveyard, Pete, someone might have seen or heard something.

Dr Kennedy's estimate is ten hours ago, give or take an hour, which gives us between ten and one.' He looked around the graveyard. 'What the hell was he doing here at that time of night? Hardly the place for an assignation.' He pointed up at the church parapet where light fittings could be seen. 'Check what time the lights are switched off. If it's before ten, they may have used torches. Someone may have seen lights moving around.'

He looked back to Edel Johnson's house. 'Her house has the best view over the churchyard. Now that we have a time frame, I'll go back and see if she can remember noticing anything.'

It took a while before the doorbell was answered and this time he wasn't asked inside.

'Sorry to bother you again,' he said smoothly. 'The pathologist has given us a time of death between ten and one. Did you happen to notice any lights or activity around that time?'

'No,' she said bluntly.

He was about to offer thanks and leave when he paused. 'Just one final question?' As she hesitated, he continued, 'Do the words, "come to good," mean anything to you?'

It was a shot in the dark and he thought he had nothing to lose by asking. He certainly didn't expect her to go weak at the knees and clutch at the door. He reached out to her, shocked at her unexpected response, but she quickly backed away, moving the door so it stood like a barrier between them.

She laughed shakily. 'I'm sorry. I think the shock is beginning to take effect. I feel a bit weak, I think I'd better go and lie down.' And with that, she closed the door softly, leaving West standing on the doorstep, a look of astonishment on his face.

He spotted Andrews in conversation with a group of gardaí. As he approached, they headed off with loud voices and back-slapping.

'When I tell Inspector O'Neill that one of his lads found the murder weapon, it will make his day,' Andrews said.

'What?' West had been looking intently around the grave-yard, watching the slow movement of men as they searched, mentally planning his strategy.

Andrews beamed in satisfaction. 'They found the murder weapon.'

At West's raised eyebrow and look of disbelief, he laughed. 'Honestly. A large-bladed, blood-stained kitchen knife, can't be anything else, can it? It wasn't even hidden, just dropped behind a shrub near the main church gate, waiting for us to find it. Come on, I'll show you where.'

Clipped box shrubs edged the pathway from the main church door to the road. Andrews stopped beside the final one and pointed to the slightly overgrown grass behind. West saw traces of blood where the knife had lain; he looked back to the crime scene and then to the gateway in front of him through which he could see a small car park and a tarmac road. 'That road leads back to the centre of the village?' he asked.

'Yes, it's just a couple of minutes' walk.'

They went through the gateway, and West eyed the concreted surface of the car park. It was crisscrossed with a multitude of tyre tracks and footprints. Was it worth trying to take impressions from every one of them, even if they could? He doubted it. 'He probably parked here,' he said. 'Arranged to meet the victim and had the knife secreted on his person somehow. After the murder, he headed back to his car, cool as you please, and just dropped it on the way. Arrogant sod didn't even attempt to hide it. I bet we'll find it's a commonly sold knife and the bastard will have worn gloves and not left a print on it.'

Both men stood a moment looking back through the grave-yard gates, the sun causing them to squint uncomfortably. 'Why here?' Andrews said. 'Why would you arrange to meet someone in a graveyard? Wouldn't the victim have been a little bit suspicious? Wouldn't he have expected trouble and have been prepared when it came? Instead, he comes dressed in an expensive suit, more appropriate for a night in a posh club than a seedy meeting in a graveyard.'

West thumped him lightly on the shoulder. 'But it's not any old graveyard. This graveyard. Right beside Edel Johnson's house.'

Andrews frowned, puzzled. West could see his mind working, wondering if he had missed something. He could almost hear all the little wheels and cogs being checked.

He put him out of his misery. 'I haven't filled you in on my final visit with her. We have a connection, albeit a loose one, between her and our victim.' Registering the relief on Andrews' face, West smiled to himself, he was so transparent.

Glancing back through the church gates again, he saw the search proceeding as planned and checked his watch. 'Let's go get some lunch, and I'll fill you in.'

3

'Y ou know Foxrock better than I do, Peter,' West said as they walked down the road from the church to the centre of the village. 'Anywhere good for lunch and a decent pint?'

'Not sure how you can refer to Guinness as being a decent pint,' Andrews said with a sniff. 'But there's a nice pub on the edge of the village.'

Sitting in the fairly quiet pub, they drank their pints and munched on the best the pub had to offer in the line of food. Since this turned out to be sandwiches of dubious origin and even more dubious date, West was glad that the pint, at least, lived up to expectation. He drank with pleasure, extolling the virtues of Guinness to the unconvinced Andrews, who was glad when the conversation turned to the much more interesting discussion of why Edel Johnson had lost it at the mention of the words *come to good*.

'If you had said "come to no good," I might have understood it better,' he said. 'I could even see where that might have a bad effect since her husband is still missing.'

West shook his head. His grey eyes glinted with certainty.

'Well I didn't. I said "come to good" and it meant something to her, that's for sure, and she wasn't sharing it with us.' He sipped his pint, thinking. 'Good detectives don't believe in coincidence, do they?' he asked finally. 'Edel Johnson moves to Foxrock, then five months later her husband goes missing and three months after that she happens to stumble on a dead body. To cap it all, she recognises words that we found written on a scrap of paper in the dead man's pocket.' He raised his pint in a salute. 'Just what we need, a good complicated case to stop us getting bored.'

Andrews placidly continued to drink his pint. 'I'm as happy to plod through a dull case as a complicated one but the missus will be happy with the overtime pay even though she'll moan about the longer hours.'

'Joyce never moans,' West remarked absent-mindedly. He was already mentally preparing a case board and preparing carefully-worded requests for extra manpower and concomitant overtime payment, both of which, he knew, would be refused. It was the way the system went; ask for extra staff and overtime payment and you would be sure to get, if not the extra staff, then at least the overtime payment for the existent team. If you didn't ask for both you wouldn't get either. He sighed resignedly. So much time wasted on petty bureaucracy. But he had learnt his lesson the hard way on his first case in Foxrock.

Eager to show his expertise in his new posting, he had refused to ask for more staff, telling the Inspector his team could manage without. Of course, the case hadn't been that simple, they'd had several problems and the team had had to work extra hours. When he then asked for extra staff his blasé remark was quoted back to him and he had had to grovel before they eventually assigned more staff and agreed to overtime payment. From then on, he had played the game, seething frequently at the stupidity of his wasted time but knowing he couldn't ever change rules chiselled in granite.

He drained his glass and set it down on the beer-glazed table and turned to Andrews who was still nursing his pint. 'You want Guinness, again?'

Andrews raised his half-full, half-pint glass slightly, and grimaced. 'I keep thinking if I try it often enough, I'll grow to like it.'

'How long have you been trying?' West asked, curious. They got on well, socialised on occasion and he frequently ate in Andrews' house, but he couldn't remember the last time they'd had a pint together.

'Years. I've even tried it with blackcurrant.'

'Blackcurrant?' West grimaced. 'Why do you bother? Why don't you just drink something else?'

Andrews shrugged. 'My father only ever drank Guinness. He bought me my first drink in our local.'

'In Tipperary?' West asked, remembering some mention of the county before.

'Yes, Thurles, to be exact. There was never any question of drinking anything else. "A real man's drink," my father used to say, and he would hold it up to the light before downing it in a couple of mouthfuls. I still remember the way he would hold the pint up, how beautiful it looked and how I was always disappointed in the taste but was afraid to tell him.' He looked at West. 'I suppose I still am.' He lifted his glass and drained the contents in one long drink.

Both men stood, and Andrews took the glasses to the bar, the barman nodding his thanks. 'I think he was glad to see us leave,' he said to West when they were back out on the street. 'I got the impression he was afraid we were putting his regular customers off their pints.'

West sniffed. 'I'd say some of his customers have a closer relationship with the gardaí than they'd like to admit.'

Back in the centre of Foxrock village, the traffic was stalled at the lights and shoppers were crossing impatiently between cars, dashing from one side of the street to the other, hopping from shop to shop. Crossing through the stationary vehicles, the two detectives walked through the village and up Wilton Road to the graveyard where they stood a moment tying up loose ends, dividing responsibilities, and making plans for the remainder of the day.

Andrews headed back to the crime scene. West watched him go with a glimmer of amusement in his eyes, knowing his head would be busy making more lists. He was lucky to have him as a partner. Solid, reliable and completely dependable. If he asked him to do something, it would be done; he never had to worry about it again.

He turned and stared up at Edel Johnson's old Victorian house. If he had hoped to catch a glimpse of her, he was disappointed. There was no sign of life at all. It was a beautiful house; he admired the architecture even as he decided that there was an ineffable sadness about it, as if it had absorbed some of the pain of the woman within.

Why had she reacted so badly to those words? What was the meaning behind *come to good*? What was the connection? Because there was one, that was a definite. They just had to find out what it was.

With a final glance, he got into the car and drove back to the station to begin the first of an almost unending morass of paperwork. As he wrote, as he filled out form after form, he tried to put sad eyes and *come to good* out of his mind.

4

E del had leaned against the closed door, listening as the footsteps faded until she was sure the garda sergeant wasn't coming back. She peered out the window beside the door, watching as he walked through the gate, before she turned to hurry down the hallway, up the stairs and into her bedroom. Pulling open the wardrobe doors, she searched frantically within, rummaging on the racks, searching the shelves. Not finding what she wanted, she dragged clothes out until they were piled in a bundle at her feet.

'Hell and damnation,' she cried and almost fell as she stepped back, her feet tangling in T-shirts and jumpers. Where had she put it? She raced into the front bedroom and wrenched the wardrobe door open so forcefully that it moved on its antique feet and threatened to topple over. Steadying it, she peered into its recesses, pulling clothes out, searching frantically for one particular yellow jacket. With a yelp she saw it, at the very back where she had buried it several weeks ago. It was the jacket she had been wearing the day she and Simon had gone to Belfast for a day's shopping. The day he had disappeared.

He used to tease her about the yellow coat, saying he'd never lose her when she was wearing it, it was so very bright. But he was the one who got lost. With a moment's anguish, she held the jacket close and remembered his smile, wondering for the hundred-millionth time what had happened to him. 'Oh God, Simon,' she whispered into the soft fabric. 'Where are you?'

How many times had she asked that question over the last few months? She rubbed her eyes, brushing away the always-ready tears and, for the moment, those searingly painful memories. They'd come back. They always did. Usually in the small hours of the morning, when she tried to sleep and imagined him slipping in beside her so clearly that she could almost feel his skin as it brushed hers. It was so real she could almost feel his warm breath stirring her hair as his face came closer. So real she could feel his lips on hers. And then she would realise again and again, the sting as sharp each time, that he wasn't there, he wasn't coming back.

Her hands gripped the jacket, knuckles white as the pain of heartache shot through her. Was it never going to ease? Tears speckled the jacket, darkness on the bright fabric that Simon had loved.

She sighed, the sound shuddering through her, and she released her grip on the jacket and searched for the pockets set deeply into side seams. Reaching inside, she found the scrap of paper she was looking for. She took it out and unfolded it. There, written in Simon's unmistakeable writing, *come to good*.

Sitting heavily on the bed, she remembered when she had first found the note. Three months ago. That train journey to Belfast. Her idea, she remembered. She had a vague memory that he hadn't really wanted to go, but she had persuaded him. They had shopped, buying this and that, a dress for her, a shirt for him. They'd had lunch in a smart and very expensive restaurant, and had sauntered through the streets to catch an early evening train home. It had been a lovely day. They had laughed and talked about... she frowned... they hadn't talked about anything important. Or had they? Had she missed something? There wasn't a day over the last three months that she hadn't gone over every moment of that day, every conversation, every nuance, trying to come up with some reason for his disappearance.

She had enjoyed the day so much, had she missed something not right with him? And, try as she might, she could never remember why it was he hadn't been keen on going. Just one of the innumerable conversations that are part of everyday living, generally forgotten as soon as finished, never meant to be remembered, never mind examined and taken apart, word by word. She had berated herself so often for not remembering, for being so self-involved that she must have missed something really important.

They had got back on the train in Belfast, several bags of shopping in tow, and had sat back in their reserved seats with a sigh. She remembered feeling happy and smugly content. Bitterness soured her stomach at the memory. The train had departed only minutes later and, almost immediately, he had got up and said he was going for coffee, did she want some. She didn't and he went, and she had sat back and closed her eyes and drifted into a doze with the sway of the train. Twenty minutes later, he hadn't returned and she remembered smiling to herself, thinking that he must have met someone he knew and wasn't it lucky she had said no to the coffee. When the train arrived in Dublin, almost two hours later, she was annoyed that he hadn't come back to help her with all the shopping, but not particularly concerned, expecting to see him on the station platform with tales of whomever he had met.

When he wasn't there, she had been surprised, then perturbed. Maybe he'd gone to the toilets; she'd kept her eyes on the door to the men's room as the train pulled away behind her and faded into the distance. The last stragglers crossed the overhead bridge and vanished. For a moment, she was alone on the platform, and all she could hear was the sound of a crumpled piece of paper being pushed scratchily along the platform by the wind that had begun to pick up. It had travelled erratically the length of the platform before being blown onto the track and, abruptly, there was silence and she had felt the first tickle of fear.

She couldn't even try his mobile, he'd left it at home, liking to get away from it when he could. It never seemed a problem, after all, she always carried hers. Now, she cursed this quirk of his as she stood waiting, hoping that he would turn up, thinking that, perhaps, for some reason he had missed the stop and would catch the next train back, or the next. Only when, two hours later, she had been assured by officials that there were no more trains, did she give up. Thankfully, she had the car keys and drove with unaccustomed speed back to their home. Even then, she had hoped to find him sitting on the doorstep with some wildly unbelievable tale to tell her. He wasn't there, of course, and she had stood, looking around, wondering what to do.

Crying, partly in frustration and partly in fear, she'd reached into her pocket, looking for a tissue, and had pulled out the scrap of paper. It had fallen to the ground and, for a moment, she had almost ignored it. Then, she'd picked it up and read what was written on it but was too worried about Simon to give it much thought and had shoved it carelessly back into her pocket.

Later, she had put the jacket away because it reminded her too much of that day and she had never wanted to see it again. She had planned to bring it to a charity shop with some other unwanted clothes but, like a lot of things recently, she hadn't done so.

Now, she stood looking at the scrap of paper and wondered what the hell was going on. She was no fool. Finding a dead body three months after her husband goes missing might just be a coincidence. A connection, between the dead body and her husband, wasn't. She knew, too, she had not fooled that tall detective garda and panic raced through her. 'Think,' she muttered. 'Calm down and think.'

Simon must have put that piece of paper in her pocket, not long before he went missing. She wore that jacket all the time and would have found it before. Her forehead furrowed. He put a scrap of paper, with *come to good* written on it, into her pocket. Three months pass without a word. Today, she sees a dead body just a short distance from their house. Almost in her back garden, for pity's sake. And, then the gardaí come and ask her about those very same three words.

For a long time, she sat there trying to think straight. Nothing made sense anymore and she rubbed her eyes wearily. She pulled her hand away, her eyes opening wide, her mouth an O of surprise as, suddenly, from some deep recess of her mind, an idea came thundering. She ran up to the attic room they had set up as an office and switched on the computer, waiting impatiently as it warmed up, her heart thumping noisily in the quiet. It seemed like hours, but minutes later she had googled *come to good* and when it came up, she felt her heart skip a beat.

How could she have forgotten? Cornwall. Their first romantic weekend away together. They had gone over on the ferry from Rosslare and had driven to Falmouth. It had rained all weekend, torrential rain that prevented even the most resilient of walkers from venturing out, and Edel and Simon had only ever been fair-weather walkers. They had driven around instead, admiring the scenery despite the rain, promising to come back again, someday in the future when the sun shone. Driving without plan, they had followed roads as the fancy took them, and had come upon a lovely old thatched inn where they had stopped for lunch.

There was a big fire burning brightly and they had sat a long time, just chatting about nothing, enjoying each other's company. She'd drunk a bottle of very good merlot, while he'd played with a pint of beer. Tempted by the menu, they'd eaten a delightful meal sitting in front of the fire as rain pitter-pattered against the windows. The inn had guest rooms; it all came rushing back to her, they had been tempted to stay, checking in as Mr and Mrs Smith just for a laugh. But they hadn't stayed. They had driven away in the dusk, rain still tumbling, and had stopped to look back at the glow of light from the mullioned windows, promising to return and stay someday. On their way out of the village, they stopped when they saw the reverse of a name sign and Simon had pulled the car over so they could read it without getting wet. It was called Come-to-Good.

They had laughed about the name the rest of the weekend, devising more and more ridiculous uses for it. He would pull her into his arms in the early morning, and whisper, *come to good*. Despite the rain, the weekend had been the most romantic she had ever had and, only a week later, she had agreed to marry him. In all the excitement of the wedding, the honeymoon in a castle in Cork, and the move to their wonderful house in Foxrock, the memories of the small village of Come-to-Good had faded, buried in so many pleasant times, in wonderful weekends away in a succession of gorgeous hotels in beautiful places.

Smoothing the scrap of paper absent-mindedly, she snapped her thoughts back to the present and wondered what to do. Three months, three months of futile sitting and waiting for an answer. Walking back to her bedroom, she went to the window and looked out. The road outside was chaotic with garda cars and a white transit van, parked every which way. At the church gate, which she could just see, two gardaí were keeping church-goers and curious children at bay. The box grave with its sad attendant wasn't visible, hidden as it was by the trees that surrounded her house and the laurel trees that encircled the graveyard.

Looking at the scrap of paper again, she realised, this time, that Simon had forgotten the hyphens between the words, *come to good*, instead of *Come-To-Good*. Probably why she hadn't recognised it immediately. She stood a moment, wondering why he would have put it in her pocket. Was he thinking of that wonderful romantic weekend in Cornwall? She remembered the promise they had made at the time to return and stay at that lovely inn.

Like a blow, the idea struck her and she looked at the piece of paper in horror. He had put the piece of paper in her pocket and disappeared. 'Oh my God,' she gasped, the knowledge coming with fully formed clarity, she was supposed to have followed. She didn't stop to think again or question it. She knew she was right. For some reason, Simon had had to leave; he had left her his address and she had stupidly ignored it.

She had a quick but refreshing shower, scrubbing away the weeks of inactivity and hopelessness along with days of grime and grease. Tying her long, wet hair back, she fished some clean clothes from the pile on the floor, pulling them on and throwing some more into a holdall. She picked up a small handbag, shoved her car keys and mobile phone inside and ran down the stairs. There, with a growl of annoyance, she dropped her bags, turned and ran back to the attic office.

She switched on her laptop, restlessly hopping from foot to foot as it powered up. Sitting, she quickly typed in Irish Ferries, and was speedily brought to their website. There was a ferry at nine-fifteen that night from Rosslare. She had loads of time; it was only... she glanced at the time on the screen... one o'clock.

Was that all? So much had happened that morning she had assumed it was much, much later.

It would only take two, maybe two and a half hours to get to Rosslare. She had plenty of time to catch the ferry. She checked the arrival time. Just after midnight. How long had it taken them to drive to Falmouth when they had gone? She couldn't remember. They had taken an early ferry and stopped for lunch on the way.

Closing the website, she typed in Google maps. Minutes later she had the information she needed. It would take her over five hours to drive to Falmouth. Adrenaline flowed through her, that wouldn't be a problem. She'd doze on the ferry and be fine. Anyway, she could sleep when she got there. Her eyes sparkled. This time tomorrow, she could be with Simon.

She didn't know how long she sat there thinking of what she would say, and what he would say, and all the ramifications of each. Finally, she blinked, shook her head with a smile and turned off her laptop. No point in hanging around, she may as well head to Rosslare now.

In the kitchen, she stopped for a drink of water, looking around the room as she drank, taking in the disorder. How Simon would laugh when he saw it. They'd tidy it together. When they came home. When Simon came home.

Leaving the mug on the dirty countertop, she turned to go. She had dropped her bag onto the cluttered table. As she grabbed hold, it sent a card that had become stuck to it spinning to the ground. Edel paused, bent and picked it up. It was one of the cards the sergeant had given her, his name and contact numbers written in plain, black typeface on a sharp white background. There was something about the starkness of it, the lack of embellishment and honest simplicity, that caught her eye and brought her back to reality with a crash.

It wasn't a romantic gesture on Simon's part that had taken

him away. It certainly wasn't a romantic gesture to leave a note where she may or may not have found it. There was nothing remotely romantic about finding a dead body. And why on earth had that garda mentioned Come-to-Good? She closed her eyes as hot tears seared and fell. Was she doing the right thing?

Looking at the card clenched in her fingers, for half a second she debated ringing the number. Then Simon's face flashed before her and she knew she would do anything... anything... to have him back. She tore the card in two and, with a half-hearted flourish, threw it on the floor. It was a childish act, raising a smile that quickly faded. She bent, picked the two halves up and dropped them into her handbag.

At the front door, she remembered with a grimace that the garda's car had been parked outside. She closed her eyes on the dart of irritation and took a deep breath before sneaking a look from the side window. There was a sigh of relief when she saw the driveway empty.

With the front door locked behind her, she hurried to her car, afraid any moment a garda would stop her and ask where she was going. Pulling out of her drive, forcing herself to take it slowly, she glanced in her rear-view mirror and saw nobody running after her or jumping into cars to give chase. She laughed for the first time in a very long time. Perhaps, she read too many detective novels. Pulling out onto the main road, she relaxed and was soon making good progress on the road to Rosslare.

The journey was uneventful and she arrived far too early at the ferry terminal. Faced with a choice of tickets to buy, she decided on an open return, not knowing what she was going to discover when she arrived in Come-to-Good or when she would be returning. She sat in her car with a takeaway coffee and watched as other vehicles arrived; articulated lorries, camper vans and caravans and an assortment of cars. The big ferry arrived and disgorged its cargo, a similar assortment of vehicles to those that were waiting to board, all eager to get going to their final destination, an air of excitement about everything.

Was she excited or scared? She was afraid to think too much. Just as long as she got Simon back.

She dozed for a moment, woken abruptly with a moment's panic when someone knocked on her window. A ferry official knocked again, louder, waving her onward with an impatient hand. Embarrassed, she started her engine and followed the signs to park her car in the belly of the ferry.

Prevented from staying in the car by the rules and regulations of ferry travel, she made her way to one of the lounges, found herself a marginally comfortable seat and tried to get some sleep. She didn't think she would, so was stunned when woken almost four hours later by the loud chatter of a group of young men who were making their way down to the car-deck.

She was briefly disorientated and felt a little nauseous. Standing, she swayed a little and then realised, with a nervous giggle that it was the ferry moving and not her. She gathered her bag, holdall and jacket and followed the line of people descending to the car-decks. Soon she was sitting back in her car, engine running, excitement mounting.

She followed the instructions to disembark and the well-signposted directions to exit Pembroke. A few miles later, she saw a sign for a service station. With an assessing glance at the petrol gauge, she indicated and took the turn. As she filled up with petrol, she caught the smell of bacon drifting from a small restaurant next door. Saliva flooded her mouth in response and she realised she was hungry, a feeling she hadn't had in a while. She found a parking space and went inside. There was only one other occupant, a dishevelled man slumped over his plate who shot her a speculative glance as he shovelled food into his mouth.

Ignoring him, she ordered breakfast from the surprisingly extensive menu. She chose a table on the other side of the restaurant next to a window that looked out over the brightly lit car park, wishing that her life was as bright, instead of filled with shades and shadows. With a toss of her head, she concentrated on the breakfast. It was good; runny eggs and crispy bacon. She finished off with some freshly-made toast and decent coffee and left the restaurant feeling better than she had in weeks.

Ferry traffic had dispersed and the roads were quiet. She checked her map, relieved to see the journey looked fairly straightforward. Soon, she was seeing signs for Swansea and Cardiff, and, almost before she knew it, was crossing the Severn Bridge from Wales to England. Darkness soon gave way to the magic half-light of early morning when the world seemed new, and as she drove, she watched it appear and take form, almost mysteriously materialising.

As Simon would.

Traffic picked up as she drove from the M4 to the M5 but it was too early in the year for the heavy tourist traffic that made driving to, and around, the south of England such a nightmare and there was only light traffic most of the way. Four hours later, she was on the A39. She pulled over to the side of the road and took out her phone. She had planned to drive into Falmouth and get directions to Come-to-Good from there but using Google maps, she guessed she'd be able to find it without going out of her way. It took a while and she'd almost given up, when she saw the right road; with a grin of satisfaction, she started on the last leg of her journey.

The inn in Come-to-Good had looked lovely when Edel had seen it in the rain but in the glow of the early morning sunlight it was stunning, the sun catching the mullioned windows and turning each into a cascade of reflections. She stopped outside it a moment, staring in admiration before continuing on to the car park. Climbing out, she held her arms above her head and stretched, stiff after the long drive, and then reached in and retrieved her belongings.

The door to the inn was solid oak, which if not original, was indisputably very old. It was worn smooth in parts from many hands opening and closing it over the years. Like many before, she ran her hands over the glossed areas, appreciating the patina of the rich wood. It opened with a soft, ancient creak and she stepped into the inn and, for a moment, back in time, remembering the last visit far too clearly.

A cheery hello from behind the bar brought her out of what could have become a painful reverie and she stepped further into the room. She recognised the tall, heavily-built man immediately and returned his greeting with a smile.

'What can I do for you, love?' the landlord asked, his hands resting on the polished brass pumps.

Give me some answers. 'I know it's very early but do you have a room for tonight?'

The landlord looked at her, unsmiling, then shrugged. 'You're in luck. We had a room ready for a couple who rang at the last minute yesterday to cancel, so I can let you have that.' He turned to take a ledger from under the counter. 'Is it just yourself?' he questioned, looking down as he flicked the pages.

He looked up at the continued silence and repeated the question.

'Yes. Just me,' Edel said, swallowing the lump in her throat.

The landlord turned the ledger toward her, and indicated for her to sign. To her irritation, it was the start of a new page and she couldn't think of any reason quickly enough, to turn the pages back. Putting the ledger beneath the bar, the landlord pulled out a set of keys and, working one off, handed it to her.

'Room eight, top of the stairs, turn right and it's the last door on the left,' he said, indicating the stairway in the corner of the room. 'Breakfast is between seven and nine,' he continued. 'And we serve evening meals here in the bar from six.' He looked at her shrewdly, seeing her pale face. 'I can give you breakfast now, if you'd like, miss.'

'That's very kind of you, but I had breakfast a while ago. I could do with some sleep though.'

'We do a good lunch, if you want it, later on.'

She checked the time on a big clock behind the bar and was stunned to see it was nearly ten o'clock. 'Is that time correct?' she asked in disbelief. 'I expected to be here around seven.'

'Never loses a minute, that clock,' the landlord replied with pride. 'Been there since I was a boy. Never stops, never goes slow.' He spoke with an accent that suggested Cornish roots and she smiled. Taking the proffered key, she picked up her bag and followed his directions.

She found her room easily and was pleasantly surprised to discover it was spacious and beautifully furnished. It was a corner room with mullioned windows looking onto the front of the inn and over a beautiful garden to the side. She spent several minutes trying to open the window to get a better view, the old latch finally giving way with a noisy groan. The double window opened wide and, leaning out, she took a deep breath as she caught the scent of magnolia from a huge tree nearby. 'Wow,' she said, seeing the extent of the garden and making a mental note to explore it before she left.

Closing the window slightly, she turned to examine the rest of the room. The bathroom was small, but clever use of space allowed both a full-size bath and separate shower. A wall unit held a pile of white towels and a small basket beside the wash-hand basin held a collection of toiletries.

She unpacked her few clothes, hanging a clean shirt in the antique wardrobe in the hopes the creases might fall out by morning and put her underwear into a drawer scented with a bunch of dried lavender. Closing the curtains, she undressed and climbed naked under the duvet. She had a moment to realise how very comfortable the bed was before she fell into a deep sleep that took her from early morning to late afternoon.

She woke confused. Where was she? The scent of lavender drifted from the open drawer and memories came flooding back. Reaching for her mobile, she checked the time. Five! Goodness, she'd slept for hours. She stretched and then lay daydreaming for a long time, playing and replaying various scenarios in her head. It was impossible to know what was going to happen, but at least she was doing something. And she knew, she just knew she was going to see Simon again.

Glancing at the time, she saw she had nearly an hour to pass before food was available so, jumping out of bed, she headed for the shower. She chose some of the toiletries to take in with her; a shower gel, shampoo and conditioner, all with the delightful name of Soft Old Rose. She hadn't bothered with conditioner when she had washed her hair earlier and she was conscious that it stood up like a badly-stacked haycock. This time, she smoothed conditioner through and left it to soak in while the hot water beat down on her shoulders, massaging away the aches, pains and stress of weeks.

Securing a dry towel around her, she used a hairdryer to dry her hair and, looking in the mirror a short while later, she was pleased to see a vast improvement. She sighed at her reflection, noticing for the first time how pale she was and how thin she had become. The stress of the last few months had taken its toll; it would take more than one good sleep to recover.

Her relative lack of wardrobe didn't give her much leeway to change so she pulled on the same jeans and T-shirt she had worn earlier and looked at herself in the mirror critically. The conditioner had done its job and her hair shone. Searching in her handbag she found a lipstick, applied it and wished she had brought some mascara. Finally, she was ready; she grabbed her handbag and went down to the bar.

Despite it being early May, there was a fire in the large inglenook fireplace. The light from it threw shadows around the room and made the brass pumps gleam. Additional lighting came from lamps and sidelights and the light was warm, glowing and flattering. It was the perfect place for a romantic meal or a passionate assignation. Several people sat chatting in its nooks and crannies and most were perusing menus so she guessed the food was still as good as she remembered. She found an empty seat in the corner near a window and sat, facing the room, looking around at the various people, seeing nobody she recognised. She berated herself silently, knowing that some small part of her had hoped to come down and find Simon sitting at the bar knocking back his usual gin and tonic. Not a day had gone by, in the last three months, that she hadn't expected him to turn up, but here, in this room where they had sat and laughed, it just seemed more possible somehow.

She shook her head, her auburn hair falling over her face and catching the light from the lamp behind her, causing a number of locals to ask the landlord who the beauty in the corner was, no amount of tiredness or stress hiding the high cheek bones or the generous mouth. Oblivious to the appreciative male eyes, she picked up the menu as one of the bar staff approached and ordered something to eat. A short while later, she was tucking into chicken stuffed with mushrooms and ham, and sipping on a glass of wine. She ate slowly, savouring the best meal she'd had in a very long time.

Finished, she sat back lingering over the last drop of wine and contemplated ordering another glass. The good food had restored her mood and optimism and she mentally prepared the question she was going to ask the landlord.

There was a contented hum in the air and the constant click-click of cutlery hitting plates. A small plump woman, who, Edel guessed, was the landlady, stood behind the bar while the landlord went from table to table chatting to his customers. He would get to her table soon. It was the perfect opportunity to ask him about Simon. She rehearsed in her mind what she was going to say, what she wanted to find out. She could feel herself breaking into a sweat, panic starting to bubble. What if... all the what-ifs... ran through her head.

Picking up the glass of water they had brought with the meal, she took a mouthful and swallowed. She willed herself not to panic, but as she saw the landlord approaching her table, she could feel all her attempts to stay calm evaporate, leaving her almost witless as he stopped and asked her a question. Nervous, but also unable to hear with all the chat around, she stuttered an apology. It worked in her favour as, instead of repeating his question while he stood beside her, he sat down.

'It's a bit noisier than usual tonight, all right,' he admitted as he squeezed his large frame into the small space left between the table and wall. 'I just wanted to make sure you had everything you needed in your room.'

'Oh yes, thank you, it's perfect. A really lovely room,' she reassured him, then hesitated before adding, 'I was here before, almost a year ago, with my husband, Simon, we had lunch here and stayed for ages chatting. We always said we would come back someday and stay here.'

'I thought you looked familiar when you arrived earlier, I have a good memory for faces. Where's your husband then, is he joining you?'

He probably expected a standard answer, the *he's had to work* or *he's coming later* or maybe *oh, we're divorced I'm afraid*. He would be more than slightly taken aback if she told the truth, *he vanished on a train and I'm following a message I think he left me three months ago.* Edel decided to tell him the story she had been rehearsing and, taking a deep breath, she began.

'We had a big row, I'm afraid, and he walked out. Nearly three months ago. I haven't heard from him.' Genuine tears came to her eyes and for a change she allowed them to fall. 'We used to talk a lot about this place and...' She held her fingers against her mouth as the tears threatened to take over. She sniffed, struggling to regain control.

The landlord put a big, gentle hand on her arm and called over to his wife. 'Another glass of wine here, Penny.' When it came, he patted her arm and told her to drink up.

She took a mouthful of wine, and with a sigh, continued. 'I hoped, maybe, he had come here. Clutching at straws, I suppose, but I have tried everything else. Nobody has seen him. We had such a lovely time here, I just hoped... maybe.' She kept her eyes on her wine, afraid to look up.

The landlord frowned. 'We get a lot of people staying here, you know, and a lot of men on their own. Sales reps most of 'em, travelling between Falmouth and St Austell. Some we know well; some just stay the one night and we never see them again.'

'So, my husband may have stayed here,' she said, trying not to sound too eager. 'His name is Simon Johnson. He's about six two, brown hair and eyes.' She was babbling but she felt so close.

'Girl, that could be every second man I see. And I haven't much of a head for names, I'm afraid, faces yes, but not names.'

'He would've had to sign in, wouldn't he?'

Without hesitating, he got to his feet, crossed to the bar and leaned over to grab the ledger. Returning, he sat and put it in front of her. She hesitated a moment, her hand resting on the cover, then slowly began to turn the pages. Starting on 19 February, the day Simon vanished, she slowly worked her way through to her entry of that morning.

'Nothing,' she whispered and bit her lip. She had been so sure.

He looked embarrassed, as if he had let her down. 'I'm so sorry, love. But it was a long shot.'

'I was positive there would be something. Are you sure everyone signs in?' She looked at him intently, wishing him to say no.

'Well no, to be honest. I'm not. My wife, Penny, has forgotten more than once,' he admitted. 'Generally, I notice and get them to sign later. But the odd one or two may have slipped through. It's a busy place.'

She jumped up, re-energised. 'You remember faces? I have a photo. I'll just run and get it. You might recognise him.'

When she came back, minutes later, the landlord was still sitting but had used the time to get himself a pint, and she noticed, another glass of wine for her. Sitting, she looked at the photo. It was a good likeness of Simon; he'd looked straight into the camera and it had captured him perfectly; his lips were curved in his habitual smile, well-cut brown hair brushed back the way he liked to wear it. He had strong white teeth, a neat nose and firm chin. She hugged the photo to her chest, reluctant to hand it over and be disappointed again. It wasn't until the landlord held his hand out for it that she let it go.

The landlord looked at it closely, his eyes narrowing. A good-looking man, he remembered him well. His name too, and it wasn't Simon Johnson. What the hell did he say now? He was no fool and his years behind the bar had shown him there were as many sides to every story as there were ants on the patio in the summer. She was a good-looking woman but he didn't believe her story about the row. She was looking for this man all right, but why, and did he want to help her? He looked at her as she watched him with an anxious expression on her face, waiting for him to say something. He didn't believe her story but he did believe the tears in her eyes to be genuine and there was a look of hope on her face. Deciding to tell her the truth, he said, 'I recognise him. But his name is not Simon Johnson, at least, it wasn't when he stayed here. He came here about three months ago and stayed about two weeks. Mostly, he stayed in his room, coming down for breakfast in the morning and dinner in the evening. Never said very much.'

He stopped, taking in the stunned look on her face. 'He was on his own, love. No woman or anything. He was using an odd name, too.' Frowning, he looked up at the ceiling and tutted. 'What was it? Ah, yes... Cyril,' he said, and then looked at her. 'Pratt. That's it, Cyril Pratt. That's why I remember it, I'm afraid. Penny and I were laughing about it, we thought it was a terrible name. And I'll tell you something else, love,' he added, 'he had a credit card in that name. That's how he paid his tab here. And there was no problem with it. That I would have remembered, believe me.'

Ignoring his wife, who was trying, vainly, to get his attention, he kept his eyes on her pale, shocked face. 'What are you going to do now?' he asked gently.

'I don't know... I really don't,' she said. 'But thank you for being honest.'

He sat a moment, watching her as she stood and edged out of the room. His missus glanced his way, a quizzical eyebrow raised, but he just shrugged his big, beefy shoulders and getting up, gathered the plates and glasses easily in his large spade-like hands and brought them to the kitchen. He'd fill her in later. Tell her more tales of folk and their strange and unfathomable ways.

5

R outine was being followed back in the police station. Leads chased, phone calls made, contacts contacted. Most led nowhere but each of the gardaí working the case knew that one of those leads, calls or contacts could hold part of the answer they sought or, at least, head them in the right direction; so, they persevered doggedly, drinking innumerable mugs of coffee, ticking off lists.

It was frustratingly slow and, by late afternoon they didn't know much more than they had done at the start. The autopsy report, when it came, confirmed what they already knew; when and how the man had died and the size and shape of the blade that killed him. The only new piece of information was that the killer was, more than likely, right-handed. That was all they knew.

So far, they had no identification for the victim.

They didn't know why he died and they were a long way from knowing who killed him.

Andrews sat in West's office shuffling pages of notes in his hands. 'Dr Kennedy puts our victim's height at six two, and weight about one ninety,' he muttered, looking at the data. 'A big man. Yet no defensive wounds at all. So, what happened? He just let himself be stabbed? Didn't expect trouble, just sat down on the gravestone for a chat?'

West tilted his chair back precariously. 'They knew each other, arranged to meet in the graveyard for some reason and had a disagreement which turned ugly. One thing led to another and, bingo, dead man.'

'If it had turned ugly then wouldn't you expect defensive wounds?'

He shrugged. 'Maybe our Armani-wearing victim is a bit of a softie. Not into violence.'

'Why would someone choose to meet in a graveyard anyway?' Andrews asked. 'And don't forget it would have been about eleven o'clock. Those church lights are turned off at ten, it would have been pitch dark in there.'

'They wanted somewhere quiet, where they wouldn't be seen by anyone?'

'They'd hardly be able to see themselves in there at night,' Andrews said, unconvinced, 'never mind anyone else seeing them. We've had no reports of lights being seen either.'

'Mmmm,' West murmured, chair rocking back and forward on two legs, grey eyes narrowed in thought.

'If you break that chair, supplies will be pretty cheesed off,' Andrews grumbled. 'It'll be the third in six months. They don't understand how they keep breaking, they would if they saw the way you abuse it.'

Ignoring him, West brought the chair down on all fours with a crash. 'Who goes to a meeting of any kind armed with a large knife? Someone who means business, expects trouble and goes prepared.' He stood and walked to the window, looking out on the grey and dismal walls of the surrounding industrial buildings. 'It doesn't look as if our victim expected trouble though. He goes to a dark, isolated spot dressed in a smart, expensive suit, sits relaxed on a box grave to talk to our murderer and puts up no resistance when attacked.'

'One streetwise man, one foolish,' Andrews said.

'On the surface anyway,' West agreed. 'We've also got that scrap of paper and its connection to Edel Johnson to think about. I know it's tenuous but there's something there, her reaction was too extreme to dismiss.'

'I agree. Do you want me to go and talk to her again? See if I can find out what's behind it?'

West sat and drummed his fingers on the desk. 'No, let's leave it for the moment. We need to concentrate our efforts on finding out who our victim is, and hopefully why he was killed will fall into place. Check with fingerprints; see if they have come up with a name. Get his photo around to missing persons and if there's nothing, check with external agencies, see if he shows up with them.' He looked up, a grin lighting his face. 'Teaching my grandmother to suck eggs again, Peter. You know what to do, just go and do it.'

They walked together to the general office where there was, as usual, a pot of coffee brewing. West poured them each a mug, adding milk and several spoons of sugar to Andrews' and, taking his own, headed back to his office to go through the data again. There wasn't much to go through but he did it anyway; he had a photographic memory and it proved a useful tool when bombarded with new information to be able to recall the old without hesitation.

Facts often came slowly, trickling from a variety of sources and, an hour later Andrews appeared with one of the crucial ones – the victim's name. He had acquired it the way information often came, through a complicated tortuous route. The usual channels had not paid up so he reached further afield, calling up favours, tapping friends, acquaintances and colleagues in various other agencies in Ireland and then abroad.

Several phone calls later, he was running out of options when an acquaintance he had made at an international symposium on terrorism, returned his call. Normally a placid man, Andrews entered West's office with a buzz of excitement.

'Remember Doug Potter, that bloke I met at the symposium last year?' Seeing he had the sergeant's interest he didn't wait for an answer. 'He has some good contacts in the FBI and got them to run our victim's prints. It seems he travelled to the States a number of times and as you know they fingerprint on entry now. That's how he came to the FBI's attention.'

'He has a record there?' West said in surprise.

'Not exactly,' Andrews hurried to explain. 'Our victim travelled to the States on a number of occasions but he also flew to a number of Middle Eastern and Far Eastern countries and that attracted the FBI's attention. Nothing overtly suspicious, he worked for a number of engineering companies as a consultant but they were always a suspicious bunch and since 9/11 they suspect everyone.'

'So, what's the name?' West asked, pen poised to write. There was silence and he looked up expectantly. A smirk split Andrews' face. 'You wanted a complicated case; I think you got one. His name is Simon Johnson.'

West sat back in stunned disbelief, pen falling from his hand. 'The missing husband? You've got to be joking. She would have recognised her husband; she was almost close enough to touch him.'

'Uh, uh, just the same name. Here are the details and photo,' he said, handing over a computer printout.

A frown gathered on West's brow as he scanned the page quickly. 'Coincidences are piling up here. Edel Johnson's husband disappears and she finds a dead body whose name happens to be the same as that of her husband. Fishy as a tin of mackerel.'

'I thought so too,' Andrews said, taking a seat, 'so I took the liberty of contacting Sergeant Clark and asked him to bring over his file on the Johnson case. He said he'd be here in about ten minutes.'

Five minutes later, the door opened with a bang. A bedraggled body filled the doorway and slouched into the room. Across the desk, West and Andrews exchanged a look as Tadgh Clark, without invitation, lowered himself into a chair designed for those with less ample proportions. Loud creaks accompanied his gruff, 'Hey, Mike, Pete.'

West had never had much time for Sergeant Clark, thinking him a lazy, boorish jerk. His opinion didn't change as Clark reached forward to hand over a very thin, scruffy file. 'This is it?' he questioned in obvious disbelief, holding the file in one hand.

'That's it,' Clark agreed with no sign of embarrassment, sitting back in the chair, ignoring the ominous creak. 'There was never much to it. Simon Johnson and his wife, Edel, got on a train in Belfast in February. He went to get coffee and never came back. Nobody saw anything out of the way. No bodies were found along the track. CCTV in the stations where the train stopped didn't show him getting off. Not that they were all working, I must admit. He hasn't been in contact since. Hasn't used his credit cards, his passport is at home.' He shrugged big shoulders. 'That's it,' he reiterated.

West opened the file. He took the photo of Simon Johnson from it and laid it side by side with the computer printout of the photo of their victim. They were definitely not the same person. Putting the photos to one side, he examined the rest of the information in Clark's file. As he expected from its size, there wasn't much in it. Credit card statements showed no activity. Interviews with the wife and train officials said little of worth. CCTV reports were all negative.

Nothing was in order, he noted with a grunt of irritation. He flicked through the file, seeing gaps in the information, formulating questions.

'Where did he work?' he asked bluntly.

Clark shrugged again. 'Some kind of engineer, his wife said. Worked on a contract basis for a number of companies and also worked, I gather, from home. Hadn't worked for any of the companies for several months.'

'How about their financial status? Any money worries? Reason for the husband to top himself? Insurance claim or anything?' West threw the questions out staccato fashion, his irritation rising in face of obvious incompetence.

Clark wasn't the kind of man to get upset easily. He lounged in his chair. 'No,' he finally answered, just as West was thinking about getting up to strangle him. 'The wife was quite clear; their finances were in order. They'd no debts. They own the house outright and have a nice comfortable lifestyle. Didn't have life insurance at all so there was no kind of scam based on that.'

'They're only in that house nine months. Where did they come from?' Andrews queried. 'That's an expensive house they live in and they have no mortgage?'

For the first time, Clark squirmed as much as he was able to, wedged into the small chair as he was, and didn't answer.

West looked at him intently. 'You don't know?'

'It wasn't relevant to my inquiry,' Clark hedged and began the slow process of extricating himself from the chair. 'All the information I needed for my investigation is there. Information you require for yours, I'm afraid, you'll have to collect yourselves.' And on that note, he left the office and closed the door on the annoyance and frustration of the two men behind it.

West took a deep breath, and let it out in a stream of colourful swear words he'd picked up over the years before opening the Johnson file again, and spreading the meagre information out on the desk. He held the enclosed photo beside the computer-generated photo of their victim again. They were different people, certainly, but there was a marked similarity. 'And look here.' He indicated the physical statistics. 'It could describe the same man. Both six two, both around one ninety, both with brown hair.'

'And both work as engineering consultants,' Andrews pointed out, leaning over the desk.

'Two men, same name, same description, same occupation. One married to Edel Johnson and disappears; the other she finds dead. Way beyond the bounds of coincidence, we have a conundrum on our hands.' West stood abruptly. 'Right, we have our work cut out. I think we can agree that the Johnson missing person case and ours are linked. I'll have a word with Inspector Duffy and get his go-ahead to take it over. I can't see Clark making any fuss about it somehow,' he added, indicating the meagre information still scattered on the desk. 'Get Garda Allen to give you a hand and start filling in the gaps on both men. And get one of the others to contact every estate agent in the area, find out who sold that house to the Johnsons and where they got the wherewithal. I'm going to head back to Mrs Johnson and see if I can fill in some blanks there. I'll call in to the inspector on my way.' He checked his watch. 'It's four o'clock; we'll have a briefing at five thirty, see where we stand.'

As Andrews left, he ran a hand over his head and frowned down at his desk before shoving everything back into the file. A quick visit to Inspector Duffy gave him permission to take over the missing person case and he headed off to Wilton Road, determined to fill in some of the gaps in their information.

Pulling up outside Edel Johnson's house, he groaned when he noticed the car that had been parked in the driveway was gone. With no idea where she was, or how long she'd be away, there didn't seem to be much point hanging around. Scribbling a note asking her to contact him, he got out to put it in her letterbox when he saw a man coming out of the driveway opposite, a recycling bin clattering noisily behind him.

'Hello,' he called, bringing the man to a halt. 'I was hoping to catch Ms Johnson, I don't suppose you know where she is?'

The man looked him up and down critically and then with a look that said West had passed muster, he said, 'Not sure where she's gone but she was in a hurry, and she was carrying a holdall, so, I guess she's gone away for a while.'

Scarpered, done a runner, vamoosed. West's expression closed down in annoyance. Thanking the neighbour, he crushed the note in his hand and got back into the car.

He still looked annoyed when he returned to the station just after five. He headed straight to his office and dropped heavily into his chair, his expression only relaxing when Andrews came through the door with two mugs of coffee, one of which he deposited on the desk in front of him. 'Cheers, Peter,' he said, picking up the mug and taking a tentative sip. Andrews had mixed up their two mugs on numerous occasions and a mouthful of oversweet coffee was something he didn't need right now. He'd got it right today though; he took a long drink of the strong, bitter coffee and sat back with a sigh.

'It looks like Edel Johnson has done a runner,' he said. 'Neighbour saw her leaving in a hurry with a holdall.'

'Maybe it was something she'd planned?'

West shook his head. 'No, that just doesn't ring true. After her reaction to "come to good," I'm convinced there's something off about her. We're just not seeing it.'

'We've managed to find some information on our murder victim, less on our missing man,' Andrews said. 'Do you want me to fill you in now?'

Sighing more loudly, West got up. 'Thanks, no, it's time for the briefing, I'll hear it all then.' They headed back into the general office where a number of gardaí were sitting on chairs and desks, comparing notes, catching up with department gossip. Sergeant Clark was also there, West noted with annoyance.

Someone had organised a large whiteboard, and photos of the victim and the missing man were fastened to it with over-large lumps of Blu-Tack.

Andrews, at a nod from West, pointed to the computer-generated photo of the victim, Simon Johnson. 'Here's what we have found out about our victim. He was a forty-two-year-old engineer who worked on a contract basis for a number of companies. He was based in Cork for a number of years and had purchased an apartment there which is presently rented out. For the last year, he was based in Dubai, flying regularly between there, other Middle Eastern countries and the USA. He hadn't been back to Ireland for the last year and was only back last week to attend a family funeral. Garda Allen spoke to his sister.' He nodded to a small, ginger-haired man who stood awkwardly.

'According to his sister, who also lives in Cork,' Garda Allen read hesitantly from his notes, 'after his aunt's funeral, Johnson spent a few days visiting friends and family. The sister said, he had some business to attend to in Cork yesterday but she has no idea what that was. After that, he had planned to catch up with some friends in Dublin today before catching an early flight to Dubai in the morning.' He fumbled to turn a page in his notes, licking his fingers to separate the pages. 'The sister says he had planned to stay in the Shelbourne. He made the reservation for two nights, but didn't show. We're still trying to contact the friends; the sister gave us a few names but she wasn't sure who he had planned to meet.'

'What about Foxrock? Does she know of any reason he might have come here?' West asked.

'She'd never heard him mention Foxrock but doesn't know where his friends live so perhaps one of them lives here. She did say, however, that as far as she knew all his friends lived in and around the Ballsbridge area.' Allen closed his notebook and sat.

'Do we have any idea what business he had intended to do?'

Andrews spoke up. 'I contacted his office. Whatever he was doing, it wasn't related to his job. I got his bank's address from the sister. They won't talk to us without a court order but that's in progress and I have an appointment to talk to them tomorrow.'

'Okay, good.' West looked over his shoulder at the whiteboard, weighing up the information, analysing it for content and relevance. 'Anything else?' he asked, looking around the room. 'What about our missing man, then?' He pointed at the other photo on the board. Silence echoed around the room, broken by the gurgle of the coffee machine and the even louder gurgle from some of the men who had skipped lunch and were anticipating a big evening meal. A few glances were directed toward Garda Jarvis, the newest member of the team, who stood self-consciously.

'I spoke to the estate agent, Kim Manners, who sold the Johnsons the house,' he began hesitantly, stopping when all eyes fixed on him.

'Go on,' Andrews called encouragingly, 'tell us what you found out.'

'She remembered them well,' Jarvis continued with more vigour. 'They went around to see the house in the morning and Simon Johnson rang and put in a full asking price offer in the afternoon. Ms Manners said they always asked potential purchasers what their situation was, if they were waiting for a mortgage approval or if they had to sell a property prior to purchase. Our missing man told her they could proceed immediately because he had won the lottery a few months before.'

The room erupted in speculation and conjecture, the noise level increasing as the conversation grew wilder.

'Okay, okay, enough,' West shouted to be heard above the hullabaloo. 'Did you check his claim with the lottery, Jarvis?' he queried and acknowledged his shake of the head, saying, 'Right, follow that up tomorrow. We want to know when he won and how much.'

'How much did they pay for the house, anyway?' Andrews asked.

Jarvis checked his notes. 'Ms Manners told me the house had been on the market for several months and the price had been substantially reduced to attract a sale. They paid five hundred grand for it but she said it was originally on the market for closer to eight hundred grand.'

West frowned thoughtfully. 'That seems cheap for the centre of Foxrock, doesn't it? Was there a reason?'

'She mentioned something about the graveyard putting people off, Sergeant,' Jarvis offered.

'Nice quiet neighbours, I'd have said,' Garda Allen put in with a gruff laugh at his own joke.

'Apart from his claim to have won the lottery what else do we know about our missing man?' West asked, looking around the room.

'I got their last address from the estate agent,' Jarvis said. 'They lived in Drumcondra.'

'Good, hit the phones tomorrow. Find out how long they lived there, when it was sold, how much for. Any information you can get. What about tax returns? He worked on a contract basis. He must have filed tax returns. Look into that too.' Jarvis nodded, anticipating a heavy day on the phone.

Andrews was looking through the information in the slim file they had received from Sergeant Clark. He took out a couple of pages, which had been stapled together, and held them up. 'Our missing man's bank statements are interesting.'

West took them, raising an eyebrow. 'What have you picked up?'

'There were no cash withdrawals made on the account,' Andrews said. 'Two thousand euro was deposited every month and then immediately went out by direct debit to pay a number of credit cards. The monthly deposit of two thousand euro, you would assume is his salary since it comes on a regular monthly basis, but he works, we've been told, on a contract basis, sometimes from home, so surely his income would differ from month to month. But that's not the only odd thing, look at this.' He pointed to a series of letters beside each deposit amount. 'These letters indicate that they are all internal transfers from another account.'

'So, he has another account?'

'He must have. If the two thousand euro were coming from an external source, they wouldn't have these letters next to it.'

'Why didn't we get the details of all his accounts when we requisitioned his bank?' West turned to Clark who leaned back in his chair, frowning.

'Because we were looking for credit card use or debit card withdrawals,' he answered indignantly. 'His debit card is linked to that account. They weren't obliged to give us data on any other account. His direct debit transactions weren't of any interest to my investigation.'

West glanced at Andrews who nodded in response to the silent request that he requisition full banking details tomorrow.

'This is getting more and more complicated,' West groaned, running his hand over his face. He looked at the clock. Almost six thirty. 'Let's leave it at that. Right, you all know what to do tomorrow,' he said, dismissing them. 'Get some rest. See you all at eight.'

Then, remembering his luck earlier, he decided to ask one

last question, halting the mass exodus in its tracks. 'One more thing, do the words "come to good" mean anything to anyone?'

He got the expected head shakes and shook his own in acknowledgement of defeat. A creak of a chair indicated movement from Sergeant Clark and West looked over dismissively.

'Come-to-Good,' Clark pronounced in a loud voice. 'It's a village in Cornwall.'

6

West, convinced that the answer to some of their questions would be found in Come-to-Good, decided that the only option was to go there. He headed to Inspector Duffy's office wishing, not for the first time, that he had one of those, rare to be sure, bosses who respected intuition. It was hard to put forward a good case, when your sole argument was *it's just a hunch.*

The inspector wasn't impressed. 'Sounds like a red herring to me, you'd be far better off focusing your attention here. But,' he conceded reluctantly, 'it's your case, Sergeant West, if you think hightailing it to Cornwall is in the best interest of your investigation, you obviously know what you are doing.' He was an expert in damning with faint praise and more confident men than West had left his office feeling an inch tall and useless with it.

The inspector had intended to retire the previous year but had been persuaded to head the detective unit in Foxrock when Inspector Morrison had gone on extended sick leave. It was supposed to have been for three months, then six. Now, a year later, he was still there. West knew he resented it, but he was a good officer and despite his objections, despite obviously thinking his idea was preposterous, he knew he could depend on him to liaise with his counterpart in the Devon and Cornwall police and obtain the usual permission.

Back in his office, he used the internet to find the nearest airport to Come-to-Good. To his surprise, Ryanair couldn't bring him further south than Bristol, a hell of a drive. Persistence paid off, and he found a flight to Plymouth with FlySouth. He checked the timetable and then his watch. There was a flight at ten; if he rushed, he'd make it. There was always a packed holdall in the trunk of his car for emergencies. He could go straight to the airport.

He had a quick conversation with Andrews who, like the inspector, considered the trip to be a waste of time. 'Stop worrying, Peter,' he said. 'I'll be back tomorrow night and at least I'll have put the Come-to-Good angle to bed. You talk to the bank, and have an alert put out for that bloody woman.'

'You never told her she couldn't go anywhere,' Andrews argued. 'Maybe she has gone on a visit somewhere. Could be something innocent, you know.'

West looked at him scathingly. 'You don't believe that for a second. There is something decidedly fishy about Ms Edel Johnson. Coincidences keep piling up, and you don't believe in them any more than I do.'

Andrews shrugged then grinned. 'You just go on your junket to Cornwall, Sergeant, and leave it all to me.'

FlySouth was an efficient airline that had him on the ground in Plymouth ten minutes ahead of schedule. There were a number of car rental offices in the arrivals area and he walked to the first of these and within minutes of form filling was in the possession of car keys for a Ford Focus. He had rented a satellite navigation system and he quickly keyed in the postcode of the only accommodation in Come-to-Good, a piece of information

Andrews had rung to tell him en route to the airport in Dublin. The sat nav quickly digested the data and displayed the information required. Arrival time would be one o'clock. He sighed wearily and hoped it would all be worth it.

He was tired and crotchety when he pulled up in front of his destination in Come-to-Good, a beautiful old public house that showed not a hint of life. He hadn't asked Andrews the name of the pub and saw, with a glimmer of amusement, that it was called simply, The Inn. He noted a sign for the car park and swung his car around, parking it in the corner of the virtually empty, unlit lot, assuming that there would be some means of entering the place. Andrews was supposed to ring and warn them of his late arrival.

Grabbing his bag, he headed for the inn door and, giving it a tentative push, was relieved when it gave easily and opened into a warm, inviting room. It was just after one and the room was empty apart from a large man behind the bar who scrutinised him as he entered.

He broke the silence. 'Good evening. I know it's late but there should have been a room booked for me. My name is West, Mike West.'

The landlord reached under the counter and, for a brief terrifying moment, West thought he was reaching for a gun and fear flashed through him, searingly painful memories following inevitably on its tail. The appearance of a disreputable ledger drew a short laugh of relief that drew a quizzical glance from the landlord.

'I'm sorry,' he hastened to explain. 'I've had a long day. I'm just relieved you are still open.'

'We wouldn't turn a traveller away this time of night. No matter how much the nuisance he was,' the landlord said bluntly. 'Anyway, your friend rang so we were expecting you.' He turned to the relevant page and turning the ledger around toward West, used a large index finger to indicate the next vacant line. 'Just sign here, please.'

West dropped his bag on a nearby bar stool and, taking the pen, started to write his name. It's a habit with most people, to read the other names in registers like this, and he was not immune to natural curiosity. The other name on the page surprised him so much, he dropped the pen and had to scrabble on the beer-sticky floor between the bar stools to retrieve it.

Putting on his best poker face, he completed the signing-in process, managing at the same time to elicit information from the landlord about business at this time of the year. Armed with the information that only two of the ten rooms were occupied that night, he settled into his surprisingly comfortable room. He toyed with the idea of going from room to room until he located the only other guest but, with a protracted yawn, and the vision of a comfortable bed in front of him, he decided that morning would be soon enough.

Moments later, he was stretching in the most incredibly soft bed he had ever been in and before the stretch finished, he was relaxed. He lay for a moment going over the events of the day, remembering clearly Edel Johnson's reaction when he had mentioned Come-to-Good. 'Perfidious female,' he murmured sleepily and, shutting his eyes on that note, he didn't open them until morning.

In another room, not far away, Edel slept through early morning deliveries and the clatter of the bottles being emptied into containers behind the inn. It was the incessant bark of squirrels in the trees outside that eventually made her open one eye, quickly followed by the other. She stretched and lay for a moment, enjoying the play of light through the windows.

Checking the time, she was surprised to see it was eight

o'clock and, suddenly hungry, she threw back the duvet and clambered out of bed, remembering that breakfast was only served until nine. Her wardrobe didn't lend itself to much choice so, after a quick shower, she donned the same jeans as yesterday and the shirt she had hung in the wardrobe from which most, if not all, the creases had fallen. She headed down the stairs to where she could hear the tinkle of cups and, even more of a giveaway, smell the aroma of coffee. Hesitating at the door, she was propelled into the room by the landlord, who came from the kitchen region bearing a well-laden tray.

'In you go, love,' he addressed her warmly, 'take a seat wherever you like, I'll be with you as soon as I have served this gentleman.' He bustled by her and, balancing the tray in one hand, he offloaded it with the other in front of a man, seated just out of her line of vision.

She chose a seat in a window embrasure with a pretty view of the garden. For a moment, as she sat looking out at tulips and early clematis, she almost forgot why she was there. The tulips were at the blowzy stage, petals falling open, showing their secrets to the world in what she'd always considered a rampantly sexual way. She loved them and had planted numerous in the garden in Foxrock, many of which were still in bloom.

She was called away from the view by a hearty, 'What can I get you?'

Quickly perusing the menu, she ordered a full breakfast with coffee. The coffee came quickly and was followed soon after by a lavish spread to which she proceeded to do justice. She was just polishing off the last mushroom when she saw movement in the far corner and, assuming the other diner was leaving, paid no more attention. So, it was with surprise that she saw the chair opposite being pulled out and it was with absolute shock that she recognised the man who sat down in it.

'Good morning,' he said with such an irritatingly smug look on his face that she wanted to slap him there and then. 'Enjoying your breakfast?' he continued, crossing his arms and tilting the chair back.

Speechless, Edel felt the breakfast gurgling in response to her increasingly rapid heartbeat. 'What are you doing here?' she managed to blurt out eventually.

West raised an eyebrow and lowered the legs of the chair. He reached into the inside pocket of his jacket and pulled out the scrap of paper he'd photocopied from the one they had found on the body. He smoothed it between two fingers, and, reaching over, placed it on the table in front of her and sat back. It was all done very slowly, a trick he used often to unnerve people. It usually worked. This time, however, he had met a worthy opponent. She looked at the scrap of paper, reached down to get her handbag and, searching for a moment, pulled out her own scrap. Smoothing it between two fingers, just as he had done, she reached over and put it on the table in front of him. 'Checkmate,' she said quietly.

At that inauspicious moment, the landlord came to remove the breakfast paraphernalia and they both hastily picked up the pieces of paper. If the landlord wondered at his two residents being known to one another, he said nothing, and soon they were alone again. West let the silence stretch as he assessed her. She looked better than the previous day, less fragile and stressed. Cleaner and prettier too. Deceitful, he reminded himself sharply.

She took the scrap of paper from West. 'Where did you get this?'

He sat back, tilted his chair and answered, 'It was in the pocket of the dead body you found. Is it your husband's writing?'

'No, this is his writing.' She raised her own scrap of paper. 'I found it in the pocket of the jacket I was wearing the day he disappeared. To be honest, it meant nothing to me at the time.'

'Really?' he said, the one word laced in disbelief.

'Nothing,' she repeated angrily. 'I read it, shoved it back into my pocket and forgot about it until yesterday.'

He stayed silent, and after a moment she continued. 'I found it in the same pocket but... you know... I still didn't understand. I had to Google it before it came back to me. As soon as I saw Cornwall, of course, I remembered this place and an afternoon we had spent here.' She stopped, laid the scraps on the table, pushing her hair roughly behind her ears.

She looked serious, intent... believable? He crossed his arms and waited for more.

'Three months I've been waiting and wondering. Have you any idea what that is like? The not-knowing eats away at you, demolishes every particle of strength and self-belief.' Her voice quivering, she stopped, took a shuddering breath and continued. 'You relive every moment you were together, looking for clues; questioning and examining every word for tone, for nuance, until you no longer trust any memory, until you try not to remember because every memory might be the key, might be the reason he went, and it is just soul destroying. So, you try to live each day, waiting all the time for the world to make sense again, but when I go out...' Her voice dropped to a whisper. '...I see him everywhere; every man wearing a certain suit, a certain jacket becomes him. When I turn a corner, I search every face in case one is his. I have stopped my car in the middle of traffic, convinced I saw him amongst the crowd. I have accosted total and bemused strangers so many times in so many places. I hear his laugh sometimes and rush to groups of people where I stand and stare, searching for him, their irritation turning to curiosity and pity when I ask them if they have seen him, when I explain that my husband has disappeared. So now, I don't go out unless I have to and even then, it doesn't end.'

With a stirring of sympathy, he watched shades of sorrow flicker across her face, turn down the corners of her full lips and settle in her pale blue eyes. 'I was digging in my garden last month,' she said, 'just moving a bush that had outgrown its place, trying to get on with my life, you know. I had to dig quite deeply to get it out. It was pretty hard going, our soil is so stony but it felt really therapeutic, the sun was shining and, for a moment... just one short moment... I wasn't thinking of Simon.'

Gardening was the same for him, he reflected. In the middle of the most difficult case, no matter how exhausting or complicated, he could spend a few hours or even minutes in his garden, digging, deadheading or weeding and suddenly he didn't feel quite so stressed and prickly.

'One of my good neighbours rang the police and told them I was digging what looked like a grave,' Edel said, meeting his eyes. 'The gardaí who called around were very apologetic and one of them even helped me. But it wasn't quite so relaxing after that.'

'Tell me why you came here?' West asked, hardening his heart against inappropriate sympathy.

Haltingly, she told him everything she knew.

'Let me get this straight,' West said. 'Your husband, under the name Cyril Pratt stayed here for two weeks?' This was something unexpected.

She leaned forward, hands clasped, elbows resting on the table. 'I think he was waiting for me. He must be in some kind of trouble and left that note in my pocket expecting me to follow him.'

He looked at her sceptically and fired a series of questions at her. 'What kind of trouble? Why be so cloak and daggerish about it? If he left you a note, why wasn't it more explicit? And when you didn't turn up, why didn't he contact you?'

'You're the bloody detective.' She glared at him in frustration. 'You tell me. My life has turned into an Agatha Christie novel and I'm just trying to make sense of it. I don't know why Simon vanished. I don't know why he's using a different name. I don't know anything and I am sick and tired of not knowing.'

Her voice rose and became shrill. It brought the landlord into the room, a frown on his face. 'Everything all right, miss?' he queried, drawing close and glaring at West.

He answered calmly, 'We're fine but some more coffee wouldn't go amiss.'

The landlord hesitated, then as Edel sat back, he delayed his departure by moving a few tables and chairs about, and, finally, with another glare at West, headed off to get the coffee.

West watched him go in amusement, the smile in his eyes dimming as he turned his attention back to Edel and speculated on her involvement. She sounded like she knew nothing but he had learned, both as a solicitor and a garda, not to take things at face value.

'Do you know what a "pushaway" is, Sergeant?'

He eyed her speculatively; he knew what she was getting at. 'Someone who is forced by circumstances to disappear,' he answered. 'You think your husband falls into this category?'

'Yes, I do,' she said, firmly. 'I've read everything there is to read about missing people, every single thing, and I've weighed up every possibility. I knew Simon. He wouldn't have chosen to leave me. He loved me.'

'Tell me about him,' West said. He saw suspicion cross her face before she took a deep breath and in a calmer voice began to speak.

'I bumped into him... literally,' she said. 'I'd been with my editor.' She looked at him with a tilt of her head. 'I don't know if you know but I write children's books.' When he shook his head, she continued. 'I rushed out the door without looking and barged straight into him. I apologised, so did he, and that was it, we went our separate ways. Then,' – she gave a soft laugh – 'amazingly, an hour later I was coming out of a shop a few streets away, and there he was, just passing by. He smiled at me. I remember I laughed, and promised not to bump into him again.' She shrugged. 'We ended up going for coffee.'

Her voice faded away and West watched countless emotions flit across her face in rapid succession as she became lost in the past. Finally, she spoke again. 'He is the kind of person who's really easy to talk to. He really listens, you know. I told him things I'd probably never told anyone else, ever. We discovered we had so much in common; we liked the same music, the same type of architecture, the same books. It was amazing. Our first proper date, he took me to a restaurant I had wanted to go to for months. We liked the same kind of food, the same type of wine. It was just so wonderful.'

The ensuing silence was broken by the arrival of the land-lord with the coffee. He seemed reassured by the quiet and set the coffee down without further ado. He had also brought unbidden, slices of what looked like homemade coffee cake. Without hesitation, they both reached for a slice, West secretly amused that they looked like any couple out for a day in the country.

He licked his fingers, sat back with a satisfied sigh, and watched as she finished off her slice, hesitating only slightly before reaching for a second with a guilty shrug. 'I just love coffee cake,' she justified. 'And this is a really good one.'

Her fabulous figure wasn't at the expense of her appetite. West administered a mental kick to remind himself why he was here and that she could well be a murderer or at least an accomplice. Time to get back on track. 'And you married after how long?'

'Three months after we met,' she said, polishing off the cake. 'We didn't see any point in waiting.' She sat back with her coffee. 'Shortly afterwards, we found the house of our dreams in Foxrock. It was a vacant possession, so things proceeded very quickly and Simon moved into it almost immediately. I stayed a few weeks longer in Drumcondra, to finalise the sale of my house there. It all fell together so perfectly,' she murmured softly, her lips curving in a smile of such sweetness that West felt something inside go *ping*.

He needed to take more control of this conversation. His voice a little harsher than was warranted, he said, 'Simon worked as an engineer, I believe?'

'Yes, he does contract work for several companies. He can do quite a lot from home, which is marvellous, as I do too.'

'What kind of engineering?' It probably didn't make any difference but the more he could learn about the missing man the better. Plus, he was curious about this paragon of a man who had swept the woman opposite off her feet.

'Chemical,' she replied, taking another sip of her coffee. 'I don't know much about it, to be honest.'

'Not the kind of stuff you'd put in children's books, I suppose. He must have earned a good living, though. Contractors tend to be better paid than average.'

'Very well,' she agreed. 'As I've said, we had a nice lifestyle. We spent one or two weekends a month away, usually in a spa or country house hotel, places a little out of the ordinary. Sometimes in Ireland, sometimes in the UK. Simon spent hours on the internet finding lovely old hotels in beautiful settings.'

West watched a slight smile of reminiscence curve her lips as she drifted down the dangerous, slippery slopes of memory lane, her face softening, eyes glowing and, for an infinitesimal moment, he felt a sharp, unexpected pang of jealousy. Then he remembered her husband's bank details; it was going to be very interesting to see his other bank account.

He put his cup down sharply, the ensuing clatter making her blink and return from wherever it was she had gone. 'Did you ever go further away?' he asked, thinking of the victim's frequent trips abroad.

'No.' Her abrupt answer startled both of them. She held both hands up, palms out. 'Sorry,' she said. 'I'm sorry, you just reminded me of an argument I had with Simon about six weeks before he disappeared. It was his birthday, and I'd surprised him with a holiday to Mauritius.' She shook her head. 'He refused categorically to go, said he hated flying. I couldn't sway him at all.'

A soft hum made West reach into his inside pocket. Pulling out his mobile, hearing Andrews' voice, he nodded an apology to Edel and left the room. Heading to the car park for privacy, he leaned on his car. 'Before you tell me what you've found out,' he said to Andrews, 'guess who's staying in The Inn?'

'Edel Johnson?'

West shook his head. 'I suppose you were bound to guess. Yes, she's here.' Quickly, he filled him in on what Edel had told him. 'Okay, now it's your turn.'

'Well, I requisitioned our missing man, Simon Johnson's full bank details. The two thousand euro is, indeed, an internal transfer from another account in Johnson's name. However, the money didn't come from any company where he worked but, in fact, appears to be coming, each month, from one individual by the name of Alberto Castlelione. It's rent,' Andrews informed him bluntly. 'Rent for a very fancy Cork apartment. And that is the only money being deposited. No money from any company or business at all.'

West frowned, digesting this news as the sound of Andrews

slurping what was probably his third or fourth mug of coffee came down the line. 'Anything else?'

A smacking of lips was heard. 'He's never submitted tax returns. In fact, Inland Revenue don't know our missing man, at all. He didn't own the house in Drumcondra, that belonged to Edel Johnson, or Edel Shaw as she was then. However,' he continued, accompanied by a rustle of paper, 'our murder victim, Simon Johnson, *did* own an apartment in Cork. I spoke to his sister; she says her brother had it let out for the last year. We're just waiting to hear if that is the same apartment our devious missing man rented out.'

'Some form of identity theft,' West surmised, with a shake of his head.

'Starting to look that way, all right. We've still a few calls to make but we should have the information we need by late this evening or, maybe, early tomorrow.'

'Cyril Pratt may well be our missing man's real name so run it through and see what you come up with. Of course,' he added, 'if identity theft is his thing, he could be using any name at this stage. Not so much missing, as metamorphosing.'

'A regular chameleon, eh? Right, I'll see what we have on Cyril Pratt, to begin with. Not sure I'd blame the bloke changing a name like that, mind you.'

'Not worth killing over though, is it?' West had the last word and, cutting the connection, headed back into the dining room. He had a moment's panic to see her gone before catching a glimpse of her through the window. Sitting, he took the opportunity to examine her more closely. Obviously relaxed in her stroll around the garden, he had to acknowledge she was a remarkably good-looking woman. Just at that moment, she turned and caught his gaze. Embarrassed, he looked away and shuffled in his chair.

'I hope you didn't think I had run away,' she said when she rejoined him a few minutes later. 'I just needed some fresh air.'

He commented on the garden. 'It looks nice out there. Tulips are a particular favourite of mine; I have a lot in my garden.'

'They remind me of voluptuous showgirls displaying their underwear to all and sundry,' she said with a smile.

He hadn't looked at tulips in that way before, he knew he would now. Dragging his wandering mind back to what Andrews had told him, he looked at her across the table. 'Your husband told the estate agent in Foxrock that he was purchasing the house with money he had won on the lottery. How much, exactly, did he win?' he asked, focused again.

'I'm sorry,' she gasped, and took a sip of water. 'Simon never won the lottery,' she finally answered. 'Where on earth did you get that idea?'

If she were lying, she was good. 'It was what he told the estate agent. He told them you would be able to move quickly on the sale because he had the cash from his win.'

'He must have been joking,' she replied with an unconvincing laugh.

'Then where did you get the money to buy the house? You hadn't sold yours.' He watched her blink and look down.

When she looked up again, he saw that her eyes were shimmering with tears. 'My parents both died when I was in my early twenties,' she said slowly, her voice thick. 'Since then, I've looked after my own affairs, paid my bills, my taxes, kept everything ticking along. We were both so excited about the Foxrock house that when Simon said we could afford it, I didn't question him.' She ran a hand over her hair, pushing it behind her ears. 'I believed him, I'd no reason not to. He told me he'd sold an apartment in Cork, just before he met me. So, the money was there, in the bank.'

West looked at her sharply. 'He had two apartments in Cork?'

She looked at him, confused. 'No, just the one. He sold it. He was staying in a hotel when I met him, doing some work for a local company.'

'You are unaware that he has been receiving money for the rental of an apartment in Cork.' He was watching her face carefully; he was almost sure she wasn't lying.

'That's impossible. Simon would have mentioned it. He had one apartment; he sold it and used the money from the sale to buy our house. Your information is incorrect.'

She held his gaze, a frown marring her smooth brow, but he noticed she was twisting the napkin she held in her hand into a knot. 'The money from the sale of your house,' he continued relentlessly, 'where did that go?'

'It's still in my account,' she explained. 'Simon wanted me to keep it.' She sighed and tried to explain. 'I don't make a lot of money from my writing, Sergeant, and deadline pressures are tough. For a long time, I've wanted to write adult fiction but haven't had the time to do so. The money has made a difference. I've reduced my workload and spend more time writing what I want.' She lifted both hands. 'I don't know if it's any good, but I've almost finished a novel.'

West's phone again intruded. He sighed and stood as he took it from his pocket. She rose at the same time. 'I just need to go to my room for a moment,' she explained, as he raised an eyebrow in query.

'I'll be five minutes,' he said, heading to the car park.

In fact, it was nearer to fifteen minutes before he sat down again following a long conversation with Andrews and then with Inspector Duffy.

Andrews had run Cyril Pratt's name as requested and hit pay dirt. 'You could make your bed with this bloke's sheet,' he informed West succinctly. 'Pratt started with petty larceny, progressing to some weighty post-office robberies. He did a few years inside for those and while there he appeared to have had lessons in the delights of extortion because he has stuck with that since. He's been put away several times but never for very long, thanks to our wonderful legal system and to the fact that our man is a real charmer and never uses violence. It seems,' he added with heavy sarcasm, 'we are now to be grateful for non-violent criminals. On a personal note,' he continued, 'he has been married three times. His current wife lives in Cork with their two children.'

'Current wife?' West repeated in disbelief. 'You're sure they're still married?'

'I rang his house and she answered. Her name is Amanda. According to her, her husband works away a lot and she's not sure when he'll be home next. I got the impression that she didn't much care. She mentioned that he took his car this time which he didn't normally do, something about needing access to paperwork that he kept in the boot of it.'

West wiped his face with his free hand. Another thread to add to the tangle. 'So, if as we suspect, the missing Simon Johnson and Cyril Pratt are one and the same, we can add bigamy to his list of crimes.' He sighed. 'Any news yet on the Cork apartment?'

Andrews hadn't heard back from the victim's sister and rang off to chase that up, leaving West to explain the increasingly complicated tale to his superior. He headed back to the dining room with a heavy sigh and a mind racing, only mildly surprised when Edel hadn't returned. The landlord came bustling in to clear the table and he asked for fresh coffee. 'For both of us, please,' he added, indicating Edel's chair and at the same time beginning to wonder what was keeping her for such a long time.

The landlord continued to clear the table, managing to balance the plates and cups easily in one enormous hand. 'She's gone,' he informed West bluntly, nodding to the empty chair.

'She's just gone to her room for a moment,' he explained. 'She'll be back. Sorry if we're being a nuisance but we'd like more coffee, we have a long journey ahead of us.' He saw the landlord's hard stare, maybe they were outstaying their welcome. Was he being too demanding asking for more? He was going to pay for it, after all.

The landlord gave a shrug and left, to return moments later with a fresh pot of coffee and one cup. West was just about to remonstrate when the landlord said, firmly, 'The lady won't want coffee. The lady settled up, about ten minutes ago, and left. She drove away in her car.'

7

A wild and wet morning didn't help to abate West's anger the next day. He slammed his office door, threw his briefcase on the floor and, sitting heavily into his chair, prepared for an embarrassing conversation with Inspector Duffy. His head ached, adding to his annoyance. He'd had a horrendous journey back from Cornwall, road works on the road to Plymouth slowing traffic down to a forty mile an hour crawl. Then, just when he thought it couldn't get worse, it stopped moving almost completely, an accident a few miles further on closing two lanes. He had sat seething for nearly two hours, alternately condemning himself for being a gullible idiot, and Edel for being a devious, conniving, manipulative... he ran out of adjectives as he inched along the road, imagining instead weird and wonderful punishments to suit the crime. He was trying to recall all he knew about the Spanish Inquisition, when the traffic began to speed up.

He had missed his flight, had no choice but to pay again to go on the next flight six hours later and had spent those hours making and taking phone calls, trying to run the case from the airport.

The first person he spoke to was an irate Inspector Duffy who criticised his decision in going to Cornwall and his incompetence in losing sight of Edel Johnson, even as he reluctantly conceded that innocent people didn't generally run, and on that basis, she must be guilty of something. He agreed, once again, to contact Devon and Cornwall police and ask them to be on the lookout for her. 'They probably won't be so cordial this time to be asked to be on the lookout for a woman who hasn't, as far as we know, committed a crime,' he said acidly. 'I don't appreciate being put in this situation, Sergeant West.'

By the time West landed in Dublin at eight o'clock that night, he was seething. He picked up his car and drove home in silence, a headache beginning to pound.

He was met at his front door by a pair of doleful, brown eyes that castigated without saying a word. 'Don't you start,' West snarled unapologetically, throwing his holdall on the hall floor. 'You can come and go as you please, you've plenty to eat. Do not give me grief.' He poured himself a large Jameson and collapsed into his favourite comfortable chair.

He had furnished his house well. Expensive sofas in a rich tapestry defying the theory that men always choose leather. Rather than modern matching furniture, he had picked up an eclectic mix from antique shops and car boot sales and the result was a pleasant comfortable home that offered an escape from the invariable seediness of his job. He thought he had pretty good taste but then again, he grunted angrily, he'd considered he had pretty good judgement and instincts too. He poured himself another whiskey, sipping slowly this time, allowing it to work its magic. Light footsteps pattered over the walnut floor and he turned his head to see the little chihuahua looking up at him again, prominent brown eyes still accusing.

He sighed and patted the sofa and the little dog jumped up and curled into a ball beside him. 'Sorry, Tyler,' he said, 'I've just had a hell of a day.' Tyler lifted his head and looked at him, gave a short, sharp yelp then curled up again. Moments later, he was snoring with a soft snuffle.

'Some day your owner is going to get tired of living the high life in San Francisco and take you home,' he addressed the sleeping dog. 'And he can take all those feeding machines with him and get rid of that damn cat flap.' Brendan, an old friend, had pleaded with him to mind the dog while he went off to *find himself*. West had pleaded long working days as an excuse but his friend had come up with the perfect solution. Three, timed-feeding machines so Tyler would never go hungry and a cat flap so he could spend as long as he wanted in West's safe, walled garden. 'Just for a month or so,' he had begged. That was over a year ago and there was still no sign of his return. West looked down at the small, hairless bundle next to him and sighed. He'd miss him when he did go but would never admit it except maybe when bone-tired, or after at least two whiskeys.

He reran the morning's conversation in his head for the umpteenth time, analysing, evaluating, looking for whatever it was that he had missed at the time. He was still mulling over it when he'd poured his third whiskey. Only when he finished that did he head to bed.

He should have stopped at the second. His head ached.

With a long-suffering sigh, he decided to get the worst part of the day over with and call in to see Inspector Duffy. His whiskey-driven headache simmered in the background as he admitted he had fallen for one of the oldest tricks in the book. Luckily, Inspector Duffy who had had a call from the Superintendent of Devon and Cornwall police first thing, apologising for his less than cordial response the previous day, was in the mood to be forgiving. He was even finding the whole episode amusing and was happy to let West see he did.

West had no doubt the inspector would tell the story of the high and mighty, university-educated, detective sergeant brought down by womanly wiles. He knew, too, that the story would grow legs and become more and more ridiculous as the weeks went on. He didn't consider himself high and mighty but being the butt of derisive stories wasn't a pleasing thought. He restrained himself from slamming the door behind him with difficulty.

In the general office, he grabbed a mug of coffee and made his way to where Andrews sat cradling a phone and scribbling rapidly. Perching on the side of the desk, he sipped the coffee and listened to one side of the conversation.

Andrews hung up and sat back with a groan. 'It's like a skein of wool this. Every time I think I've got it unravelled, I get another knot to untie. It's your fault, Mike, you wanted a nice complicated case.'

'Fill me in,' West said, pulling up a chair. 'You have to have had a better day yesterday than I did.' He was pleased that Andrews had the good sense not to laugh.

Picking up a folder that lay on the desk in front of him, Andrews handed it over and summarised bluntly. 'Our friend Cyril Pratt is a five-star con artist.'

Putting down his half-empty mug, West opened it, raising his eyebrows in disbelief as he read.

'Makes interesting reading, doesn't it?' Andrews said with a grin. 'I've arranged a briefing at nine. Some of the lads are out tying up a few loose ends.'

He glanced at his watch. It was ten to the hour. He finished reading the collated information just as the rest of the team assembled. 'Okay, listen up everyone,' he started without ceremony. 'We've done well. I'll let Garda Andrews bring you all up to speed.' He waved the folder at him to indicate that he take over.

Andrews stood and pointed to the photo of the missing man stuck on the whiteboard. 'Simon Johnson. Also known as Cyril Pratt, Paul Stokes, John Fisher, and so on. Altogether, we have six aliases listed for him. And they're the ones that we know of. According to our various sources, our Cyril, as I'll call him for the moment, worked for a cleaning company, called, with a distinct lack of imagination, Industry Cleaning Company. It appears that it's cheaper, for big companies and industries, to hire a team to go in and clean on a regular basis than it is for them to hire their own cleaners. They have a headquarters in Cork and send teams of cleaners to various parts of the country where they stay, sometimes for a number of days, and do several premises before moving on to the next area. One of the premises they clean, on a regular basis, is Bareton Industries in Cork.' He waited a beat and then pointed to the photograph of the murder victim. 'The same Bareton Industries, where our victim, Simon Johnson, worked on a contract basis, two or three days a month, until last year.'

Andrews checked his notes and continued. 'According to his sister, Jennifer, Mr Johnson signed a two-year contract to work in the Middle East and decided to rent out his Cork apartment.' He looked up. Some of the younger officers were eagerly jotting things down while the more experienced just listened, mentally filing information away. He knew they would recall information instantly while the youngsters were still trying to find their notebooks. They'd learn, he hoped. 'Jennifer describes her brother as being, quote "too trusting for his own good" unquote. Rather than give his apartment to an agency, which would have been the sensible thing to do, he stuck an advert up on a notice board in the office in Bareton Industries. According to the receptionist, the advert listed address, contact phone number and also mentioned that he would be out of the country for two years.'

A collective groan filled the room, with much head shaking and frowns of disbelief at the continuing stupidity of relatively intelligent people.

'Yeah, yeah, yeah,' Andrews agreed. 'We all know how clueless these highly educated, university-softened people can be.' His sideways glance at West drew a guffaw from the room. Most, at this stage, had heard about Come-to-Good and the disappearance of Edel Johnson. West gave an obligatory grin and a half bow to his appreciative team before nodding a *get on with it* to Andrews.

'The receptionist remembers the advert and thinks it was only there a day or two. Unfortunately, she can't remember what days or if the cleaning team were in while it was there but we are drawing our own conclusions based on what follows.

'Adam Fletcher,' Andrews continued, 'also works on a contract basis, for Bareton Industries. According to Jennifer Johnson, her brother was contacted by Mr Fletcher about the apartment; he subsequently met him for lunch and, found him' – he checked his notes briefly –'to be, quote "utterly charming" unquote.' He looked around the room, noting the grunts of expectation. 'So charming did he find this Mr Fletcher that, when a crisis arose in the Middle East and he had to go two weeks earlier than planned, he didn't hesitate. On the basis of their lunch meeting, and a reference from Bareton Industries, he gave him the keys of the apartment. According to Jennifer, Mr Fletcher agreed to pack all his belongings and put them into storage for him. Simon had asked Jennifer to make sure that this was done and to check with his bank that the agreed rent was paid. She checked for a couple of months, there appeared to be no problems, and that was that. She guiltily admitted she didn't check again.'

Andrews stopped and took a mouthful of what West assumed was cold, sweet coffee.

He liked to listen to him giving the update. It helped clear things in his head and frequently brought up questions that he hadn't thought about before.

Andrews cleared his throat noisily, bringing the murmurs to a close as he again opened his notes. 'For those of you who haven't already guessed, the real Adam Fletcher has never rented an apartment and lives, happily, with his wife and two children in Cork. Mr Fletcher says he knew of Simon Johnson, but as they worked different contractual hours they had never met.' He closed his notes, sat comfortably on his desk and turned his gaze on Sergeant West. We're like an old married couple, West thought wryly, as he stepped up to the board.

'Right,' he started, looking up at the photos of the two men. 'So, this is what we know.' He pointed at the first photo. 'Our murder victim, Simon Johnson, rents his apartment to a man claiming to be Adam Fletcher and goes abroad for two years. The deposits that were made to his account – three in all – were cash lodgements, lodged according to the bank by a Cyril Pratt. So, we can probably surmise that Pratt doesn't have banking or other identification in Adam Fletcher's name, it's not one of the aliases he has used before according to our files. It is likely that he acquired the name while he worked as a cleaner in Bareton Industries and used it for the sole purpose of fooling Simon Johnson.

'In Johnson's apartment, however, Pratt had access to sufficient personal data to allow him to create a complete identity including banking facilities. Alberto Castelione, who rented the apartment two months later from Simon Johnson, identifies this man' – he pointed to the photo of Cyril Pratt – 'as being Simon.'

He paced back and forward, thinking and working things out as he spoke. He turned to the room and continued. 'The real

Simon Johnson comes home for a family funeral and discovers his bank account to be a lot lighter than he'd expected. Garda Andrews spoke to his bank in Cork yesterday and it appears that this is where he had business on the Monday before leaving for Dublin. This is where he learns that only three month's rent had been deposited into his account. He then went to his apartment looking for answers from Adam Fletcher where he met instead the current tenant, Alberto Castelione who told him he was renting his apartment from a Simon Johnson, and denied any knowledge of Fletcher. Mr Castelione was able to show him direct debit arrangements and even, believe it or not, a signed rental agreement. Mr Castelione describes Simon as being shocked and upset. He invited him in but Johnson refused and left immediately.'

West looked around, taking in the animated faces of his team. 'Mr Castelione estimates the time Johnson left the apartment to be about 6pm.' He turned and pointed at the photo of a handsome, vibrant Simon. 'Approximately thirty hours later, someone drove a very large, sharp knife deep into his stomach and left him to bleed to death on our doorstep. Was it this man?' He turned to point at the photo of Cyril Pratt. 'Our missing husband, con artist and bigamist? If so, how did Simon Johnson contact him?' Something occurred to him. 'Who spoke to Adam Fletcher?' He looked around for a response, nodding at Garda Jarvis as he stood. 'Get back on to him. See if he has had any strange phone calls over the last few days.' Jarvis moved immediately to a corner of the room and opening his notebook, dialled and was soon deep in conversation.

'What about Pratt's claim he had won the lottery?' West continued. Garda Allen answered swiftly. 'They say no one by the name of Pratt or Johnson won it over that period. I spoke to the bank the Johnsons use here in Foxrock. They say the money to buy the house was lodged in cash. According to their files, it is the proceeds of a house sale in Drumcondra. They maintain that Simon Johnson submitted all the correct paperwork.'

'I just bet he did,' West said, perching on the side of the desk as Jarvis rejoined the group. 'Well?'

'Mr Fletcher and his wife were away for a few days in the Achill Islands and only arrived back late last night. His children were staying with his mother so the house was empty. He said there was the usual assortment of hang-ups on his answerphone but nothing out of the ordinary.'

'Okay, so we don't know if Johnson tried to contact him or not. We still have any number of questions we need answered. If our victim was murdered by Pratt, how did he meet him?' West asked, and expecting no response continued, 'Edel Johnson states that the money from the Drumcondra house sale is still in her account. Find out if she is telling us the truth.'

'And what has the village of Come-to-Good got to do with anything, and why did Edel Johnson do a runner?' Andrews added to the mix. 'Let's find some answers. Allen, you and Jarvis hit the phones. I want to know if our murdered man hired a car. He had to have come to Foxrock in some form of transport. If you have no luck there, show his photo at the local DART and Luas train and tram stations, you might get lucky.'

Both men moved to the far desk and got down to work.

West was still staring at the photos of the two men. He turned when he saw Andrews. 'You got the warrant to search the Johnson house without problem?'

'Yes, I'll take Baxter and Edwards with me. Unless you want to come?'

'No,' West said, rubbing a hand over his head. 'I spoke to Jennifer Johnson yesterday; she's agreed to meet me to allow me to go through the stuff belonging to her brother that's in storage.' Reaching out, he tapped the photo of the missing man. 'I'm just wondering did he bite off more than he could chew. All that cash, did he try to outsmart the wrong person? Is that why he had to run?'

'When I get back, I'll have a word with the Drumcondra lads, see if they can come up with anything,' Andrews said. 'Maybe our friend Cyril left a trail there. It's worth a shot.'

West wiped his face with his hands and rubbed his eyes, wishing again that he'd passed on the damn whiskey and gone to bed earlier.

'You're sure you fancy another long drive. I could go to Cork.'

Noticing the concern in his eyes, West clasped his arm briefly. 'Thanks, Pete, I'm fine. No, you do the Johnson house.' He checked the time. 'It's ten; I should be back here by six. I'll talk to Falmouth on the way and see if they have had any sightings of Edel Johnson. Keep me informed if anything shows up in the house.'

Andrews left as he lingered a minute more, staring at the photos of the two men. Picking up the A4 size photo of Edel Johnson that he had taken from Clarke's old file, he placed it between them. He remembered she had compared her life to an Agatha Christie novel. There were a lot of conniving women in those novels.

'*You* should remember though, Edel,' he murmured softly, 'in those books, the murderer and his accomplice always got caught.'

8

The journey to Cork, where Simon Johnson had rented storage facilities in an industrial area just outside the city, was uneventful. Jennifer Johnson, an attractive, blonde woman in her early fifties, was waiting when he arrived. She accepted his condolences graciously and handed him the key to the storage shed.

The door opened easily. Inside, there were a number of boxes neatly piled at the entrance but the remainder appeared to be various items of furniture. A mountain bike and a road bike balanced themselves against one wall.

Jennifer pointed to them. 'They were the real reason he rented the storage facility in the first place,' she explained. 'He loved to cycle. When he decided to rent the apartment, it seemed like a good idea to store extra furniture and stuff here. There isn't much, as you can see, my brother wasn't a hoarder.' She indicated the boxes. 'All the personal papers he left behind are in those boxes. You are welcome to take them with you, if you so wish. I trust you to return them to me when you can.'

West smiled at her gratefully. 'That would make it a lot easier, thank you. I'll have the contents inventoried and returned to you as soon as possible.' He quickly transferred the four boxes to the boot of his car and, relocking the storage door, he handed her back the key.

'There was something Simon said that puzzled me, Sergeant,' she began. 'He said that he hoped all his clothes wouldn't get damp here. When I said there weren't any clothes, he laughed and said maybe Adam Fletcher thought his Armani suits were too valuable for a lock-up. He said, he would ask him where they were, when he spoke to him.'

'Do you know if he did?'

'Not when he was here. He never mentioned it again and I forgot about it until now. Simon had very expensive taste, Sergeant, and the money to indulge it. He only wore Armani; he swore nobody made suits so well. He wore dark suits in London and lighter suits in the Middle East. All his dark suits, several of them, would have been in his apartment and, of course, all the shirts and shoes to match.' She smiled suddenly. 'Simon loved his shoes; he had them handmade in Italy.'

'Maybe that was the other business he had to attend to, contacting Adam Fletcher?' West queried.

'It is a possibility, I suppose. He only mentioned having business. I'm afraid I didn't inquire. Simon was a very kind, indulgent brother but he kept his business to himself, as I do.'

'Just one last question, Ms Johnson, before I go. How long was the man you knew as Adam Fletcher in possession of these boxes?'

A chill breeze blew Jennifer's expensively streaked blonde hair across her face where it caught tears she had been trying hard to contain. 'You think it was him, don't you?' she asked in reply. 'Simon hadn't a bad bone in him.' She struggled a moment before continuing, her voice thick with unshed tears. 'He saw people as invariably good and kind because he himself was. He trusted that man without knowing him at all. Did he trust a monster, Sergeant West?'

He reached out and took her hand, holding it a moment. 'I don't know, Ms Johnson. Not yet anyway. But we'll catch whoever killed Simon, believe me,' he said, instilling his voice with a confidence he didn't feel, giving her the answer he knew she needed to hear.

'Thank you, Sergeant; I know you'll do your best.' She took a step towards her car and then looking back at him, she answered his question. 'Those boxes... they were in the apartment about a week before they were moved here.'

He waved his thanks but she had already turned away to walk to her car. Climbing into his own, he once again headed for the long drive to Foxrock.

There were no hold-ups on the journey home and it was just after five when he pulled into his designated parking spot outside the station. Climbing out, he stretched his tired muscles, feeling every one of his forty years as they adapted to a standing position. He'd spent too many hours, over too few days, on the road. His stomach joined the chorus of protest, gurgling loudly enough to remind him he had missed not only lunch, but breakfast as well. He hailed a young garda he recognised and instructed him to have the boxes in the boot brought to his office.

Avoiding the desk sergeant's eye, to bypass any messages that might have come for him, particularly ones from Inspector Duffy looking for an update, he made his way to the station canteen. This was a badly lit, uncomfortable room that he generally tried to avoid but he was hungry and tired, a combination he knew could lead to frayed tempers at best and mistakes at worst. It was quiet and West took the canteen's version of shepherd's pie and sat with a sigh, enjoying a seat that wasn't moving at sixty miles an hour. He ate the pie without tasting, a trick he had learned long ago to cope with institutional food, and soon sat with an empty plate. For a few minutes, he relaxed, enjoying the comfort of a full belly, listening to the murmuring of the canteen staff.

Had he known the murmuring issued from the smitten lips of two of the younger canteen staff he wouldn't have lingered so unconcernedly. He took his good looks for granted, had his hair cut at a local barber shop for fifteen euro every six weeks, and, generally, wore clothes he got as presents from his mother, sisters and, occasionally, girlfriends. His smartly-tailored suits were handmade, however, a relic of his days in law and they hung well on his six-foot frame. The gifts from his mother, sisters and girlfriends were invariably expensive so, despite himself, he always looked smartly dressed and stylish. His manners matched, effortlessly charming and generally agreeable. Women loved him, responding as much to his manners as to his looks, and he enjoyed them, while taking their love very much for granted and on his terms completely. So it was, that he was still single at forty and currently unattached.

Pushing away from the table, he took his tray and left it on the rack, completely unaware of the admiring and flirtatious giggles of the two young women who watched him pass.

Most of the rest of the afternoon passed in a flurry of mindless paperwork, done with an ill will because it had to be done. The powers that be, he often criticised, delighted in adopting new and more ludicrous forms to complete for every aspect of his working day. He was scribbling his initials on the final piece of drivel when Andrews knocked and entered. He threw it in his out tray and, with an exaggerated sigh of relief, threw his pen on top and sat back in his chair.

Andrews patted the pile of forms. 'Who told you being a detective was more exciting than law, eh?'

He tilted his chair back on two legs. 'All the criminals I

locked away, perhaps I shouldn't have believed them. Sit down, tell me what you've got.'

Moving a pile of folders from the only spare chair to the floor where they toppled immediately into another dustier pile, Andrews sat, opened the folder in front of him and proceeded to update him on the day's work.

At the end, West raised his eyebrows in exasperation. 'Nothing,' he muttered in annoyance.

'Nothing,' Andrews echoed calmly, 'the lads have chased every lead so far and have come up with exactly that... nothing.'

'What about Drumcondra?'

'They have no current file on our Mr Pratt or any of his aliases. There is always the possibility, I suppose, that he used another temporary alias that we know nothing about. I put the five hundred grand into the mix but, still nothing. No report of any swindle or scam. Mind you,' he added, 'not everyone is willing, or able, to come to the police if they have been ripped off. There is always the possibility, like you said, that he tried to rip off the wrong person.'

'What about the house?'

'Again, nothing. We found personal papers in the name of Simon Johnson but nothing in any other name. No further bank accounts apart from what we have. We found a couple of accounts in her name and it seems she was telling the truth, there is a balance of three hundred thousand which is almost what she received for her house in Drumcondra.'

'Did you talk to her bank?'

'Got a court order this morning. If she uses her card, we have her.'

'I spoke to Falmouth earlier,' West said tiredly, stretching his arms over his head and making the chair creak as it strained to balance on two legs. 'No sign of her, or her car as yet, but they'll continue to be on the lookout. I still can't believe she ran out on me,' he muttered.

Andrews' eyes narrowed in a smile. 'We'll get her,' he said consolingly before West's chair came down on all four feet with a crash, startling him into dropping his folder to the floor, the contents scattering.

'Sorry.' West helped him pick up the contents, rescuing one gory shot of the victim from under his desk and returning it to him. He waved at the boxes piled beside the door. 'Our victim's. Want to give me a hand to go through them?'

Andrews looked at his watch pointedly.

'It's only six thirty,' West complained. 'Give me a hand and I'll buy you a pint.'

Muttering imprecations against Guinness, Andrews opened the nearest box. Thirty minutes later, they had found nothing of any consequence and he rang his wife to tell her he'd be home in half an hour.

'No later,' he promised, looking pointedly at the sergeant, and hung up.

In the last box, they found a reference from Bareton Industries for one Adam Fletcher. West read it quickly. 'It's signed Tom Bareton. I'm sure it'll prove to be a forgery but we'd better get it checked out tomorrow, just to be sure,' he said, handing it over to Andrews.

Looking at it with little interest, Andrews frowned. 'Might be easier to go down to them, Mike.'

'Dammit, I'm only back from Cork. It's a long journey just to find out something we already know, isn't it?'

'Well,' Andrews said slowly, 'I was thinking about paying a visit to Amanda Pratt, anyway. I might get a better feel for our Cyril, if I saw where he came from. We know about his life as Simon Johnson, I'd like to see how it differed, why he lived the lie.'

West nodded thoughtfully. Peter was right, it would help. He had been in Cork, why hadn't he gone to see her? That bloody woman, she was filling his mind with distractions he didn't need. 'I should have done that,' he conceded, rubbing a weary hand over his face. 'Fine, you go down. Check out Bareton Industries, and Amanda. The lads can handle anything that turns up here.'

'I'll leave around 5am,' Andrews said. 'I hate driving in Cork; the traffic is a nightmare and that one-way system is dreadful. Every time I drive there, I break the law, driving up one-way streets the wrong way.' He sighed heavily. 'At least if I'm early, I can catch Amanda Pratt before she leaves to do, whatever it is she does.'

West's face relaxed. 'She is going to love you arriving on her doorstep at eight.'

'I'm expecting breakfast, Mike.' He grinned and then shrugged his shoulders. 'Well, maybe coffee. I can go straight to Bareton Industries afterwards and have a word with' – he glanced at the reference – 'Tom Bareton. I might have a word with this Adam Fletcher too; see if he has remembered anything of relevance.'

There was certainly nothing else of relevance among Simon Johnson's papers and they quickly returned the flotsam and jetsam of the victim's life to four sad-looking cardboard boxes.

'Doesn't amount to much, does it?' West said as he taped up the last box.

Andrews obviously wasn't in the mood to get philosophical. 'You're forgetting his Armani suits and his handmade Italian shoes – they're still walking around enjoying life.'

West could never stay miserable and introspective when Peter Andrews was around.

They left together, walking in companionable silence to the car park.

'You want that pint, Peter?' West asked, knowing as he did so the answer he would get, and wondering, not for the first time, what it must be like to have someone to rush home to.

'I'd better get home; Joyce will have dinner waiting.' He hesitated. 'You're welcome to join us; she always makes too much.'

He shook his head. 'Thanks, another time maybe. And we'll go for that pint another time too. I'm going to make it a personal mission to teach you to appreciate a good pint of Guinness.'

Andrews opened his car and bent his tall frame into the seat. 'Maybe I'll convert you to the joys of a pint of Heineken instead,' were his parting words as he sped off, exceeding the car park speed limit by one hundred per cent.

West grimaced at the thought as he climbed into his own car. He decided to drive to the Stillorgan Orchard for a pint knowing he was unlikely to meet any of his colleagues there and could enjoy it without the usual shoptalk. He knew the story of the Come-to-Good fiasco would be doing the rounds and he definitely didn't want to be the butt of jokes about that. He closed his eyes briefly; in a few days, maybe he could laugh about it, but not tonight.

He laid his head back against the headrest, remembering her smile. Damn the woman, how many lies had she told him? What a fool she had made of him.

He started his car, hearing his mobile hum as he reached for the gearstick. What now? Leaving the car in neutral, he fished in his jacket pocket and, with a weary sigh of exasperation, answered it.

9

Almost five hundred miles away, a storm battered the coast of Cornwall. The ground, sodden after an exceptionally wet winter, gave up in defeat and water flooded roads and fields. Weather warnings were issued. Police and rescue services advised people to stay indoors unless a journey was absolutely necessary.

Worried householders hastily piled sandbags at vulnerable doorways remembering the last time when floodwater had swirled in and destroyed everything before it. Optimists said they'd be fine; pessimists carried everything of value to the highest point in the building, securing against flood and, in the worst-case scenario, against looting should they need to be evacuated.

Two miles from Come-to-Good, the wind howled up a narrow, high-hedged, private laneway, chasing rain before it and making the hedges sway drunkenly. Where the lane branched off the narrow road, a To Let sign stood, its paint peeled and fading, its wood rotting from long exposure to Cornish wind and rain. Tenacious fingers of ivy and bramble had reached out and, slowly but surely, were pulling it in. Soon it would vanish altogether, devoured by the multitude of woodlice and beetles that scuttled in and out of the rot.

The two-storied cottage that the sign referred to lay at the end of the lane and was, itself, showing signs of decay. Six-foot rhododendrons, planted by some well-meaning, but woefully ignorant, previous tenant or owner, encircled it. Nothing grew under their dense foliage except the ubiquitous brambles and ivy that pushed damp, destructive fingers into the brickwork, the window frames and under the corrugated roof, intent on claiming the cottage for their own.

Sufficient space had been roughly hacked through the shrubbery to allow access to the weather-beaten front door but already new growth was edging its way across the gap. The windows, small by design, were made smaller again by the encroaching greenery and let in very little light during the day and at night the cottage was in total darkness. Electricity had been cut off after the departure of the last official tenant over two years before and now there were just a few flickering candles to battle the night.

Edel Johnson sat at one of the windows peering out at the impenetrable darkness, wondering what on earth she was going to do. Wondering if he would really come.

Yesterday morning, at the Inn, all the coffee she had drunk had necessitated a visit to her room. She'd left the sergeant, expecting to be back with him within minutes. She hadn't bothered locking her room when she went for breakfast and, turning the handle, she had opened the door with her mind elsewhere. Her knees had gone weak and she had had to grasp the door for support when she saw Simon, sitting on the bed. She had conjured him out of thin air so often, she thought she had done so again. Then he stood up, and she realised he was real. It was Simon. All six-foot two of him, whole and healthy, standing there, grinning at her. As if nothing had happened. As if she hadn't spent the last three months in anguish, imagining every possible outcome.

Her heart had reacted, the way a heart in love will. She had hugged him, kissed him and filled her eyes with him, feeling her love for him bubbling over. He hadn't changed a bit, maybe a little thinner, maybe a grey hair had sneaked in among the brown, but otherwise, just Simon. She held him close; smelling his scent, allowing herself the luxury of thinking it would all be okay now. Everything would be the way it used to be, and she'd held him even closer, trying to absorb him into the heart of her, back where he belonged.

They had both laughed and begun to talk at the same time.

'You first,' she laughed, sitting on the bed, the laugh fading into confusion as she looked at him. 'Where have you been, what happened to you?'

He sat down briefly, then jumped up again. 'Edel,' his lips curled in the smile she remembered so well, the smile she had searched for in every face the last three months. 'God, I have missed you. I have so much to tell you, but not here. Pack your things and meet me in the car park. We have to get out of here.'

'What?' she cried. 'What are you talking about?' The bubble of relief and pleasure at seeing him burst with a loud bang, leaving confusion, worry and stress fighting for control.

'We have to get out of here,' he said again, his eyes flitting to the door, to the window.

She stood back, looking at him. There was something different about him, a shiftiness that she had never seen before, an unwillingness to meet her eyes. 'We have to get out of here? I don't understand,' she pleaded quietly, suddenly afraid, the ground wobbling precariously under her feet.

He paced the room, running his hand impatiently through his hair. 'Listen, I can't explain now. It was only by luck that I was passing by and saw your car. It's too long a story to tell you now and... well, to be honest, it's not safe here.'

She stood and faced him, reaching out to hold his arm, almost relieved to feel warm flesh. It wasn't a dream. 'I don't understand, Simon. Not safe, why?'

'Oh, for God's sake, will you just do as I ask,' he shouted, brushing her hand away roughly, a frown creasing his forehead. 'We have to get out of here.'

'You don't understand,' she tried to reason with him. 'There's a garda sergeant downstairs, from Ireland. He's... well, interviewing me, I suppose you'd say... I found a dead man, you see, in the churchyard yesterday. He's a garda, Simon; he'll be able to help with whatever it is, whatever trouble you are in.' She reached out, trying to instil some reassurance into her voice. 'You'll be safe now.'

He interrupted angrily, 'No, you fool, you just don't understand, we can't trust anyone, not the gardaí, not anyone.' He took a deep breath and continued in a calmer voice. 'Listen, love, we need to get out of here. When we are safe, I'll tell you everything and then you'll understand. Trust me. I love you, remember.'

He reached out and took her into his arms. She rested her head against his chest, hearing the reassuring thump of his heart. 'I do trust you,' she said, ignoring the voice of doubt that hammered in her head. Of course, she trusted him. She loved him; they were back together where they belonged. Everything would be all right now. It took less than a minute to throw her belongings back into the holdall and she was ready to go.

Simon opened the bedroom door quietly, listened and then shut it. 'I have a car in the car park, right beside yours. Give me a minute and then follow quickly, okay?'

She watched him go and then, calculating how much she owed for her stay, she withdrew sufficient cash from her purse, holding it in one hand with her room key. Making her way down the stairs, she cast an apprehensive glance at the dining room door then made her way to the bar where she was in luck, the landlady took her key and cash without question and she made a dash for the car park.

Simon had his engine running already and his car started to move toward the exit when he saw her. Throwing her bag onto the passenger seat and putting the car into gear, she followed.

They drove for what seemed to be miles, up and down narrow and narrower country roads and lanes. She indicated when he indicated, turned when he turned. Finally, she saw his indicator light flash again and she followed his car down an even narrower lane lined with high hedges that brushed the sides of the car as she passed.

Suddenly his car stopped. She pulled up behind him, opened her car door slowly and got out, looking on in amazement as Simon seemed to disappear into a large shrub. He moved back into sight, beckoned to her and she realised there was a building lurking behind it. She grabbed her bag and holdall, took a deep steadying breath and followed him.

He stood at the doorway holding a nasty-looking bramble out of the way with one hand. Seeing her, he pushed it back behind the branch of a rhododendron, winding it around to stop it springing back. 'Dreadful things, brambles,' he commented calmly.

Inside the cottage was dark and damp. Her eyes wide, she watched as he lit a number of candles that were scattered about and put a match to a fire that had been set. It was obvious from his self-congratulatory smile that he thought he'd created a cosy atmosphere; but the candles threw huge shadows on the grubby, white walls and illuminated large spider's webs, while the struggling fire hissed and crackled, too small to warm the room and too smoky to provide much additional light. Her nose crinkled at the combined odour of smoky damp and candle wax as her eyes peered into the gloomy corners wondering if there were mice. She regretted not wearing boots, she could have tucked her jeans in and felt a little safer.

'It'll warm up soon,' Simon said heartily, refusing to look in her direction. He poked another log into the spluttering fire sending sparks shooting into the room. They landed on the damp wooden floor and quickly fizzled out.

'Simon,' she started and stopped, horrified to hear the pathetic pleading note in her voice.

He rose from the fire and came to her, ignoring her evident distaste and distress. 'I'll show you the bedroom,' he said and took the holdall from her stiff fingers. Without another word he headed up the stairs, her bag in one hand and a flickering candle in the other.

Reluctantly, she followed him. Cobwebs hung from the handrail, and each step of the stairs creaked ominously as they climbed. It was ghastly and macabre and she wanted to cry as the fear she had managed to dismiss earlier returned to squeeze her heart until she could feel it thumping.

He led her into a small bedroom and lit a number of other candles from the one he held, turning to her with a smile. 'It's not the Ritz,' he said, with an understatement that took her breath away, 'but the bed is comfortable and once you're under the duvet, you'll be nice and cosy. Don't forget to blow out the candles before you go to sleep though. These wooden beams,' he pointed up into the gloom where the outline of beams draped with a lacework of webs could be seen, 'they'd go up like tinder.'

'Simon,' she said and this time she persevered, her voice stronger. 'What is going on? What are we doing in this... this...' she looked around in despair, '...this awful place?'

He was still holding her bag and he swung it onto the bed, expending more energy than it required, the bag bouncing and landing on the floor. He left it there and turned to her, annoyance shading his face.

'You've had it so soft all your bloody life, Edel,' he sneered unattractively. 'There's nothing wrong with this place. It's clean and warm enough if you make some effort. I've been here the best part of three months and I've survived.'

He picked up her bag and put it back on the bed, looking at her from the corner of his eye as she registered what he had said.

It took a moment. 'You've been here the whole time?' was all she could manage and she leaned against the bed, needing the support. 'You've been here the whole time,' she repeated, her voice rising as she assimilated the fact. 'While I have been out of my mind with worry, while I have had the guards questioning me, and neighbours doubting me, you've been here?'

He came around the bed to her and tried to take her into his arms but she knocked his hands away. 'Listen, I can explain–'

'Well explain,' she interrupted angrily. 'Go on. How can you explain disappearing for three months? Not a word. Not a phone call. Nothing.'

He sighed heavily and reached for her, quickly dropping his hands at her warning look. 'I did leave you a message,' he explained with a shrug. 'I expected you at The Inn months ago.'

'Message?' She almost shrieked in angry frustration. 'You mean that scrap of paper you put in my pocket? I didn't get it until yesterday.'

Annoyance flickered again, hardening in his eyes. 'I did wonder why you hadn't come. I put it in that jacket you wore all the time, that yellow one; you should have found it after I left.' His face took on an accusing look, quick to blame her. 'I waited two weeks at The Inn for you.'

Wind rattled the windowpane, startling them both. 'You waited...?' Edel cried. 'You vanished. I haven't worn that jacket since then. I have just wondered, waited and worried every day; always expecting a knock on the door to tell me they'd found your body. Why didn't you ring me when I didn't come?'

The shifty look she had seen earlier returned. 'I can explain,' he said, looking at his watch. 'But not now, I have to meet someone. It's important.'

She glared at him in disbelief. 'You have to meet someone? You must be joking! Nothing,' she said, rising anger replacing every other emotion, 'nothing is more important than explaining to me what is going on.'

The wind howled again and a draught from the window made the candles flicker, causing shadows to chase across the room. For a brief moment, one lingered on Simon's face and now, it wasn't fear she felt, it was spine-tingling terror.

He smiled but his smile held little warmth. 'Later, I promise. I'll tell you everything later. I have to meet this man. Then... well, then we should be able to get back to normal. I promise. I'll have things sorted and be able to tell you everything and,' he added hesitantly, 'I hope you'll understand.' He looked beseechingly at her, as if anticipating a difficulty with either the telling or the understanding. 'I know you will,' he said more determinedly. He moved closer to her and put a finger under her chin, forcing her to look at him.

'Marrying you was the best thing I ever did, Edel.' This time there was warmth in his smile. 'Ever,' he repeated. 'I wanted you from the first moment we met, when you bumped into me. I knew then you were everything I had always wished for.'

This was, once more, the man she loved, his words effectively dampening down the anger and the fear. 'Oh Simon,' she said, taking a step closer to him, desperately wanting his arms around her again.

He put his finger gently on her lips, stopping her. 'I have to go. We'll get through this, I promise, and if I have to spend the rest of my life trying to make you understand, trying to make it up to you, I will. Just for now, remember I love you.' Leaning in, he kissed her gently on the lips.

Then he was gone.

Edel waited a moment and then, with a cry ran after him. She couldn't let him go like that. Not without telling him that she loved him too; not without telling him that, of course, she would understand, whatever it was he had to tell her, whatever it was he had done. They could sort things out, they could do anything. What was there to understand?

'Simon, wait,' she shouted, hurrying down the stairs, hearing a car door slam as she pulled the front door open and stepped outside in time to see her car being driven away at speed. She stood there, seeing the lights flicker on and off in the gloom like some unknown Morse code as the car negotiated the twists and turns of the road.

Leaves rustled around her feet, blown by gentle winds that were the precursor of the storm to come and a distant relation to the menacing clouds that hovered with intent over the cottage. She eyed them with rising anxiety, suddenly realising that Simon hadn't mentioned what time he would return. A shiver ran through her, causing her skin to prickle with goosebumps and the fear to spark back into life.

Turning back to the cottage, she eyed it with disfavour. How incredibly ugly it was. The roof had probably once been thatched but some misguided or uncaring person had replaced it with a corrugated roof that sat on the cottage's four walls like an ill-fitting toupee. The two downstairs windows were small and, oddly, set at different heights, as if the builder had put the second window in as an afterthought, not bothering with something as foolish as symmetry. She knew there was at least one upstairs window, there may have been more but she couldn't see past the bramble and ivy.

It didn't matter, ugly as it was, she had no choice but to go back inside. Gritting her teeth, she ducked under the rhododendron and bramble arch and shut the door behind her. She looked around the dank, miserable room with a lump in her throat and wondered how much worse her day could get.

10

Edel had told Sergeant West that her life had turned into an Agatha Christie novel, but that was yesterday. Today, it felt more like a Stephen King novel, with the obligatory isolated cottage, no electricity, a dying fire, huge cobwebs and, she glanced around anxiously, probably huge spiders. At least, there was no dead body to contend with. It was an attempt at humour that misfired as she realised, she couldn't be sure of that. She hadn't, after all, seen all the rooms yet. Who knew what waited in them?

'Great,' she said aloud, feeling that flicker of fear flame a little higher as her voice echoed in the near empty room. 'I'm doing a marvellous job of scaring myself witless.' It was hard to believe he'd been here all this time; she couldn't even begin to wonder what it was that had happened.

She sat in the only chair in the gloomy room, the chill settling in around her, adding to her discomfort as the darkness intensified. Moving the chair closer to the fire, she tried to draw some heat and comfort from it as she mulled over her brief time with Simon. It seemed she had been right; he had been forced to go missing by some unknown circumstances.

When he explained what had happened, she would under-stand, they could put all this behind them and get back to their real life. She would understand. After all, how bad could it be?

A soft hiss came from the fire and she regarded its death throes with alarm. If it went out, it would get very, very cold. 'Don't do this to me,' she entreated, her voice echoing around the room. She jumped up and, holding a candle high, looked frantically for more logs. There were none inside but she remembered seeing some outside close to where she had parked her car. Eyeing the dying fire, she knew she had to go out and bring some in.

The door opened with a scary-movie screech and she looked out in horror. There was only dense blackness beyond the door-frame, the jaws of death couldn't be any darker. Fear leapt into her throat, almost choking her. Stepping back quickly, she shut the door, turned the key in the lock and leaned against it. She wasn't afraid of *normal darkness,* but that emptiness outside, that lack of everything as though nothing existed now outside the cottage. Bloody hell, she wasn't going out there.

Definitely more Stephen King than Agatha Christie, she laughed shakily, trying to regain some self-control. If she'd just brought some wood in earlier instead of sitting there like an idiot, feeling sorry for herself. She shivered as she imagined the wildlife and insects scurrying around in the shadows of the woodpile. She'd prefer the cold. Pulling her jacket tighter, she tucked her hands up the sleeves and sat reviewing her situation. Tired, cold, hungry and scared. And angry, yes, definitely angry. Where the hell had Simon gone?

Her mind wandered over the last couple of hours, analysing every word. None of it made sense. She frowned. He had been here all the time, why on earth couldn't he have rung her? She told him she would understand, but she knew it would take a lot of explaining. She looked around the room and shivered. A hell of a lot of explaining.

She sighed and the sound echoed eerily; stood and the floorboards creaked loudly. With a gulp, she made her way across the darkened room to the stairway and peered up. It was too dark to see anything. The candles Simon had lit must have blown out. She reached for the wall, pulling her hand back in horror and biting her lips to contain the shriek when her fingers felt something soft. Probably just a spider's web, she reassured herself as she retreated and sat to look at the now critically ill fire. She sat unmoving, elbows resting on her knees, hands cupping her face, feeling choking tears forming. Resolutely, she tried to think of something positive or, at least, something different.

She wondered how long Sergeant West had waited in the dining room before he got suspicious about her absence. It brought a quick wicked smile to her face. She'd bet he was pissed off and wondered if she would ever get the chance to explain, if he would even listen. Suddenly, in the silence, the sound of a car in the distance made her jump up and rush to the door, unlocking it and pulling it open. *He was back*. Relief surged through her and she waited expectantly, peering into the darkness, trying to catch a glimpse of approaching beams. But there was nothing to be seen, the sound faded and the heavy silence enveloped her again.

Shutting the door, she gave in to a moment's despair, leaned her forehead against the door and wondered again what she was supposed to do. She had her mobile with her but, for the second time in as many days, she realised there was nobody to phone. How foolish she had been to lose touch with friends. When this was all over, she resolved to build bridges, mend fences, break down walls, whatever construction term was suitable, to change things in the future. But that wasn't going to help her now.

She sat back in the extremely uncomfortable chair and, as

she did so, one of the candles that held back the impenetrable darkness sputtered and died. Two more followed in quick succession causing her to jump up with a yelp. Four candles remained but all, she realised quickly, were in the latter stages of life.

'Idiot, idiot, idiot,' she berated herself. Hastily, she blew all but one of the candles out while she frantically searched the meagrely furnished room for more. She quelled the rising panic when she found none, but discovered a door to the rear of the room, which on opening led into a tiny, cluttered kitchen. She put the candle down on the cooker top, the only free surface available, and looked around in distaste. It was not only cluttered and untidy but incredibly dirty; what wasn't covered in dust was layered in grime. She was beginning to find it increasingly difficult to merge the memories of her glamorous, sophisticated husband with the man who would live in such squalor, a man who would abandon her in such a place.

Had she a more active imagination, she could almost have believed he was an imposter, an evil twin or something equally ridiculous. But she knew beyond doubt, he was her husband, Simon. It was his smile she saw, when she went into the bedroom at The Inn, his arms that held her, his smell, his kiss. She banged a cupboard door, shutting away the clutter and pushing away memories.

She had to find candles.

Her mind was instantly focused when the candle she had brought into the kitchen began to sputter. She ran back and grabbed one of the other candle ends and quickly lit it from the faltering flame. For a frantic second, she thought she'd left it too late, the candles seemed reluctant to cooperate. With a soft hiss the first candle died just as the second, petulantly, took up the flame. With a sigh of relief, galvanised by the near calamity, she opened and searched cupboards and drawers, giving a longer sigh moments later when she opened a drawer full of candles. Matches too, she noted with relief, putting a box into her pocket.

Back in the main room, she pulled her chair closer again to the fireplace and lit a couple of new candles in an attempt to brighten, if not warm the room. She shivered as she watched the fire splutter and die. There were two choices available to her. To go out and get some firewood or go up to bed and climb under the duvet. She contemplated for a moment or two a third choice of bringing the duvet down and staying in her chair but then she thought of mice, and of mice scurrying up and under the duvet from the floor, and she shivered.

The storm clouds she had seen earlier were making themselves felt now and the wind hurled rain against the windows. The cold was beginning to seep into her bones and she knew she had to decide. She was hungry too. Heading back to the kitchen, she sniffed an open milk bottle, drawing back hurriedly at the rancid smell. Undeterred, she opened the cupboards again, searching this time for something to eat. 'Eureka,' she said, puffing mist into the cold air as she discovered tins of soup. She turned with determination to the cooker. Surely, if he had soup, he had a way to heat it. She was right and the gas cooker worked at the turn of a knob. With a crow of pleasure, she turned on all four rings and searched for a can opener and saucepan. The gas flames soon made inroads in the chilly air of the kitchen and Edel tucked into two tins of hot and tasty soup. She ate it straight from the saucepan, with a huge serving spoon she had found in a drawer, choosing to ignore the food-encrusted bowls and cutlery lying in the sink.

Feeling warm and with her hunger satisfied, it was easier to make a decision. She'd go up to bed, at least she would be warm, she might get some sleep and, she decided a bit fatalistically, she might need a clear head in the morning. Switching off the cooker, she put several candles into a bag and went back into the main room. She kept one candle lit, extinguished the others and walked in the small circle of light up the stairs to the room she had been in earlier.

As she reached the top of the stairs, she noticed there were two other doors. She dropped the bag of candles onto the bed and, because she knew she couldn't settle until she had, explored the other rooms. One door led to a small, old-fashioned, exceedingly dirty bathroom and the other to a second bedroom strewn with boxes and bags. She laughed as she realised she had been holding her breath. 'Did you really expect to find a dead body?' she asked herself with a shake of her head, her voice echoing in the room. Or should she say another dead body? She gave a ghoulish giggle.

She used the bathroom facilities, washing her hands and face in the icy water that gurgled with a marked lack of haste from the taps and drying them on the end of her shirt rather than the stiff, exceedingly grubby towel that hung from a nail on the back of the door. Returning to the bedroom, she was grateful to see a key in the lock and turned it decisively, hearing the click with relief.

The room was small and untidy, there were no curtains on the one small, dirty window and the floorboards were bare. But the bed, Edel saw with relief, was relatively new. Or at least not ancient, she amended on closer examination when she had lit a few candles and positioned them around the room. The sheets were grubby and stained but the duvet was a heavy feather one that promised warmth. She hesitated a moment. Even fully clothed, she couldn't bring herself to climb between those sheets. She stripped the bed, flung the sheets and pillowcases into a corner of the room and, removing only her shoes, climbed onto the bed wrapping the duvet around her. Soon, she was snug and cosy, listening to the escalating storm swirl rain and wind against the windows and roof. She had left two candles burning and their flames flickered in numerous draughts causing shadows to dance across the ceiling and walls. With hunger and cold dispelled, and feeling secure behind the locked door, she suddenly realised, to her surprise, that she felt more relaxed than she had in a long time.

Unravelling herself from the duvet's warmth, she clambered from the bed and extinguished the candles. As crazy as her life was, she had no intention of setting fire to herself. Back in bed, buried once more in warmth, she gave a sudden chuckle, her life had become so fantastic, so completely bizarre, it seemed unreal. 'Ridiculous,' she whispered into the night. 'My life has become ridiculous.'

The rain on the corrugated roof was incredibly noisy. She'd never sleep through it. Anyway, she was waiting for Simon to come home. She couldn't sleep until he did. On that final thought, her eyes closed and sleep, reluctant at first, claimed her for the night.

11

The storm, as storms do, exhausted itself overnight and departed, leaving behind a crystal clear blue sky. The morning was cold but the sun hinted at warmth to follow and the birds sang their pleasure and ate the insects unwise enough to venture forth. All around the cottage lay the evidence of the storm; leaves and small branches littering the laneway, bluebells flattened. The air had that wonderful clean, rich, after-the-storm smell.

Edel took a deep breath when she opened the cottage door, the early morning sun making her squint. She looked around with unexpected pleasure. What a lovely morning. To her surprise, she had slept incredibly well, and had awoken refreshed and ready to face whatever Simon had to tell her. Whenever he returned. Why hadn't he come back last night? The pleasure in the morning dimmed in the face of rising anxiety.

One thing was certain, she was definitely not spending another night here. Turning back to the kitchen, she decided, for want of anything better, to have soup again for breakfast. She would kill for a cup of coffee. She sighed as she put the soup in the same saucepan she had used the previous evening.

After her makeshift breakfast, her restlessness took her for a walk up the laneway to the road. Walking briskly along, she appreciated how isolated the cottage was. It was the only dwelling on it, the lane ending in the woods just behind. She saw no other houses or even buildings in the distance. The road at the end was, she guessed, only a very minor one and she wondered exactly where she was. She had followed Simon up and down so many roads they could be several miles away from The Inn or only a couple.

Turning back, she noticed an old road sign on the laneway, held together with bramble and ivy. Reaching carefully through the bramble, but still managing to get scratched by vicious thorns, she pushed enough ivy out of the way to read the name. 'Hedgesparrow Lane,' she read aloud. She stepped back, examining and quickly dismissing the bramble scratches, and said in amusement, 'Hedgesparrow Lane. Goodness, it sounds like something from a Winnie-the-Pooh novel.'

She headed back to the cottage but the walk hadn't relieved her restlessness. How much longer would she have to wait? And what would she do if Simon didn't turn up? 'He will,' she said, trying to reassure herself but failing miserably. Her good mood was proving to have a short life. What did he do here for three months, she wondered, and then decided to see if she could find answers in the cottage. She had only a moment's indecision, torn between the need to know and the fear of what she would find. The ethical considerations she dismissed; a man who vanished for three months didn't deserve any. She started opening letters, and sifting through papers and anything else she could find.

Most of the papers she found in the living room were the mundane detritus of modern living; bank statements, credit card bills, store card statements. All of the paperwork was in the name of Simon Johnson. Looking through statements, she was amazed at how many store cards he had, one for almost every store she could think of. Some of them were final demands, the red writing standing out. She was shocked at how much he owed as she swiftly, and very roughly, calculated that he owed about twenty-five thousand on store cards alone. Looking at his credit card statements, for three different cards, she added another thirty thousand to the total. 'Fifty-five thousand euro,' she gasped. Was this why he vanished? Why didn't he tell her? They could have paid these off with the money from the sale of her house.

A million things ran through her mind, as she sat with the statements in her hand. Was she such a terrible wife that she hadn't realised her husband was in trouble? She didn't care what it was; they could have sorted it out together. What kind of a person was she, that he hadn't come to her and asked for help? Was running away and living in this squalor preferable? She tried to remember if there were signs that she just didn't see, or worse, saw but ignored. But she couldn't remember anything untoward.

She glanced through the statements again, confused. He earned good money. How could he have built up such a debt? She picked up the nearest statement, a store card for that wonderful Armani shop in London. She remembered going into it with Simon before Christmas and persuading him to buy a trench coat. 'The one you have is getting a little worn,' she had said, and he had needed no more persuasion. Was it really twenty-five hundred? She cringed as she read on. Had he really spent another two thousand on shirts, jeans and socks?

She picked up a credit card bill, and saw with horror how much a recent weekend away had cost. Did they really need to drink two bottles of champagne at two hundred and fifty euro a bottle? In fact, she wondered, as she skimmed through his credit card bills, did they drink anything else apart from incredibly expensive champagne?

Another glance at the statements showed her that he rarely paid more than the interest each month. 'I don't understand,' she muttered. 'He *had* a good income, didn't he?' A bolt hit her, and she sat back on her ankles in sudden shock. She had absolutely no idea how much he earned. She had always just assumed, from his expensive clothes and lifestyle, that he earned good money. That irritating expression about *assume* came to mind, *it makes an ass out of u and me* – had she been an ass?

Leaving the bills on the chair, she headed up to the second bedroom, where she had seen boxes and bags the night before. Despondent now, she opened boxes carelessly. The first box held sheets and pillowcases still in their shop wrapping. The second held a quantity of clothes neatly folded. The first bag she opened appeared to hold dirty laundry and she hastily closed it with a grimace of disgust. She had had enough. Simon was in debt, that was all it was about; she could cope with that.

Closing the door behind her, she went back to the first bedroom where she lay glumly on the bed for a long time, trying not to think. She tried so hard she felt a headache taking over, slowly pounding to a crescendo. Struggling to her feet, she searched for her bag and, finding it, fumbled inside for a moment before fishing out some paracetamol. She headed to the bathroom to get a drink to swallow them but, passing the wardrobe, some inexplicable urge, an unexplained sense of dread made her stop and then, of course, she just couldn't go on until she had looked inside.

She put her hand on the handle and pulled the door open. Inside, hanging innocently, were Simon's clothes.

Idiot! Her head pounding, she started to close the door when she saw a briefcase on the bottom and pulling it out, she took it downstairs. She dropped it beside the chair while she went to the kitchen for a drink, tossing the pills back with one mouthful of icy water.

Back in the living room, she stood looking at the briefcase but she couldn't face opening it with her head pounding as it was. She dragged herself back up the stairs and lay down again, shielding her eyes from the light with her hand, and waited till the hammering in her head eased to a bearable thump. As the pain eased, her sense of dread grew disproportionately large. The briefcase, there was something in the briefcase. She didn't know what, she didn't know how she knew, but she knew she was going to find something terrible inside.

She sat up slowly, holding her head stiffly, waiting for the pounding to resume. When it didn't, she relaxed, stood up and stretched. The bedroom window looked over the front of the house – she glanced out, part of her hoping to see Simon arriving and part of her hoping he wouldn't arrive, not yet. Determinedly, despite her fear of whatever lay inside, she headed down, opened the briefcase and emptied it. It had been jammed full and the contents formed a pile that slid to the floor in a puddle around her feet. Kneeling down among them, she picked up the first sheet of paper. Another credit card statement, she saw in despair – how many did he have?

There was only a few thousand on this one, she saw with an element of relief, which quickly turned to puzzlement when she realised the statement was not in Simon's name at all but in the name of Cyril Pratt.

'The name he used at The Inn,' she muttered, putting the paper to one side and picking up the next. Another statement in the same name, but dated the month before he vanished. It took several more statements for her to realise that Simon had been using the name, Cyril Pratt, for a long time. Before he met her, she realised in amazement, noting the date on the last one she picked up. Most of the rest of the papers were correspondence with people she had never heard of; some seemed work-related. She started to pile the rest back into the briefcase, having become quickly disillusioned with amateur detective work, when a photo appeared amongst the letters. She picked it up with curiosity, half expecting it to be one of her.

It was a studio shot, well-lit and artistically arranged, of a heavily made-up, attractive woman, a handsome man and two adorable children. She recognised the handsome man as her husband, but the woman wasn't her, and the two adorable children... she could feel her heart struggling not to break... well, the two adorable children obviously belonged to the handsome man and the unknown woman. She turned the photo over and read the date. Two years ago. She could taste the bitterness, thick on her tongue. So, she had been right, there was something terrible in the briefcase; the truth. Whoever it was who had said truth was beauty, well, they didn't know anything; truth was ugly, ugly, ugly.

She collapsed in the chair and wept. She hadn't wept when Simon vanished. And she hadn't wept when he had left her alone last night in this god-forsaken cottage. So she wept for all the lies and the deceit, for dreams destroyed, a future jeopardised. Hot tears of rage and frustration, quick tears of pity and sorrow because she really didn't know what to do, or who to trust.

When the tears stopped, exhaustion took hold and she sat on that uncomfortable chair so long she was stiff when she eventually stood. 'What to do, what to do?' she muttered, wringing her hands and pacing the room like one of Macbeth's witches. Then, as if released from a spell, she moved.

Running up the stairs, she threw her few belongings into her holdall and, slamming the door after her, she headed for her car, almost without thinking, before remembering that Simon had taken it. Swearing in frustration, she went to his. It wasn't locked and, typical of Simon, he had left the keys in the ignition. She turned the key and then realised why Simon had taken her car, his engine was dead.

So, she was stuck here. She banged her clenched hands down on the steering wheel in anger before getting out of the car and looking around. She could walk, but where to and how far was it to anywhere? All she remembered from the journey were miles of narrow winding roads and innumerable turns. She didn't remember seeing houses on the way, and there were certainly none to be seen around the cottage.

Checking her watch, she was horrified at the time. She should have left that morning when Simon hadn't returned. It was too late to go anywhere now; she was going to be stuck here again for another night.

Her headache, which had retreated to a dull throb, turned up the volume and tempo and she rummaged hurriedly in her bag for more paracetamol. In her panic, she couldn't find any and, in exasperation, she emptied the contents of her bag onto the chair, breathing a sigh of relief when she saw the familiar blue box. She picked up the packet, popped two pills into her hand and headed to the kitchen for a drink.

Returning, she picked up her bag and began stuffing the contents back inside. A torn piece of card caught her eye and she picked it up. Quickly, she found its partner and stood for a moment holding the two pieces in her hand. It seemed like aeons ago. *Keep it anyway, just in case,* the sergeant had said. She had torn it up and almost thrown it away and now here it was when she was desperate. Karma, she wondered with a faltering smile. She looked at it for a moment, remembering his intelligence and his obvious... she searched for a word... decency, she decided.

Then she remembered abandoning him without explanation. It didn't seem quite so amusing to her now. He would have been understandably incensed. She felt a twinge of guilt. Would he understand? For some reason beyond her comprehension, she thought he might.

Again, she faced the depressing truth. She really had no one else to turn to. Oh yes, she had learned her lesson, she was going to change. When life returned to some semblance of order. When she faced the reality of returning to her life before Simon. Simon... had he ever loved her? Had he?

Her breath caught on a sob and she shook herself. She refused to go there. Shaking her head, she reached into her bag for her mobile, relieved to see it was still charged and grateful to see that, despite the isolation, she had a strong signal. Nervously, she punched in Sergeant West's number with unsteady fingers, cursing when she misdialled and had to start again. Finally, she heard the ring tone.

12

The journey back to Cornwall was quick and uneventful but it was still nearly midnight before Sergeant West turned his car down Hedgesparrow Lane. Nothing much surprised him these days, but the call from Edel certainly had. He had been so stunned to hear her voice asking for help that he had dropped the phone and had to scrabble in the footwell to pick it up, explaining the commotion to her as a difficulty with the signal.

The conversation had been short. She asked for help, he agreed, and here he was, almost unbelievably, in the wilds of Cornwall again. He had rung Andrews on the way to Dublin airport.

'You're joking,' Andrews had said in disbelief. 'Inspector Duffy will hit the roof.'

West manoeuvred his car into a parking space and, grabbing his bag, jumped out still explaining, or at least trying to. 'I'll give the inspector a ring in the morning, Peter, don't panic. Meanwhile, have to go. Have a plane to catch.'

No doubt Andrews would be wondering if he'd lost his marbles and, unfortunately, he'd bear the brunt of Inspector

Duffy's annoyance in the morning. Then West remembered he was going to Cork first thing and smiled. Duffy would be chewing at the bit and the only person he could take it out on would be Sergeant Clarke. Couldn't happen to a better person.

Hours later, he stopped at the end of a narrow lane. The headlights of the rental car picked out a building partially submerged in a tangle of overgrown shrubs. It looked to him like a building that had been abandoned a long time ago and for a moment he thought the satnav had led him astray. He checked but it said the same thing, *you have reached your destination.*

There was a car parked but it wasn't the one Edel had been driving, and it looked as abandoned as the house. He peered out, looking for some sign of life but saw none. Finally, in frustration, he opened the glove compartment, searching for the flashlight the car came equipped with. Leaving the engine running, he got out of the car to investigate further but, just as he did, he heard the creak of a door and Edel appeared from the middle of the shrub. She raised her hand and stepped forward into the circle of light thrown by the car's headlights.

'There's no electricity, I'm afraid,' she said by way of greeting, pointing back to the darkness of the cottage where he could now see a faint glimmer of light through the ivy cloaked window.

In the relatively poor light of the car, West could see she looked more drawn and haggard than the day before. Her clothes, the same ones she was wearing the previous day, were creased and decidedly grubby. Lank, greasy hair was scraped back into a severe ponytail with what looked like a piece of twine. Although she hadn't struck him as the tearful type, her eyes were red-rimmed and swollen, as though she had cried all the saved-up tears of months.

She stood clasping and unclasping her hands, waiting for him to speak, shivering slightly in the cool night air.

They stood for a moment longer, each weighing the other up.

He was surprised he wasn't angry, after all, this woman had run out on him, made him the butt of jokes at the station. Embarrassed and humiliated him. He reached into the car and turned off the engine. The headlights dimmed and he spoke at last. 'They'll go out in a minute; we'd better get inside.'

She turned back to the cottage, leading the way through the foliage-festooned door, holding back a particularly long, barbed bramble that sprang back as she tried to fix it out of the way. West took it from her gingerly, reaching up and looping it over a branch that overhung the door, cursing as the bramble took its revenge.

Sucking on the bloody scratch at the base of his thumb, he crossed the threshold into the cottage, a look of disgust written clearly across his handsome face. The smell hit him first, damp and something... rodents, maybe? He wasn't sure he wanted to know. The log fire added to the problem, the damp logs giving off more smoke than flame and the small amount of heat intensifying the unpleasant smell. He was determined not to spend more than a minute inside.

'You spent last night here?' he asked in astonishment. 'This is a hovel. Why on earth did you leave The Inn to come here?' He waited for her answer, watching as she moved to sit in the solitary chair and clasped her arms around herself. It seemed to be half in comfort, half to ward off the chill that the smoky fire did little to dispel.

'It's a long story,' she said.

He looked around the room grimly. It wasn't a place to listen to long stories.

Edel tilted her head and looked at him. 'Simon said I was being precious when I condemned it. It is pretty awful, isn't it?'

His eyebrows rose at the mention of her husband's name but

he said nothing. He took in the paltry cheap chair, the inadequate fire and sputtering candles. 'Pretty damn awful,' he agreed with a slight smile. 'You've a lot to tell me, I think, but I don't fancy hearing it here.'

She nodded and waited for him to continue.

'I rang the landlord at The Inn on the way here. He has rooms available and agreed to stay open until we get there. It's not far really, about four miles. Get your things, you can fill me in when we get there. Okay?'

She indicated her bags on the floor. 'I'm ready to go.' With a grim expression on her face, she pointed to the briefcase lying beside them. 'I think you'll need to take that, there are some papers and things...'

Hearing in her voice more than she knew, he grabbed the briefcase, brought it out to the car and locked it into the boot. Back in the cottage, he checked the fire, guessed it would soon burn itself out, and extinguished the remaining candles as Edel picked up her bags. 'Let's go,' he said gently, and he shut the door of the cottage behind them.

Concentrating on the twists and turns of the road back to Come-to-Good, he had little time to consider the implications of what she had said. He pulled up in The Inn's car park and parked in the exact spot he had done before, in what felt like weeks ago but, in fact, was only two nights. He sighed. He had done far too much travelling in too short a space of time and he was bone tired. Almost reluctantly, he stepped out of the car, trying to delay the start of what would, he presumed, be a long and complicated conversation.

He heard the passenger door open and turned to watch Edel. She too stood wearily, leaning for a moment against the car. Events certainly seem to have cowed her; he felt more sympathy than was healthy in his position. He gave himself a mental kick and opening the boot, ignored the briefcase and took out his overnight bag. With a glance at her, he turned and headed for the door, leaving her to follow in his wake.

Paul Murphy, the landlord, commonly called Murphy by all and sundry including his wife, was polishing the last of a pile of glasses. West saw curiosity flicker across his face when he saw them. But he was a good landlord, and West guessed he'd seen his fair share of oddities over the years so rather than ask what they were up to he tilted a pint glass at him in silent invitation.

He shot him a look of sheer gratitude. 'A pint of whatever you recommend would go down well,' he said.

'Good evening, miss,' Murphy said, pulling the pint. 'What can I get you? Glass of wine?'

'Perfect.' Edel smiled slightly and moved over to a seat near the glowing embers of the fire.

West waited at the bar as Murphy topped off the pint and filled a large wine glass from an open bottle in the fridge. 'You have the same rooms as you had last time,' Murphy informed the sergeant, handing him two keys. 'You're welcome to stay in the lounge as long as you wish. Throw some more logs on the fire, if you need to. And,' he added, 'if you want another drink, help yourself. You can settle up in the morning. There's nobody else staying tonight, you won't be disturbed.' With a final wave, Murphy called a *goodnight* to Edel and left.

West took their drinks over and sat in the seat opposite her. Outside, he could hear the wind picking up. It was going to be another stormy night; he hoped it would be clear by the morning. He threw another couple of logs on the fire, took a long drink of his beer and sat back with a sigh.

He watched Edel for a moment as she hugged her glass of wine. 'Well?' he asked, too tired to provide foreplay for what was bound to be a long story.

'Where do I start?' she asked, her voice suddenly thick with tears.

He started to say 'the beginning' but, hesitated and surprised himself by asking instead, 'Why did you run away yesterday?'

She looked at him, a pleading light in her eyes. 'It wasn't planned, believe me. I really did go up to my room just for a minute but when I got there Simon was there. I was so stunned. He was alive, you have no idea...'

A log spat suddenly, startling them both. West reached forward and poked it further into the fire where it rewarded him with a wave of flame. Resting the poker against the fireplace, he sat back with his beer.

Edel swallowed a large mouthful of wine and continued. 'I told him you were here, you know, but he became very anxious, told me we couldn't trust anyone, not even the gardaí.' She took another sip of her wine and drew a long shaky breath. 'He said he would explain when we got to that terrible cottage.' She shivered at the memory. 'As soon as we arrived, he told me he had to go. I couldn't believe it. He said he had an important meeting, that he'd explain when he got back.' She gulped noisily, took a mouthful of wine, sniffed and continued. 'I sat and waited. Then it got dark and cold and he didn't come. I had to sleep in that awful place and when I woke, he still hadn't come back. I waited and waited.'

West watched as her lower lip trembled. Tears, women's inevitable weapon. He was strangely disappointed and waited for them to come. But as he did, he saw her sniff, chew on that quivering lip and lift her chin.

'It was the most awful day, so terrible that after a while it began to feel unreal, a page from a book I had read, a scene from a movie.' She put her glass down and looked across the low table at him. 'I didn't know what to do. I discovered, at the last minute, that Simon had taken my car because his had broken down, so I was stuck there. And I really couldn't bring myself to spend another night at that place. When I found your card...

well, I...' Her voice faded from a mixture of embarrassment and guilt.

He sat a moment, a frown between his eyes, trying to digest what he had heard. She wasn't confessing or admitting guilt or complicity. 'Let me get this clear,' he said. 'Are you telling me that you hadn't seen your husband since he was supposed to have vanished three months ago? That you hadn't, in fact, planned the meeting here?'

'No, of course I hadn't. You think I'd have chosen to go to that awful place?'

'You didn't know that Simon Johnson was really a man called Cyril Pratt?'

Edel lifted her glass and drained it. 'Can I have another, please?'

He hissed in annoyance, but went behind the bar and removed the white wine bottle from the fridge. Returning, he filled her glass, left the bottle within reach and sat back expectantly.

'The first time I heard that name was here,' she said quietly. 'I told you about that, didn't I?' She looked to him for confirmation and continued when he nodded. 'I had never heard it before, I swear. Then, when I was hanging around that awful cottage, waiting for Simon to return, I decided to do a little sleuthing of my own and went through his stuff. I found credit card and store card statements for Simon. He owes about fifty thousand euro.' She stopped talking for a long minute and stared into the fire.

'I was shocked and upset that he hadn't told me,' she said. 'Horrified he had run away for that reason, so sad that he hadn't felt able to tell me. I wondered what kind of woman I was that her own husband couldn't trust her to help, and felt so sorry that he'd had to go through all that on his own, that he'd had to live in that terrible place all these months. Oh, yes,' she said bitterly when he sat forward to interrupt, 'he has been there all this time.' She had another drink of her wine, slowly this time, as if to delay the next disclosure till the alcohol numbed the telling.

'When I found the briefcase,' she began hesitantly, 'I knew it would tell me something more. It did.' She gave a short, sad laugh. 'But not what I expected.' Reaching into her pocket, she pulled out the photo she had taken from the briefcase. 'I've looked at this several times while I was waiting for you; examining it in anger, in frustration, in deep, stomach-churning sorrow.' She straightened it out, smoothing the creases, almost caressing the family group it portrayed before handing it over.

He took it and gave the family portrait a brief look, too weary to assume surprise.

She drew a sharp breath. 'You knew?'

'Yes,' he said, putting the photo down on the table between them. 'When you gave me the name yesterday, I had my office run it and they got back to me with the information. That was,' he added pointedly, 'the call I was taking while you were sneaking out the door.' He hesitated a moment, wondering how much to tell her. 'Cyril Pratt used yet another alias to trick Simon Johnson... the real Simon Johnson... into renting him his Cork apartment. He then set about using his name and identity for his own ends. He sublet the apartment and pocketed the two grand a month.'

Edel had drained her glass and sat back, both arms wrapped around herself.

'Perhaps we should stop there?' he suggested, but she shook her head emphatically.

'Please, I need to know,' she said in a whisper, 'please.' She reached for the bottle and filled her glass again.

He shrugged and went on. 'According to our records, Cyril Pratt has been in prison a number of times, mostly for petty crime and extortion, nothing in the last few years. His current marriage is his third. His wife says he works away for long periods.'

He watched her face tighten at the mention of Cyril Pratt's wife and, ignoring the sympathy that was natural to him, he said roughly, 'The night he supposedly vanished we think he went home to her. According to her, he stayed there a few days around that time and she hasn't seen him since. She has, however, had the odd phone call from him and regular money by post. She said that was the way things always were when he was away.'

'So, Simon, or Cyril as I suppose I should call him, is hiding from this man Simon Johnson?'

He looked at her intently. 'Simon Johnson is dead, Edel.'

She sat forward suddenly, putting the wine glass down, wine slopping over the rim, eyes wide. 'Dead,' she cried. West watched as the truth, slowed by the wine she had taken, eventually dawned. 'The dead man? Oh my God, *he* was Simon Johnson?'

He watched her expression change, realisation hitting her hard, her body curling in on itself as it weathered the blows. 'So... did my hus... did Cyril Pratt kill him?'

The fire suddenly sparked loudly again, making both jump and drawing a gasp from Edel. He took the poker and moved the embers around in the fireplace, getting soot on his hands in the process. There was something infinitely soothing about poking a fire, he always lit one in his own place when he could. He sat back on his heels for a moment, relaxing a little in the resurgent flames, allowing his weariness off the tight leash he'd kept it on, for what seemed like hours, and closed his eyes for a nanosecond.

He could feel her eyes on him and turned to say simply, 'I like fires,' before getting up and sitting back into the chair with a sigh. 'We don't know who killed Simon Johnson yet,' he said. 'At the moment, Pratt is just wanted for questioning.' He rubbed his hand over his face wearily. 'He doesn't have any history of violence but there is the matter of where he got the money to buy your house; he didn't get it from Simon Johnson.' He yawned suddenly, quickly covering his mouth with one hand while he waved the other in apology. 'That's all I can tell you at the moment, Edel. All we know, to be honest.'

He rested his head on the wing of the chair, his eyes drifting shut again. The hiss and crackle of the fire was a pleasant lullaby, he could have fallen asleep right there but, then he heard her loud sigh.

'Yesterday, when I saw him again,' she said, 'when I saw him smile at me, I thought everything was going to be all right. I couldn't have been more wrong, could I?'

'That one may smile,' he murmured sleepily, lifting his head and opening his eyes to look at her.

'And smile, and be a villain?' Edel finished the quotation, causing him to raise an appreciative eyebrow. 'I know my Shakespeare. Better, obviously, than I knew the man I married.' She grimaced. 'Perhaps I should be relieved that he is, in fact, not my husband. I take it,' she added, 'he will be charged with bigamy, too? It is still a crime, isn't it?'

'Yes, under Section 57, Offences Against the Person Act. I must admit it is seldom prosecuted unless it is done with intent to defraud.' He stood. 'We will be questioning him on a number of things, it will certainly be one of them. It's one o'clock. We need to get some sleep and make an early start back to Dublin tomorrow.' He hesitated before looking down on her. 'No more running away, eh?'

'I wasn't running away,' she bristled. 'I told you what happened.'

'Okay, okay, we're tired, let's just get some sleep.' He took both glasses and put them on the bar and returned the almost empty wine bottle to the fridge. Opening the door, he waved her through. At her bedroom door, he handed her the key, holding on as she reached for it. For a moment they stood silently, joined by the key, each weighing the other up

'Goodnight, Edel,' West said, releasing the key and turning away, hearing her soft, 'Goodnight, Sergeant' as he opened his bedroom door.

13

West made an early call to Andrews, filling him in on the previous night's events and outlining the plans for the day. He hoped to be back in the office by early afternoon, he told him finally, and rang off as both Edel and a very well-laden plate arrived. He tucked in appreciatively and they breakfasted together in almost companionable silence.

'What happens next?' she said, cradling a coffee cup in her hands.

He looked up from his breakfast in surprise. 'I go back to the station and get on with the investigation and you... well, you go home, and wait until we find Cyril Pratt.'

'My husband, by any other name, or should I say *every other*,' she commented with some bitterness. 'Although, legally, we were never married, so I can't really call him that anymore, can I?' Her eyes widened. 'I've just had a horrifying thought. If I'm not married, the house isn't mine, is it?'

He frowned, putting down his knife and fork. 'Are both your names on the deeds?'

It was her turn to frown. 'I don't know. The purchase all

happened so quickly. I remember signing whatever I was asked to but, to be honest, I never read anything.'

He opened his mouth to ask how she could have been so stupid as to sign something without reading it but there was no point. It was done; damage limitation was needed now, not criticism. 'If both your names are on the deeds, you can argue you have a right to stay in the home as you entered into the relationship in good faith. If your name is not on the deeds, well, then that's a bit of a problem.' He refilled his coffee cup. 'There is the bigger problem of where the money came from. It may need to be repaid. When you get back, get yourself a good solicitor, give him the whole story. If you know where the deeds are, take them with you.'

He finished his coffee and stood. 'We'd better get going. I'll settle up with the landlord and meet you out front in ten minutes.' He waited for her nod of agreement, picked up his bag and headed to where he could hear the landlord chatting to a delivery man.

Tossing his bag into the boot beside Pratt's overfull briefcase, he settled himself behind the steering wheel for another long journey. Minutes passed. Finally, with a hiss of frustration he got out of the car to head in search of her. He had just banged the car door shut when she appeared at the door of the inn with the landlord. He watched as she rose up on her toes to give the much taller Murphy a kiss on the cheek.

When they were both sat in the car, he gave her a quizzical look. 'You told him everything, didn't you?'

'An edited version,' she admitted. 'He deserved an explanation; he's been very kind to me.'

West's Ford started with a diesel growl and he turned out of The Inn's car park onto the narrow main street of Come-to-Good. He predicted making good time, the weather was good and there were no roadworks on his planned route to the airport. Just as he had finished this mental prediction his mobile rang. He slowed, pulled to the side of the road, and stopped. 'West,' he answered and listened. Years of practice had taught him how to acquire a poker face when he needed it, so that a listener couldn't tell if he were hearing good or bad news. He tried hard, too, to resist a sideways glance at the woman sitting so unconcernedly at his side, even while the fingers of one hand white-knuckled on the steering wheel as he muttered an agreement to what he was being told. Hanging up, he kept his eyes averted from Edel who had turned to look at him, an arrested expression on her face. But he couldn't put it off any longer and turned to her. His poker face mustn't have been any good because he saw her eyes widen and her hand moving to cover her suddenly trembling mouth.

'It's Simon, isn't it?' she said. 'Or Cyril, I suppose, to be absolutely correct, maybe I should just refer to him as my husband, although I suppose...' She stopped and slapped a hand over her mouth again, holding it there as tears gathered and started their slow descent. 'Please,' she begged, taking her hand away. 'Just tell me, whatever it is.'

West drew a breath. He had had to give bad news many times, but never before in the too close confines of a car. 'They found your car,' he started gently. He saw that for a minute, she thought that was it, and there was the beginning of relief that it was no more than that, and then the dawning realisation that of course there was more. 'They found the body of a male answering the description of your husband, Edel, I'm sorry.'

Tears ran down her cheeks, but she stayed eerily quiet. 'Do you know, I'd just been thinking of the times we had laughed together; long romantic walks, trips to the theatre, leisurely breakfasts, dining by candlelight; a million moments that were, each of them, precious. And I was thinking, that it didn't matter what name he went by or that we weren't legally married; he was my husband, I loved him and had felt loved by him in return.' She lifted a hand and brushed away the tears. 'Nothing is going to change that; not the things I have found out, nor the law that will dictate that our marriage was void. I married him, missed him and now, I will mourn him.'

He reached over and took her hand. 'I am so sorry for your loss,' he said simply. What more could he say? He held her hand another moment before letting it go and restarting the engine. 'I'm afraid they have asked for you to identify the body. Do you feel up to that?'

'Yes, of course,' she said. 'I need to see him, to say goodbye. What's that overused expression? Oh yes, closure. Isn't that what I'm supposed to look for now? I'll go and see his poor, dead body, get closure and it will all be okay.'

West heard the bitterness lacing her voice and knew the reason. She'd never get the answers she needed now. He bit his lip and looked away.

Her voice was suddenly stronger, sharper. 'I know what you're thinking, Sergeant West, you're thinking you'll never get the answers you want from him, never be able to solve your case now that he is dead. That's all you're worried about now.' Her voice rose as she spoke, growing shrill. Her eyes were filled with anger and hatred as she looked at him.

He considered saying nothing, letting her believe what she wanted. It was mostly grief talking anyway, he knew that. But he couldn't let her believe his only interest was the damn case. 'I was thinking that *you* won't get the answers you wanted, Edel. My case will be ongoing; your husband's death just makes it more complicated, that's all.' His calm, gentle tone of voice seemed to work. He saw the anger and hatred fade as quickly as they'd come, replaced by sadness and weary resignation.

'There's no point in shooting you, is there?' she muttered, then sniffed and searched her bag for a tissue. He indicated the glove compartment; she opened it and pulled out a handful of tissues, rubbing her eyes and blowing her nose. 'It was a car crash, wasn't it? That's why he never came back to the cottage. That's why he didn't come back to me and explain. He drove away from the cottage so fast; I saw the car speeding down those narrow roads, saw the tail lights flashing.' She blew her nose again and gulped. 'He always did drive too fast. I was constantly asking him to slow down. Poor Simon. I've been criticising him, condemning him for not having come back and, all along, he'd been lying injured and dying somewhere.'

She turned away from him, burying her face in the wad of tissues.

'I'll be back in a sec,' he said, getting out and walking out of earshot to make some calls. To his annoyance, he couldn't get hold of Andrews so he was forced to ring Inspector Duffy and fill him in on his late-night dash to Cornwall. He interrupted the inspector's tongue-lashing to tell him of the discovery of Cyril Pratt's body.

'At least, I am here on the spot, Inspector,' he offered. 'He was our main suspect in Simon Johnson's murder. We will need the continued cooperation of the Devon and Cornwall constabulary in order to identify any suspects they may have.' He paused and then offered a very large olive branch. 'I know that is your forte, Inspector, so I would be grateful if you could make some calls.'

Inspector Duffy wasn't immune to flattery and agreed. West, who had learned the hard way to lick ass if he had to, finished the conversation and hung up as quickly as he could before he was asked for an explanation as to why he'd gone careering off to Cornwall in the first place. Duffy would think of it later, be aggrieved that he'd been played and take it out on West in some form. Probably with more damn paperwork or one of his interminable audits. Shaking his head, he tried Andrews' number again, inordinately thankful that it was answered on the second ring and to hear the reassuring Tipperary accent of his partner. 'Peter,' he said quickly, 'Where are you?'

Andrews had just returned to his car after visiting Bareton Industries, and was still in the car park. He turned off the engine. 'Just leaving Bareton Industries, Mike. Something wrong?'

West gave him a quick rundown on the evening and morning's events culminating in the news that Cyril Pratt had been found murdered.

'Bloody hell,' Andrews retorted. 'I only left his wife a couple of hours ago. Do you want me to go back and break the news?'

'No, leave it to the locals, they can handle it. Give them a buzz and fill them in. Devon and Cornwall will probably be in contact with them anyway, if they haven't already. I need you back in Dublin to stop Duffy going ballistic.'

'Great,' Andrews said sarcastically. West chuckled and hung up.

Climbing back into the car, he cast a glance over Edel who appeared calmer. Ignoring her for the moment, he concentrated on turning the car in the narrow road. They had to drive to Falmouth, to the Divisional Headquarters whose morgue now held the body of Cyril Pratt aka Simon Johnson.

'Where did it happen?' she asked, once the car was heading in the right direction. 'I can't get it out of my head, him lying injured, maybe calling for me.' She closed her eyes tightly on the image.

He flicked a look in her direction. There was no point in leaving her with that idea torturing her. 'It wasn't a car crash,' he said. There was no easy way to tell her, as there never was when bad news needed to be told. She was going to find out soon enough. 'Your car was found on the outskirts of Falmouth, yesterday evening. Simon was sitting in the front seat. He had been strangled.'

'He was murdered?' She gave a high-pitched hysterical laugh and wrung her hands together in distress, tears now flowing freely down her face. 'Simon was murdered.' Her voice caught on a cry, a sad sorrowful sound that seemed to echo inside the car.

He threw a glance her way and then with a soft inaudible oath, he pulled the car over again, and parked. Undoing both their seatbelts, without ceremony, he pulled her into his arms where she sobbed against his shoulder. Words were superfluous; he just held her until the sobs became soft snuffles.

With a final gulp she pulled herself away, sitting back in her seat and wiping her face with the quickly disintegrating wad of paper tissue.

West watched her withdrawing into herself, her body instinctively going into self-protection mode. He had seen it too many times to be surprised – shutters and barricades going up; the polite charade of civilised behaviour, the stiff upper lip so beloved of old-fashioned manners. He was never too sure if he didn't prefer the weeping and wailing and gnashing of teeth that were its polar opposite. Holding it all in or letting it all out, why was life lived in extremes? He heard her gulp and clear her throat; now would come the apology. Sorry for being human, for having emotions, for daring to show them in public, in front of a stranger no less, how vulgar. He could almost hear his grandmother's voice echoing in his ear, *boys don't cry, be a man*, when he had fallen and returned with painful, bloody knees looking for comfort that never came. Not from her anyway. His own mother, as if in reaction to her mother's ideology, had cosseted and loved him, cried over him, for him and once, *just once*, with him. His own philosophy was a combination of both his grandmother's stoicism and his mother's compassion; it worked for him.

Once again, however, Edel proved she wasn't going to fit into that round hole he had chosen for her. Instead of an apology, she fastened her seatbelt and blurted out tersely, 'Let's get it over with,' before turning her face to the window and sitting silently until they reached Falmouth.

He parked in the visitor car park outside the mortuary building. The drab old building did nothing to disguise its function. Utilitarian and grey, it fused with the dark storm clouds gathering sullenly behind it. He opened the passenger door and Edel stepped out, her eyes puffy from the constant tears that waited furtively to slip out from under her control like an errant child and wind their way down her cheek. She held onto the door a moment as if clutching onto a solid mass in her shattered world, before she stepped away from it with a look of grim determination held firmly, if precariously, in place.

West, ignoring her first withdrawal, held her elbow in a supportive grip and walked with her to the reception desk, feeling her tremble as they approached it.

'Sergeant West,' he introduced himself to the middle-aged receptionist. 'DI Pengelly is expecting us.'

Experienced and sympathetic, but unfortunately ill-informed, the receptionist looked at the sergeant and then at the pale, distressed lady beside him and jumped to the wrong conclusion. 'I am sorry for your loss, Mrs Pratt,' she said politely, continuing oblivious to her faux pas, 'I'll let DI Pengelly know you're here. Please,' she indicated seating behind them, 'take a seat.'

Edel sat, leaving West to have a discreet word with the receptionist who blushed scarlet and stumbled an apology before looking over to where she sat. He shook his head emphatically before returning to take the seat beside her.

'I'm sorry about that, she should have known.'

'That the dead body in their morgue is a bigamist, how could she have known? I think, Sergeant, I have more to be worried about than a receptionist's well-meaning mistake.' She turned on the uncomfortably hard seat to face him. 'I feel like an imposter and I know I have no reason to, but somewhere, there is a woman with two young children who is being told that her husband is never coming home. A woman who then has to explain to those children, that their father is never coming home.'

One of those annoying tears slipped down and she dashed it angrily away. 'Do you know the worst thing? I hate her.' She shuddered. 'I hate her because she was really married to him, she had his children. I'll never have that. All I am left with is questions.' Her voice, rising sharply as she spoke, failed on a sob and she held her hands over her face.

Unaccustomedly speechless, West was relieved to see the approach of a large-boned, well-fleshed man that he recognised immediately as Detective Inspector Pengelly. He rose to shake his hand, drawing him away as he did so, giving Edel a moment to recover.

They'd met, several years before, at a conference on international crime in London and over the course of the three days had developed a friendship that had survived infrequent meetings. He gave him a quick precis of the case and Edel's part in it. Watching her from the corner of his eye, he saw she had pulled herself together so he turned and introduced her to the detective.

'Detective Inspector Pengelly, this is Cyril Pratt's wife, Edel Johnson,' West said smoothly, determined to avoid any further confusion or embarrassment.

'I'm sorry for your loss, Ms Johnson,' DI Pengelly said in his Cornish burr. 'Are you sure you are able for this?' he asked, looking at her keenly.

'This is something I have to do, Detective Inspector, so perhaps we could just get on with it.'

He didn't appear to take umbrage at the sharp words. 'If you'd like to follow me.' Without further ado, he walked ahead of them, through double doors and on to a room reserved for the purpose.

It was all very straightforward and almost matter-of-fact. West knew they tried to make it as unemotional as possible, as painless as they could; cold, clinical and scientific rather than an emotional maelstrom. He wondered how many railed against the clinical coldness of it all; how many screamed *this is the person I loved* as they tore at their clothes and hair and ran into the cold sterile walls until their bones cracked, shrieking their pain and loss until the echoes joined in the chorus, to bleed, break and lay with their beloved. He knew it would be that way for him, if he ever lost the woman he loved. He knew this despite never having met her.

From the corner of his eye, he watched Edel's rigid body. She seemed to be numb, her face set and cold. It was only when she turned to him that he saw the pain etched in it, the tight line of her mouth, the tear-filled eyes, the tightly clenched fists held stiffly by her side. 'Yes,' she said, and then, lifting her chin, she added firm words of affirmation, each word carefully pronounced. 'That is my husband.'

West escorted her to the visitors' room, a small airless place well supplied with the paraphernalia for making hot drinks, plus a cold-water dispenser. 'I need to have a quick word with the inspector,' he said, as she sank into a chair and rubbed her eyes with a tissue. Filling a glass with cold water, he left it within her reach. 'I won't be long.'

Detective Inspector Pengelly was waiting outside, holding two coffees, one of which he held out. 'Milk, no sugar, I remembered,' he said, and then indicated down the corridor with a jerk of his head. 'We can use an office here. No point in dragging you down to the station.'

The office West was taken to was a large, neat one. Pengelly lowered his big frame into the comfortably-worn chair behind the desk and took a noisy slurp of his coffee before opening the slim folder in front of him.

West hesitated, wondering whose office they had invaded. Pengelly looked up and saw his anxious expression. 'Sit down, Mike. Stop worrying, you haven't changed a bit.'

'Neither have you, Joe, and that's what I'm afraid of,' he returned, remembering practical jokes the big detective had played on him and other attendees at the conference back in London.

'Relax, seriously. This office belongs to the Mortuary Director. Her name is Sara Pengelly.'

West's face lit up with pleasure. 'Sara? Sara Baker? You persuaded that beautiful, gorgeous woman to marry you? I don't believe it.'

Pengelly reached out, picked up a photograph frame and turned it around. 'Just over a year ago. There she is, and that's our boy, JJ.'

West took the frame in his hand to look closer. 'She's still stunning and, luckily, your son takes after her and not you. I don't know how I missed that news.' Then of course, he did know. Just over a year ago. 'I suppose I had a bit on my mind back then,' he said.

'Just a bit,' Pengelly agreed. 'Enough to contend with, without knowing that I had married the most beautiful girl in the world.'

The shadow that had descended on West when he remembered those days, dispersed. 'Yes, that would have made my situation absolutely unbearable, Joe. Thank you for sparing me.'

'We moved down here round the same time you moved to Foxrock. Suits both of us. Sara is away on a course today. She'll be sorry to have missed you,' he said, and then, switching from personal to professional, he opened the folder in front of him.

'We have nothing yet,' he admitted, closing the folder and tossing it across the desk to him. 'Forensics has the car. The murderer is a casual bugger, he tossed the rope he used on the ground as he walked away. Forensics are working on it but I wouldn't hold out much hope, looked like common buy-anywhere fishing rope to me.' He took another slurp of coffee. 'There's no money in the wallet but the wallet was there, so I don't see this as a robbery.'

'No,' West agreed, knowing a thief would have taken the wallet, not wasted time looking through it. The file was given a cursory glance before he threw it back on the desk and gave Pengelly a rundown on his case to date. 'Our victim, Simon Johnson, went to a meeting with an unknown person and was stabbed to death, the murder weapon casually dropped not far from his body. Cyril Pratt went to a meeting with an unknown and was strangled, the murder weapon thrown away nearby.' He sat back with a groan. It was blindingly obvious; they didn't need forensics to tell them what was poking them in the face.

'They were killed by the same person. We had been looking at Pratt for Johnson's murder.' He stood and stretched tiredly. 'It looks like we were on the wrong track, doesn't it? There's something we're missing. Some connection between the two men that we haven't found yet.'

Pengelly sat back, sipping his coffee. 'Our dead man conned your dead man out of two grand a month, then meets and marries this Edel what's 'er name, without bothering to divorce his wife.' He looked across the desk at West. 'It's hard keeping one wife happy and this bugger wants two.' He frowned. 'She's on her way in, by the way.'

West looked puzzled. 'Who?'

Pengelly looked slightly embarrassed. 'We identified Pratt

from his fingerprints and obtained his next of kin details. His wife, the other one I mean, was contacted first thing and is on her way. There was a slight mix-up in the communication; Edel Johnson wasn't really required for identification. She isn't legally married to him after all, as you know.'

West looked suitably annoyed. 'So, Edel didn't have to go through that?'

'What would you have had me do?' Pengelly said with a shrug of muscular shoulders. 'Tell her she wasn't any use to us because her marriage was bigamous? It seemed to me, to be better to let her identify him. She probably wanted to see him anyway. It is supposed to be healthier. Closure and all that crap.'

Edel had said something similar, West remembered, frowning.

'Getting back to your case, you were running with the theory that Simon Johnson had gone to Foxrock to confront Pratt, and Pratt had killed him?'

'Yes,' West said, rubbing a hand over his face. 'We've been trying to join the dots with the admittedly sparse information we've managed to acquire. We know Johnson found out about the scam but we don't know, yet, how or even if, he found out it was Pratt. The scrap of paper we found in Johnson's pocket had Come-to-Good written on it and, we know now, Pratt had been living there for the last three months, so he must have had the name from him. But how did he contact him? Johnson was found in the graveyard beside Pratt's house, so it looks like he was able to trace where he lived, too. How? He'd been missing for three months. We had a trace on his bank accounts and nothing turned up and yet this guy arrives home and within days has found him. It's a bit galling for the team.'

'And if Johnson knew Pratt was in Come-to-Good, why did he go to Foxrock?' Inspector Pengelly finished.

'Exactly.' West sat back restlessly. 'All we have are questions.

And then, apart from the dead bodies piling up, there's the money. Somewhere, Pratt got his mitts on five hundred thousand euro and we have no idea where from. But nowhere legal, I'm sure. Maybe our unknown is connected to the money but then what's his connection to Johnson? From all accounts, Johnson was a law-abiding, upright, model citizen.' He ran a tired hand over his face. 'We just need a bit of luck on our side.'

The Cornish detective smiled. Luck had a big part in their work, asking the right questions; being in the right place; talking to the right person. Sometimes, both men knew, luck was on the other side.

'The wife wasn't involved, was she?' he asked.

'Which one?' West replied grimly.

Pengelly looked momentarily flummoxed. 'First? The legal one... the one in Cork.'

'Third to be exact, if you mean the current Mrs Pratt. No. We've had her checked out. As far as she was aware, he was working away. He sent her money every week or so. They've been married six years. Two kids. We got the impression she didn't particularly care if he came back or not, as long as he sent the money. The officer who went to interview her described her as a bottle-blonde battleaxe.'

'A different sort to Edel Johnson then, eh? Wonder why he didn't just divorce her?'

West stared into his coffee. What had made Cyril Pratt marry Edel and live a lie? He had an idea but didn't know if he was indulging in psycho-babble or whether the idea had real merit. He tried to put his idea into words now, tried it out on the big, gruff, plain-talking detective sitting opposite.

'I think it might have started out as a scam. He had lived in Simon Johnson's apartment, was wearing his Armani suits and living his expensive lifestyle for about a week before he bumped, accidentally into a beautiful woman. He followed her and manipulated another *accidental* meeting. She laughed at the coincidence, he invited her for coffee, they had dinner and she told him all about herself.

'He may have planned a scam but instead he finds himself with the perfect woman to match his newly-acquired lifestyle. A glamorous, attractive, successful woman who finds him, Simon Johnson, successful engineer, attractive. A woman who probably wouldn't have looked twice at Cyril Pratt, ex-con.

'Edel said he was very easy to talk to, she told him things she had never told anyone. He used the information to become the man of her dreams, and he got deeper and deeper into his dream lifestyle, far too deep to turn around and admit the truth. The pinnacle of his dream, of course, was when she agreed to marry him. There was no choice but to continue the deception, he was so immersed in his dream that he didn't see it was doomed.'

'It only fell apart when Simon Johnson came home?' Joe Pengelly asked.

West shrugged. 'He was supposed to be away for two years, but an aunt, who was a favourite of his, died suddenly and he came home for the funeral. At that stage, Pratt had already gone missing, so something must have happened earlier, something we don't know about.'

'But Pratt must have known he couldn't keep it going indefinitely, anyway.'

'He was a con man, a scam artist, Joe. I suppose he hoped something would turn up to save the day. You know the way they work, living from scam to scam.'

Pengelly nodded, making his chair creak, then leaned forward over his desk. 'You are sure wife number three isn't in the picture. She might have found out about his other life and resented it.'

West sat back in his chair with a groan. 'I'm tired. No, the local officers say she had a cast-iron alibi, brings the kids to school every day, picks 'em up. School confirms it.'

'Just leaves us one candidate for his murder then, doesn't it?' Pengelly concluded, draining the last of his coffee. 'Wife number four. She finds out her beloved husband is a con-artist, and that her marriage is as legal as a nine-pound note.'

West stood and moved to the window. He watched as a large seagull banked and shimmied, using the breeze to lift itself above the harbour below. He had stayed in Falmouth once, years before, and the noise of the seagulls had woken him at some ungodly hour and he had cursed them roundly. Now he watched in admiration as the bird soared and vanished from view.

He turned reluctantly. 'Time of death would leave her without an alibi for Pratt's death, certainly. She could have driven to Falmouth and back to the cottage. She says his car had broken down, I suppose she could have sabotaged it after she returned from Falmouth and called me to establish an alibi of sorts. She certainly has a motive, Joe, but I don't see her as a murderer.'

Pengelly sat back in his chair and looked grim. 'She had motive, opportunity and no alibi. She looks pretty good for it to me. Pratt was strangled by someone who got into the car in the seat behind. *Her* car, Mike. Pratt wasn't an innocent; it had to have been someone who didn't make him suspicious, someone he knew.

'The pathologist said it could have been a woman; insists it would have taken dexterity rather than strength. And your murder victim, Simon Johnson, he didn't expect trouble, she could have done that too. She certainly had the motive. He knew her husband was a con-artist and was going to expose her life-style for what it was.'

West stood restlessly. Was he wrong? Was Edel guilty of two murders? He sensed the hidden warning behind Pengelly's words, knew what he was thinking, why he was being circumspect in what he said. They'd both heard of officers getting involved with suspects, it happened, a bit like actors falling for their leading ladies. But falling for a suspect could be dangerous, it could cloud your judgement, make you lose track of the case and could lose you your job.

He needed to address and dispense with the issue. 'You're wrong, Joe,' he said bluntly, continuing in the face of the other officer's innocent expression. 'I'm not blind to her attractions but they haven't blinded me. I just don't think she did it. We haven't found the source of the money; I think that's where we'll find our answer.'

Pengelly considered a moment and then stood, holding out his hand. 'Cherchez la dosh, eh? I hope you're right, Mike. You always did have good instincts, I'll admit, and by all accounts you've never gone wrong following them before. But,' he continued as they shook hands, 'you be careful.'

'Always,' West said with a smile.

'And come back and stay with us next time. Bring a friend,' Pengelly said, always liking to have the last word.

14

West stood a moment looking through the window of the visitors' room door, watching Edel as she sat and stared without moving. Death and its consequences were an accepted part of his job, but that didn't make it any easier. He checked his watch. Three, he saw with annoyance. He opened the door quietly, giving her time to come back from wherever it was she had gone. She rose when she saw him and came to the door.

'We can head back now,' he said, reaching out to take her arm.

Outside the building, she hesitated. 'My car,' she began with an interrogative glance in his direction, 'am I allowed take it?'

'I'm afraid not for the moment,' he apologised. 'I'll arrange to get it sent back to Dublin when they've finished with it but that won't be for some time. Maybe you should get a hire car for the time being.'

'Maybe,' she replied vaguely. She sat into his car without further comment and buckling up, she leaned her head back against the headrest, sighed and closed her eyes.

The drive to the airport was fast and uneventful and she kept her eyes closed throughout the journey. Whether to prevent conversation or because she was tired, West didn't know, but he maintained the silence she seemed to prefer. He was honest enough to admit it suited him too, gave him time to think. He was running through the day's events when he remembered the briefcase and groaned, he should have turned it over to Pengelly. They were almost at the airport but if he insisted, he'd have to go back. He saw a lay-by sign ahead and, indicating, he pulled in. Dialling Falmouth station, he tapped on the steering wheel as he waited to be put through.

'I can go back with it,' he said, after giving a quick explanation.

'No, that's okay,' Pengelly said. 'A briefcase full of papers, eh? Sounds like I had a lucky escape. If you find anything of interest, copy it and send it to me, okay?'

Swallowing a sigh of relief, West assured him that he would, and cut the connection. Back on the road, he glanced in Edel's direction to find her staring intently at him. Slightly unnerved, he concentrated on the road ahead. A brief glance, moments later, found her still staring and he felt irritation beginning to prickle.

It turned to surprise when she finally spoke. 'Are you a good detective?' she asked.

Taken aback, he gave the question some consideration before answering. He'd been a good solicitor, was he a good detective? He didn't like the paperwork or the politics and struggled sometimes to remain objective, but he loved the puzzle of it all, the search for the end of the string in an attempt to find the right one to pull to untangle the knot. He railed at the revolving door of crime, seeing criminals he'd put away last year, back to their tricks the next. But he never grew tired, he never became bored and, in every case, he was doggedly determined to get the answers he needed. 'Yes,' he said, 'I am.'

'Do you think my Simon killed your Simon Johnson?'

He sighed and decided he had nothing to lose by telling her. 'Cyril Pratt had a record; he had the means, motive and opportunity. He certainly *was* a suspect in the murder of Simon Johnson but now, well, now we're not so sure.'

'Because he was murdered too.' It was a statement, not a question and he didn't comment. 'Means, motive and opportunity,' she repeated.

He gave her a quizzical glance before concentrating on the road ahead.

In the airport, FlySouth were very accommodating. They changed West's flight without extra charge and happily sold the adjacent seat to Edel. Flying at thirty thousand feet, his head resting against the headrest, gritty eyes closing, he was, once again, aware of her eyes on him. He tried to ignore the feeling. Dammit, he was tired; he just wanted an hour's rest. Impossible, he could feel her eyes boring into him. In exasperation he threw her a look. 'What?' he asked gruffly.

'Two men are dead. If, as you say, Simon... or as I suppose I must get used to calling him, Cyril Pratt... had means, motive and opportunity to murder Simon Johnson, but didn't, then who did?' She continued to stare at him intently for a long moment then laughed shortly. 'You think Cyril and Simon were killed by the same person.' Again, this appeared to be a statement rather than a question and West said nothing.

'Means, motive and opportunity,' she repeated quietly. 'If it were just Cyril, you might have suspected me of having killed him.'

He looked at her, seeing the expectant look as she waited for him to remonstrate, to reassure her. It was tempting, but could he be one hundred per cent sure she wasn't involved? Instead, his eyes fixed on hers. He asked, 'Did you?' He watched her jaw drop open in shock. 'It is very unlikely that Cyril's death is unconnected to that of Simon Johnson's. Let's just say there are certain elements in common,' he continued, ignoring her shocked silence. 'You did have means, and opportunity and, you certainly had motive. I think you were probably genuinely unaware of your husband's deceit and were shocked by it, but you were probably more horrified by his bigamy. That's a much more intimate crime, destroys your belief in what you had, what you were. Made you question yourself.' He hesitated. 'I think when you found that photo it was the last straw.'

She pressed trembling lips together and stared at him with wide eyes. 'You think I drove into Falmouth, murdered him, drove back, sabotaged the car and then phoned you to provide myself with an alibi?'

Since this was exactly the scenario purported by Inspector Pengelly, he refused to answer, resting his head back again, wishing he could get her shocked face out of his mind. Did he really think she was involved? He had to admit that he was attracted to her and struggled to remain objective. He was venturing into very dangerous territory and he knew it. It was a classic scenario to fall for a suspect, one most good detectives steered well clear of. He had been a smug bastard to think he was immune to such stupidity, so above making an idiot of himself.

No, he decided, he didn't think she was involved but he had to prove it. He turned to look at her. 'What I think doesn't matter,' he replied eventually, choosing his words with care. 'We'll do what we do. Investigate, examine all evidence and then, and only then, draw our conclusions.' He watched as her face fell, a look of disappointment in her eyes, as if he'd failed her.

'I didn't kill him. I couldn't have,' she said quietly. She struggled to maintain control, biting her lower lip, but a sad, pathetic sob escaped. Just one. She drew a deep shuddering breath, wiped her face on the sleeve of her jacket, and turned red, swollen eyes to him, her lips resolutely firming the quiver that still threatened. 'You have to believe me.'

He justified himself by thinking that stronger men than he would have caved at the sight of her sad, vulnerable face and he stepped over the line dividing personal and professional without further ado. 'I believe you,' he said. 'I don't think you murdered anyone. I don't think you were involved at all. Over the next few days, I'm sure, forensic evidence will prove it. Until that happens, I have to do my job, and that means, unfortunately, investigating our only suspect.'

'Me,' she said quietly, with drying tears like snail tracks down her cheeks.

'You,' he agreed, the lift of his lips not quite a smile as he reached out to wipe away first one tear, and then the other with the soft pad of his thumb. He forced down the quick flush of desire the small gesture brought to the surface, and he held it down until it gurgled. One final mental reminder of the conse-quences of any involvement with Edel rendered it not dead, but completely inert. For the moment anyway.

He sat back and the rest of the flight passed in silence. In Dublin airport, they retrieved West's car and drove across the city. Feeling the quiet becoming oppressive, he searched for something neutral to talk about and remembered she had told him she was a writer of children's books.

'What age group do you write for?' he asked now. A question without agenda.

She looked at him. 'You don't have to make conversation, Sergeant West. This isn't a date.'

He shrugged. 'I was curious, that's all. I've never met a writer of any sort.'

Silence continued for several minutes.

'Well, to satisfy your curiosity,' she said, eventually, 'I write for the pre-teenage group. I got into it by accident really, I won a competition. What I really want to do, as I think I already told you, is to write adult fiction.' She shrugged. 'That was why Simon insisted I keep the money from the sale of my house. It was supposed to enable me to write what I wanted to and not be at the beck and call of my publisher who wants a variation of what I have been writing for years. Their motto is, if it sells, don't change, just keep churning the same thing out, year after year.' She gave a derisive, dismissive snort. Seconds later, changing the subject, she asked, 'Do you think, when this is all over, I'll be able to remember the good times?'

The question was unexpected and West wasn't sure how to answer it. He decided on the truth as he knew it. 'I had a rough time before I transferred to Foxrock,' he said. 'The details don't matter; suffice to say it was difficult. I still remember the bad times but they have lost their ability to hurt.' He stopped a moment, gathering his thoughts. 'Not their ability to disturb me, or make me sad, because they still do that; just their ability to sting.' He gave a grunt. 'I wanted to kill people who told me that time was a great healer, so I won't tell you that now, but the fact is, they were right, it is. If you can get through the first few days, then the first few weeks and the months well, you'll be okay. And as for the good times, they never fade, Edel. They will be with you long after the bad times have become a misty memory, I promise.'

Neither said a word as he pulled up outside her house and switched off the engine. They sat a moment, unmoving. Finally, undoing her seatbelt, she turned to him. 'What now?' she asked quietly.

Undoing his belt, he opened the car door and got out, waiting as she followed suit before replying. 'Try and get some sleep.' He stopped as she gave a tired grunt. 'Try, at least,' he continued. 'We'll be in touch tomorrow.' He waited as she found her keys and opened her front door, before he added, 'You need to be here when we call, Edel.'

She stood framed in her doorway by the light of the hall and gave a tired smile. 'Is this what you call house arrest?'

He returned the smile. 'House arrest entails having a garda on your doorstep. I don't think we need go that far.' He raised his hand in salute. 'I'll talk to you tomorrow.'

He walked back to his car; for the first time in a long time, he was looking forward to the next day.

15

West drove home in silence. It had been a hell of a day. A hell of a week, since he was being honest. He pulled up outside his house in Greystones, sitting a moment as exhaustion hit him with a sledgehammer before pushing the door open and climbing out.

The garden gate opened with a squeak, the sound loud in the quiet of the late night, and he made a mental note to oil it, adding it to a growing list of things to do whenever he had a chance. He knew how Edel felt about her house; he felt the same about this one. He'd been lucky; his parents lived a short walk away and had heard it was going on the market; he'd approached the vendor and made them an offer they, and he, knew they'd be foolish to refuse. Within a short space of time the house was his.

An old Edwardian redbrick, it had needed work but luckily had many of the original features intact. He'd hoped to do a lot of the refurbishment it needed himself but when he had the house two years, and still hadn't found the time, he gave up and got in the experts. They'd done a good job and it was as near perfect as could be.

He wasn't sure at the time how he felt about living so near to his parents but it had never been a problem. In fact, when he had that trouble last year his mother had been... he smiled slowly, she'd been a mother.

He opened the door, listened and almost at once heard the pitter-patter that announced Tyler's every arrival. The little dog looked up at him, big brown eyes asking the usual question. 'Where *have* you been?'

He sat on the sofa and the dog sat beside him; West told him about his day and Tyler listened in companionable silence. It was too late to bother about food, but never too late for a whiskey – just one – he wasn't going to work with a hangover twice in one week. Tongues would begin to wag. He could tell them, if they were really concerned, that if he hadn't hit the bottle last year, he never would.

He sipped the whiskey, savouring the expensive single malt that had been a gift from somebody back when he had been a highly paid solicitor and gifts of expensive malt whiskeys were commonplace. Now as a garda, if someone gave him an expensive bottle of whiskey, he knew it would come with conditions and he'd have to say, thanks, but no thanks. He knew not all his colleagues believed as he did and were happy to pull a few strings here and there, but he wasn't going down that road. The thin edge of the wedge and all that.

His reputation for being as straight as an arrow held to him last year. Helped him get through it a little easier. Not easily, but definitely a little easier.

What had Edel asked him? *When this was over would she be able to remember the good times?*

He sipped his whiskey. He hadn't lied to her. It had got easier with time. What he hadn't told her was how difficult those first few days, weeks and months had been. The pain that hit at the most unexpected moments and left him gasping for air; the sympathetic looks from people that too quickly turned to frowns of impatience accompanied with a grunt that said, clearly, *get over it*; the complete inability to carry on with anything.

He rested his head back against the sofa. Tyler, spotting a moment's weakness, climbed into his lap, curled up and, within minutes, was snoring softly.

West reached for the whiskey bottle and poured another. To hell with it. If he was going to start thinking about Glasnevin, he needed it.

He'd spent a year in Garda Headquarters before begging for a transfer. He hadn't left his lucrative career as a solicitor to sit in an office formulating strategy for a fraction of the money. That wasn't why he'd joined up. He wanted to be on the streets, investigating, solving crimes, putting the bad guys away.

His insistent requests for transfer to an active assignment paid off eventually and he was offered the choice of two posts, one in Foxrock or one, further from home, in the north city suburb of Glasnevin. He'd decided on Glasnevin, an area he didn't know very well, hoping for more diversity of crime than in upmarket Foxrock and he supposed, looking back, he just wanted a complete change.

How many hours had he been there before it happened? One or two at the most. The call had come through just as he arrived, early as usual, and there was nobody available to take it apart from him. A report of a disturbance. The desk sergeant had given him the address, told him how to get there and he had gone. On his own, simple as that. Wasn't that always the way things happened?

But he couldn't find the house. He drove around for thirty minutes, got completely lost and had to ask for directions back to the station. Brian Dunphy, the garda assigned to be his partner, had arrived for his shift and West, totally embarrassed, had explained his predicament.

'Don't worry about it,' Dunphy had said with a laugh of genuine amusement. 'We get so many of that type of call. Usually, they turn out to be nothing. We'll have a word with the desk sergeant, see if they rang again.'

They checked and no further calls had come through but West insisted they go, just to check it out. Dunphy had laughed again and called him an eager beaver, but had shrugged and agreed.

He had driven, listening as his passenger regaled him with tales of the happenings in Glasnevin, all of which were amusing and, although he'd obviously told them several times before, Dunphy laughed at each one, a full-on belly laugh that filled the car with sound. And that's how West remembered him, laughing heartily at his own stories.

They had arrived at the address. It wasn't far from the station; he would have been there in five minutes if he hadn't got lost. He parked the car at the kerb and Dunphy got out and stood looking around the quiet, well-maintained suburban street.

He had unbuckled his seat belt to follow.

'I wouldn't bother getting out, mate. I'll just give the door a knock and see if they know anything about the call, okay?'

Just then, West's mobile rang and with a wave to Dunphy, he answered. It had been some query about paperwork at headquarters. He'd finished the call and was just about to get out of the car when the front door of the house opened.

He'd looked towards the door in time to see a middle-aged man wielding a gun. There wasn't time to move, or shout a warning. He heard the crack and watched his partner fall, then saw the man look across to him and taking aim, with a blank look of horror that was clear even at a distance, he reversed the weapon, wedged it under his chin and fired.

West sat stunned for what seemed like hours but it was probably only seconds before he ran to Dunphy, stepping over a pool of blood to turn him over carefully. His eyes were open, but he didn't have to feel for a pulse to know he was dead. He'd never had a chance.

The other man had fallen backward into the house. West checked, but he too was dead.

The shots had brought neighbours out and there were screams of horror. One woman came rushing up to him. 'Can I help?' she asked simply, her eyes wide with shock.

'Do you know this man?' West asked, indicating the body in the hall. It was a stupid question; there was little of the man's face left to identify him.

But the woman, keeping her eyes averted from the body, nodded. 'I live next door,' she said, pointing. 'Our houses share walls, you know, and I could hear him earlier. He was shouting at his wife and kids, screaming actually. I rang the gardaí then, but nobody came.'

'We are the gardaí,' West replied, indicating the fallen man at his feet.

'Pity you didn't get here sooner, then,' she said sadly.

'You mentioned a wife and children?' he asked, trying to stay focused, feeling shock seeping in and paralysing.

'Yeah, they should be here.' Her shocked face took on a new look of horror. 'You don't think he hurt them, do you? God, no.'

He shook his head. 'I don't know. I need you to go back home, and ring the gardaí and for an ambulance. Tell them an officer has been shot. Tell them his name, Brian Dunphy. Have you got that?' He gave her Brian's name rather than his own. The local gardaí would know the name and respond quickly.

'Brian Dunphy,' she repeated before running off, shouting at people to get out of the way.

He stood, swaying a little, and looked around. There appeared to be a million faces looking back at him, all reflecting the look of shock he knew they saw on his. He pointed at one man, older than the rest, and called him over.

'I'm Sergeant West,' he said. 'My partner's been shot. I need someone to stay here and stop anyone else going into the house, can you do that for me, while I go and see where the wife and kids are?'

The man nodded curtly, said nothing but took a handkerchief from his pocket and draped it over Brian Dunphy's open eyes.

The tears that sprang to West's eyes were sharp and sudden. He blinked them away. He had to find the wife and children. 'Damn,' he muttered, as he stepped over the body of the man in the hall, he hadn't thought to ask her how many children there were.

The hall led directly to the kitchen. A quick look showed him it was empty. The back door was locked, the key on the inside. Retracing his steps, he tried the first door – it was empty as was an understairs toilet.

He had to climb over the dead body to gain access to the stairway, carefully avoiding stepping into the brain tissue that was spattered around the area. Taking the stairs two at a time, he stopped at the top and listened. He heard nothing. 'Hello,' he called. 'Is there anyone here? My name is Mike West, I'm a Garda Síochána.'

He opened the first door; an empty bathroom. Slowly, he opened the first bedroom door and then the second. Nothing. Perhaps they had gone out, he hoped, his hand reaching for the last doorknob. He stood there a moment, hearing the distant sound of sirens, knowing help was on its way, wondering if he should wait until it arrived. But he didn't, he pushed the door open and, then it was too late. Inside the small room, there was carnage. The man hadn't used a gun here; he'd used a knife.

Frozen in the doorway, he looked around. He could make out

four bodies, although there was so much blood... so much blood. He felt his vision going, a blackness creeping in around the edges. Four bodies. He had slit the mother's throat; it gaped like a wide toothless smile... the children... the three children... so very small, so very, very small.

The blackness crept in and claimed him. He folded like a concertina just as he heard a yell from below announcing the arrival of gardaí and ambulance crew.

When he woke, he was in a private room in a local hospital, a drip in his arm, a monitor beep-beeping behind him. He felt a fraud; he hadn't been hurt, hadn't been shot; hadn't even been shot at. 'I'm okay,' he told the doctor who came to see him. He wasn't aware of the tears that spilled down his cheeks until he noticed the drops peppering the blue hospital gown he wore. When he saw them, he couldn't understand where they were coming from, pointing them out to the doctor who said nothing, just told him to sit tight.

It wasn't until his mother came in twenty minutes later, and said in distress, 'Oh Michael, don't cry,' that he realised he had been crying the whole time, his tears soaking the hospital gown so much they had to change it. His mother sat with him, holding his hand, telling him it would be okay, that he would be okay.

He didn't believe her; he didn't think he would ever be okay again.

The inquest into the deaths exonerated him completely. The coroner told the court the wife and children had been dead several hours and had, more than likely, been killed while they slept. Had West arrived earlier, the inquest decided, he may have prevented the death of Brian Dunphy but only at the cost of his own.

He was free to carry on as if nothing had happened. As if he hadn't seen two men die in front of his eyes, one of whom was laughing and joking only moments before. As if he hadn't seen those tiny, bloody bodies.

He received counselling from the department psychologist and advice from friends and colleagues. From his mother he got unconditional love and support, and it was that that got him through. That and time.

He still woke up in a sweat sometimes and saw the gun pointing at him. Sometimes, walking down the street or standing in a crowded place, he heard a laugh and thought of Brian Dunphy. Sometimes, when he saw a small child, he remembered those small, bloody bodies and wondered if they had known what was happening to them. But sometimes now, he didn't think about it at all.

He had returned to Glasnevin two weeks after the event, had stood in the car park and knew he couldn't work there again. He went home and requested an immediate transfer. It was granted within hours and the next day he started in Foxrock.

Before he reported for duty, he bought a satellite navigation system for his car; he was never going to get lost again.

And it was working out all right for him in Foxrock. Of course, if he had taken the position there in the first place... well, how many times could he play the *what if* game.

Tyler growled softly, a dog-dream of who-knows-what. West ran a hand over his head and smiled. He had told Edel the truth; it had taken a while but he had regained the pleasure in his house, his garden, friends and family. He tried to build up a store of things that brought happiness, things he could dip into when the sadness came sweeping over him, as it still did now and then. Edel Johnson's smile came to mind and on that pleasing memory, he emptied his glass. He picked Tyler up without waking him and put him on the sofa, then got up, stretched his long body and took himself to bed.

16

For a short, sweet moment when Edel woke early the next morning, she forgot her problems and stretched with the warm contentment of a good night's sleep. Before the stretch was over, reality had forced its sticky fingers between her closed eyes and it all came rushing back. Eyes wide, she considered her predicament.

'My husband has been murdered, I am a suspect, my marriage wasn't legal and this house may not be my home.' Hearing it aloud didn't make it any less preposterous nor did it offer any solutions. She curled up under the duvet, pulling it over her head as if it would protect her against the reality she had to face, and tried to force her unwilling body to go back to sleep. If she did doze, it wasn't for long and when she looked at the clock it was still only six. There was no getting away from it, the cold hard reality of her situation had to be faced.

Nothing made any sense. Refusing to lie there another moment, she threw back the duvet and swung her feet to the floor. She sat on the edge of her bed looking down with a frown at the dirty, wrinkled jeans and the even dirtier creased shirt she'd been too weary to remove the night before. Raising her eyes, she looked around the room. Articles of discarded clothing lay everywhere, testifying to her inability to cope, to how she had completely fallen apart in the last few months.

So, what now? Simon was dead. Simon, who never really existed, was dead. How much farther could she fall apart? How much more could he take from her in death?

A tear ran slowly down one cheek and then the other. Silent, sad tears of self-pity. She stood, wrapping her arms around herself, the comforting embrace she needed, self-applied but comforting nevertheless. As she stood, arms tight, something stirred inside, a small frisson of determination to get through this. It wouldn't be easy. She had been looked at suspiciously when Simon had disappeared. When the truth came out, what would people say? That she must have known, how could she not?

How could she not? She winced. How could she have been so trusting, so gullible? The little voice that answered *because you loved him* was ignored. She was going to ignore that voice for a long time to come.

Anger, a healthier emotion than self-pity, rose to the surface and she bent and gathered up clothes from the floor. It took three trips to bring them all down to the utility room where she loaded the washing machine with some, piling the rest on a worktop to be done later. Bringing a black rubbish bag up with her, she stripped the grubby sheets from the bed, rolled them up and pushed them into it, refusing to think, trying not to breathe the last scent of Simon.

She tied the bag tightly and left it by the front door before pulling out the vacuum cleaner and bringing it up with her to suck up the dust and debris of months. The restoration of order to at least a small part of her world gave her immeasurable pleasure.

Taking fresh linen from the airing cupboard, she remade the

bed, and with sad determination piled the pillows one on top of the other instead of side by side. She turned away abruptly from the sight.

Coffee was in order, she decided, and headed downstairs. Waiting for the kettle to boil forced her to consider the state of the kitchen. Her nose wrinkled in disgust as the smell of sour milk and stale food wafted toward her. She felt the stickiness beneath her bare feet and cringed. *My God, the place is disgusting.*

Instead of making coffee, she pulled another rubbish bag from the roll and started tidying up. She put any letters to one side and discarded months of circulars and free newspapers. Crumbs, stale bread, withered fruit, old tea bags. Mugs were emptied of their gloop and put steeping in hot soapy water. Worktops were wiped. The floor was swept and washed. Edel had to go on hands and knees to scrub some of the more noisome and resistant stains but, she did so with a re-emergence of pride in herself and her surroundings.

Then she laughed as she surveyed her jeans and shirt. She was filthy and needed a long shower but first she'd have that coffee. The kettle boiled again and she spooned coffee into the freshly-washed mug. She walked, sipping it, to her bedroom where she stripped off the filthy clothes she had worn since... no, she wasn't going to think of that. Throwing the clothes into yet another rubbish bag, she tied a knot in it and threw it down the stairs, watching as it bounced and landed with a fat splat.

She was still standing looking down, naked and lost in thought, when the phone rang.

17

To his surprise, West slept well; usually, thinking of Glasnevin led to a sleepless night, but with the memory of Edel's smile on his mind, he'd slept soundly and peacefully. Maybe her smile could be his talisman.

Events in Glasnevin hadn't altered his habit of being early to work and he was there pouring over data when the rest of the team trickled in. Noisy sounds of morning greetings soon subsided into the working day's business. Information was sourced, acquired, collated from a variety of sources with the tempo of a tango – slow-slow, quick-quick frustratingly slow.

Forensics in Cornwall contacted them mid-morning. 'We've been asked by DI Pengelly to give you our findings directly, Sergeant West,' a forensic officer by the name of Cubert Baragwanath said slowly, with a Cornish burr so soft and low that West had to press the phone tightly to his ear to catch. 'We have finished our examination of the car found in Falmouth, but we haven't much to give you I'm afraid,' the man continued, 'all fingerprints we collected proved to be from Cyril Pratt's and one other person. We don't, unfortunately, have fingerprints from the car's owner, a Mrs Edel Johnson, but from the ubiquity of the second prints we assume they belong to her. We would appreciate if you could obtain her fingerprints so we could clarify that point.'

'Okay,' West agreed. 'We can get them done and have them sent directly to you.'

'Thank you, Sergeant,' Baragwanath replied and continued his report. 'The rope that was found on the pathway outside the car was definitely the murder weapon. There were traces of Cyril Pratt's DNA on it, unfortunately that was all and, also unfortunately Sergeant, it is a common variety of rope, you can buy it anywhere.

'We also collected a number of hairs and fibres from a variety of fabrics. We might, just might be able to match them if you have a suspect,' he said, but West heard the doubt in his voice and knew it was a remote possibility. 'Otherwise...' he concluded.

'I understand, thank you for keeping us informed.' Great, another dead end.

Mid-morning, Pengelly rang to pass on the results of the autopsy. 'Did Baragwanath ring you, Mike?' he asked.

'Yes, he did, thanks. Not that he had anything to tell us, as you know.'

'Thanks for nothing, eh? I'm afraid the autopsy report isn't going to set any bells ringing either. It didn't tell us anything we didn't already know. He was strangled; they've matched the marks on his neck to the rope that was found, so that's conclusive. Skin under the victim's nails is his own; he'd tried to prise the rope away evidently, there are deep scratches on his throat, above and below the rope mark. They also found some fibres under his nails.' West heard loud slurping on the line before Pengelly continued. 'Leather, probably from gloves the assailant was wearing.'

There was a loud crackling of paper, the clunk as a mug was

placed carelessly on a wooden surface and a soft curse as the Cornish detective searched for the next page in the notes.

'Don't know why they can't ever put these damn reports in the right order,' he complained, and then, with a sigh of relief. 'Right, here it is. The pathologist reckons the murderer was right-handed and from the rope marks on Pratt's neck, he extrapolated that it would have taken minimal effort to strangle him; in other words, it could have been done by a man or woman. They just had to twist it, and hold on.' There was a long pause before Pengelly concluded with, 'There're some other details but nothing pertinent. I'll have the lot faxed to you.'

'Thanks, Joe, that'd be great,' West replied, knowing the information hadn't added much. 'We've nothing further to add from our end yet but, I'll keep you informed. We've promised your forensic office Edel Johnson's fingerprints, to confirm hers are the second set they found in the car. We'll get the prints to them as soon as we can organise it.'

'Ah, your lovely lady friend, nothing new on her?' Pengelly asked, the smirk in his voice obvious.

Irritated, West answered sharply. 'Ms Johnson is not my lady friend, she is a suspect in a murder case, and, no, we have no further information on *any* aspect of the case.' He took a deep breath. Pengelly was only trying to get a rise out of him. And he had succeeded so well. 'You're having one of your men check the car outside the cottage, aren't you?' he continued in a calmer tone, refusing to give him any further ammunition.

'Yes, they should be there now. I'll let you know as soon as. Don't fret, we'll get your la... I mean Ms Johnson, in the clear.' He wisely didn't wait for a reply and hung up, leaving West no outlet for his annoyance except to bang down the handset, which he did, knocking it and the pile of papers it balanced on, onto the floor. He gave an exasperated grimace and left them where they fell.

Restless, he stepped over the mess and headed to the general office. A mug of coffee in hand, he stood in front of the case board and ran his eyes over the data. The photos of the two victims headed the board, copies of relevant information pinned under each for the team's convenience. It allowed quick identification of connections, efficient correlation of facts, a focus for thinking, a spur for ideas. West perused dates and forensic results, going over all the details they had collated. Some pieces were new to him. One in particular caught his attention, as he recognised the logo of the Property Registration Authority of Ireland. Edel's house, it appeared, was in her name alone.

Filing that information away in his head, he moved on, noting that Simon Johnson had flown from Cork to Dublin, and had hired a car at Dublin airport for the drive to Foxrock. Recognising the writing, he turned to look for its owner, spotting him deep in conversation, the phone tucked under his chin as he scribbled furiously. He wandered over, waiting while he finished the call and hung up with a grin of satisfaction.

West knew the signs. 'Something interesting?'

Garda Jarvis struggled to cover his excitement at having uncovered an important piece in the puzzle that was their case. 'I was thinking last night about that Italian bloke, Castelione,' he began, 'you know? The guy who rented the apartment from Cyril Pratt.'

At West's nod he continued. 'Well, I just wondered if there was something else he could tell us.' Excitement came to the fore and he continued, waving his hands as he spoke. 'I asked him to go over what happened again and he said exactly the same as the last time, and I was just about to hang up when I remembered something.' He looked expectantly at the sergeant.

Deciding to humour his infectious excitement, West played along. 'And what was that?' he asked, hiding a smile.

'Well, sir,' Jarvis continued, standing up. 'I rent a flat and I have the landlord's mobile number, in case there is any problem. So, I asked Mr Castelione if he had the same facility and, of course, he admitted he did. I asked him if perhaps he had given this number to Simon Johnson and...' Jarvis hesitated for effect before finishing, relishing his moment in the spotlight of his sergeant's gaze. 'He had, he just hadn't thought to tell us.'

West raised his eyes in exasperation. 'He didn't think it was an important piece of information? Good work, Sam. So, now we know, at least how Johnson managed to contact Pratt when we couldn't find the bloke.'

'Castelione said Pratt didn't give him the mobile number immediately. When he moved into the apartment, he asked for one, but Pratt told him he was changing his phone provider and would get back to him. Sounds like he went and bought a phone especially for that use.'

'I agree,' West said, 'they had no luck tracing the mobile number Edel Johnson had for him. He must have tossed that one.' He indicated the case board and continued. 'Simon Johnson must have contacted Pratt on his mobile and got the name of the village in Cornwall from him.'

'That explains the scrap of paper we found in his pocket,' Jarvis said.

'Yes, but not why he came to Foxrock. If he planned to go to Come-to-Good what made him change his mind and end up here?' West turned to Jarvis. 'We'll get there, bit by bit. You did well, Sam, that was good thinking, an important piece of the jigsaw to find.'

Jarvis, obviously preening, returned to his desk.

West was still standing reviewing various other pieces of information when Andrews appeared at his side with a mug of steaming coffee in each hand. With a smile, he put his cold one down on a nearby table and, indicating his office with a tilt of his head, took the fresh mug of coffee, went through and slumped behind his desk. Andrews, raising an eyebrow at the mess on the floor, picked up the phone and placed it on a corner of the desk before sitting opposite. He put his coffee on the floor and sat back, an expectant look on his face.

'Jarvis found the link between Johnson and Pratt,' West began. 'Mr Castelione neglected to tell us that he'd given Pratt's mobile number to Johnson.'

'Well done, Jarvis,' Andrews said, impressed. 'So, Johnson rang Pratt, probably looking for an explanation, only to discover he was in Cornwall. Since he'd scribbled down the name of the town, maybe he'd planned to go there?'

'Maybe he did. So, what on earth took him to Foxrock? Who was he meeting here?' West ran fingers through his hair.

'Edel Johnson is still in the picture, isn't she? I know you don't like her for the murders, Mike, but we have to consider her as a suspect. Plus, we still haven't traced the source of the money.'

Yawning, West linked his hands behind his head and stretched. 'I haven't ruled her out,' he said firmly. 'Yes, the money. Cherchez la Dosh, as Joe Pengelly put it. Oh blast,' he muttered, annoyed. 'The briefcase, I'd forgotten the briefcase.' He got up, waving Andrews to stay seated. 'I have Cyril Pratt's briefcase in my car; Edel gave it to me yesterday. She found it in the cottage. I'll go fetch it and we can go through it while you fill me in on your interview with Amanda Pratt.'

18

'Amanda Pratt,' Andrews muttered to himself as West left the office. Now there was a hard-faced cow.

He had left home at five am the previous day to make the most of the traffic-free roads and arrived in Cork shortly after eight. Amanda Pratt lived in a huge estate on the north side of the city, one that appeared to be made up of innumerable cul-de-sacs and winding roads. He'd groaned when he'd driven into dead end after dead end. He really should get a satellite navigation system for the car to save this messing about. Joyce had wanted to buy him one for Christmas but he'd said no; he didn't want someone talking to him while he drove, he liked peace and quiet, it gave him time to think. He wasn't a quick thinker like Mike West, he needed to go over things in his head, the aspects of a case that puzzled him and the various characters and personalities involved. There were so many unknowns in this case, it was like trying to do a jigsaw without having the edge pieces and he had worried various aspects of it to death on the drive down.

Finally, after a number of wrong turns, he'd spotted the road sign for Delaney Crescent.

It was similar to other roads he had driven along on the estate and probably similar to hundreds of housing-estate roads throughout the country. The houses were semi-detached and solid, lacking any decorative features or architectural merit. To counter the sameness, many of the residents had concentrated on the front gardens, and here decorative features abounded, with evidence that a local garden centre was making a killing selling gnomes.

Number seven lacked even this attempt at diversity. Its front garden, a small square that had probably been grass at some time in its dim and distant past, was filled with weeds. Curtains were still pulled across the windows but they hung from poles that dipped badly in the middle so that a crescent of light showed above.

Andrews had checked his notes again. This was it. He'd climbed out, locked his car and walked slowly up the path to the house, listening for signs of life as he reached the door. If they were awake, they were very quiet. He checked his watch. Ten minutes past eight. The kids were of school age; surely they would be up having breakfast at this stage. His son, Petey, would be sitting at the table with his cereal by this time. He hated missing breakfast with his family but that was the job.

If the Pratt family weren't awake, they soon would be. There was a doorbell on the wall to the right of the glass-panelled uPVC door. He'd pressed his finger to it, and waited. Unable to hear it ring, he waited patiently for a few minutes before ringing again. This time he pressed his ear to the door as he pushed it; he couldn't hear a thing. He'd bet it wasn't working. The letterbox had an integrated knocker, he lifted it and rapped it sharply, hearing the noise reverberate in the quiet house. After a few more minutes, he rapped it again, this time with more vigour.

He was just about to look around the house for a back door

when a light appeared at the top of the stairs. Peering through the glass, he saw a figure silhouetted against it. It disappeared for a few seconds only to reappear and come quickly down the stairs.

There was the grating sound of a key being turned in the lock and then the door opened, a safety chain still firmly in place. A dishevelled woman had peered through the gap and glared at him. 'What the fuck do you want at this hour of the morning?'

The gratingly aggressive greeting wasn't what he'd expected. Keeping his voice even, he'd shown his identification and said, 'I'm sorry to bother you, Mrs Pratt. I wanted to ask you some questions about your husband.'

'Cyril?' Amanda Pratt queried, picking sleep from her eyes with a dirty fingernail.

Just how many husbands did she have? He kept his mouth shut. When looking for information, sarcasm didn't help.

With a loud, irritated sigh, Amanda Pratt had closed the door and he heard the rattle of the safety chain as it was removed and the door reopened. 'You'd better come in, I suppose, before someone sees you. You couldn't be anything but a policeman, you know that?' She led the way into a cluttered, untidy kitchen and waved him to a chair while she filled the kettle and lit a cigarette, coughing loudly and throatily with the first inhalation, letting the smoke come out her nose in two long trails.

It was the nearest thing to a fire-breathing dragon Andrews had ever seen, and he couldn't take his eyes off her. She was so involved in filling her lungs with as much nicotine as possible with each drag, she was oblivious to his bemused stare. Hearing the kettle boil, she turned to make coffee and broke the spell he was under. With a shake of his head, he filed it away as a story to tell Petey who was particularly keen on dragons.

She hadn't offered him coffee, making a mug for herself and standing, coffee in one hand and cigarette in the other, glaring down at him. 'What's Cyril been up to then? I answered a pile of questions yesterday, and now I have a copper on my doorstep at a ridiculous time. Must be something serious?'

Andrews gave her the standard reply that gave nothing away. 'We're interested in talking to him, that's all. He may be able to help us with our inquiries.'

'D'you think I'm a fucking idiot?' she barked at him. 'Interested in talking to him, right! He's been up to his old tricks, hasn't he?'

Andrews didn't see the point in lying. Pratt may not have murdered Simon Johnson but they had him for identity theft, no matter what happened. They also had him for bigamy, but he kept that to himself.

'I'm afraid he is involved in some shady dealings, Mrs Pratt,' Andrews conceded, hoping she would accept the euphemism without demanding details he didn't want to share.

'The bastard,' she growled. 'I warned him if he started messing around again, he was on his own.'

Andrews had spent the next twenty minutes trying to see if Amanda Pratt knew anything about the five hundred thousand euros and quickly came to the conclusion that she knew nothing. If Cyril had got his hands on a lot of money, none of it had ended up in Delaney Crescent.

'Is that your son?' he asked finally, pointing to a framed newspaper cutting of Cyril and a small skinny child.

She puffed smoke. 'That's my Trevor,' she said without any pride or pleasure. 'Cyril dragged him to a festival of some sorts and they took that. He wasn't happy with it being in the paper, said they'd never asked permission.' A laugh ended on a hacking cough. 'You'd have expected him to be delighted, him with his celebrity complex, to be in the Cork *Echo*, but no, he went on and on about it until I told him to fuck off.' She laughed again. 'Funnily enough, that was the last time I saw him.'

'I'd better let you get on with your day, Mrs Pratt,' he said, conscious time was getting on and wondering where her children were.

'Nothing to do today,' she informed him. 'The school is closed so the kids will be under my feet.'

In the tiny hallway, he stopped to admire studio shots of the Pratt family that lined the walls. 'These are really good,' he said sincerely.

She gave a throaty laugh. 'They can do wonders these days. Cyril wanted to have these done, I only agreed if they'd make me look slimmer. Worked well, didn't it?' She stood admiring herself for a moment.

'Why did he want them so much?' Andrews asked, curious.

Instead of answering, Amanda opened a door into a small sitting room and pointed to a mountainous pile of magazines.

'Those are Cyril's,' she explained with a sneer. 'He is too embarrassed to go into the shop to buy them so he has them delivered.'

Andrews picked up the first few; they were all popular celebrity magazines. 'Cyril likes these?' he asked in surprise.

Another throaty laugh. 'Yeah, sad, isn't he? He'd have liked that lifestyle. That's why he wanted those photos done, to prove we could be as good. Sad bastard. When he started wearing those fancy Armani suits, he really thought he was going somewhere. I used to laugh at him for being a fool.'

His ears pricked up at the mention of the Armani suits. 'He must have earned a lot of money to be able to afford Armani, Mrs Pratt?'

She looked at him as if he were an idiot and then waved a hand to encompass the house. 'Do we look as if we have that kind of money? He got those suits at some charity shop in

Dublin when he was there on a job. I've read about them myself, ones where rich people donate their cast-offs. Cyril happened to visit one just as some stuff was left in and he bought the lot. Shoes and shirts too, all barely worn.'

She lit another cigarette and puffed smoke at him. 'He thought wearing those clothes made a difference, that his shit didn't stink, but he was still the same stupid fucker he was when I married him.'

Andrews, normally unshockable, hid a grimace at her vulgarity. He was embarrassed by the sneering tone in her voice, the contempt she obviously held for her husband. 'Why do you stay married to him?' he dared to ask, curious as to why they stayed together. Wouldn't it have made more sense for Cyril to divorce this woman and marry Edel properly?

She considered him a moment through smoke-narrowed eyes as if wondering if she should tell him the truth, and then gave a careless shrug. 'As a married woman, I can have all the male company I like. Men know I'm not looking for anything permanent, so I have a good time, no strings attached, no questions asked. As a divorcee, they would think I was looking for something more and they'd vanish into the woodwork. Cyril asked me for a divorce about a year ago. I told him to get stuffed; I was in it for keeps. Third time lucky, you know.'

Andrews looked puzzled and she laughed.

'I was his third wife, didn't you know? His first marriage when he was seventeen was annulled after six weeks.' She laughed raucously. 'I think his young wife was frigid. The second wife was killed in a car crash when he was twenty-four and then he was lucky enough to meet me. So, you see, third time lucky.'

Cyril *had* wanted a divorce. He'd seen a way out of his life here and he had wanted to take it. Andrews looked at the pile of magazines and at the smoke that poured from Amanda Pratt's nose.

He didn't blame Cyril a bit.

At the front door, he was thanking Amanda for her help when two small, thin children appeared at the top of the stairs. Big eyes stared at him wordlessly before the two wraiths vanished to wherever they had come from.

He looked at the fleshy, well-fed body of Amanda Pratt.

No, he didn't blame Cyril a bit. Except, perhaps, for leaving two small children in her care.

19

West was back from his car within minutes, carrying the overfilled briefcase with difficulty. He hefted it onto his desk with a grunt. Seeing the grim look on Andrews' face, he paused and said in some concern, 'You okay?

The grim look lightened. 'Oh, it was that Pratt woman, yesterday. She was a piece of work.'

'Tell me about it, Pete, we can tackle this' – he indicated the bulging briefcase – 'afterwards.'

Without glancing at his notes, Andrews quickly filled him in on the previous day's interview with Amanda. 'She didn't have much regard for him, according to her he was a lousy husband and even lousier father, spent more time away from home than he did in it, and could be gone months at a time.

'As far as I could tell, she didn't care, as long as he sent money home, which he did at irregular intervals. He never told her where he would be working; she said she could sometimes tell where he was, from the postmark on the envelope he sent the cheque in, but I doubt if she really cared where he was.'

'Not exactly a happily married couple, eh?' West said.

'Not exactly. She mentioned having other men, was quite blatant about it.'

'I wonder if Pratt knew.'

'I don't think he would have cared, she said he'd asked her for a divorce.'

West opened his eyes wide at that. 'So that he could marry Edel?'

'She said he asked her about a year ago, and that ties in with when he met her, so I suppose so. She wasn't letting him go though.' He explained Amanda's reasoning.

West's face clearly showed his disgust. 'She wanted to stay married because it was easier to be married and have extramarital affairs than to be a divorcee? Bloody hell, Peter, what a bitch.' And what a contrast to his bigamous marriage to Edel. He remembered how happy she'd said they were, and sighed. 'When was Cyril home last?'

'About three months ago. Dates match when he went missing from Foxrock. Up to that point, he was home a couple of nights a month. I'd guess if we questioned Edel Johnson, we'd find the dates he was in Cork correlate with dates he said he was working away.'

'Edel said they went away two or three times a month to hotels around Ireland and the UK,' West said. 'I bet if we had the envelopes he sent to Amanda, we could match the dates there too. What a conniving so-and-so he was.' He shook his head. He had met so many shady types, he shouldn't really be surprised. But he always was. 'Any indication Amanda knew about his many and varied scams?'

'She says he was honest about his past when she met him six years ago.' Andrews struggled but failed to keep a weary cynicism from his voice as he continued. 'He promised he was a reformed character, so she married him, and as far as she was aware, he had been straight since. Certainly, from all appearances there is no money to spare in the Pratt house. It's a too-small house in need of refurbishment and,' he added, remembering the house in detail, 'a good cleaning. Kids look small, undernourished; any spare money isn't being spent on them.'

The two men sat a moment, thinking. West broke the silence first. 'Big contrast between his two lives, wasn't there?'

'Definitely,' Andrews agreed. He told him about the celebrity magazines and the press cutting from the Cork *Echo*. 'He was fascinated by the lifestyles of the rich and famous. He had studio photographs taken a few years ago and they're hanging in their hallway. Amanda said he wanted to show everyone they could look as good as any celebrity family.' Shaking his head, he finished, 'About a year ago he brought home a pile of fancy designer clothes. He said he bought them in a great charity shop he had found. That he happened to be there when they were left in, and he bought the lot.'

'And she believed him?' West asked with a raised eyebrow. 'Armani suits, shirts and handmade Italian shoes.'

'She said the clothes were obviously not new and she had read about charity shops where you could buy designer stuff cheaply.'

'Simon Johnson's wardrobe,' West said, rubbing a hand over his face. 'All the clothes he had left behind, all the Armani suits and other stuff. Johnson had very expensive taste. Pratt must have thought he'd died and gone to heaven, when he found they all fitted him. Of course,' he added, 'Pratt was passing himself off as Simon Johnson so he had to look the part. Then he met Edel; glamorous, attractive – and the play went on, the actor continuing to dress the part.'

Andrews shuffled in his seat and crossed his arms. 'He must have known it would come falling down when Johnson came home.'

'But he wasn't supposed to be home for another year,

remember? Anyway, don't forget, Pratt had already gone missing by the time Johnson discovered the scam. Something else caused his world to come crashing down. He'd finally got what he had wanted, beautiful, classy wife...' He stopped abruptly, noticing the half-smile hovering on Andrews' lips. 'What?' he demanded. 'You don't think she's beautiful?'

Andrews hastily made a backing off gesture with his hands and, tucking the smile away for another time, agreed. 'Absolutely stunning, no doubt about it. At least,' he reconsidered, 'she is in her photographs. Don't forget, I haven't met her yet, and Morgan's description wasn't that great. Skinny, he called her; I don't like skinny women myself.'

West eyed him in irritation but with a shrug continued. 'Beautiful house, designer clothes and respect... don't underestimate the desire for respect. Something must have happened to threaten it all, he would have been exposed as a fraud, a failure to everyone, especially to the woman he had fallen in love with.' He stood and paced the room. 'I think that was Pratt's downfall, the reason he couldn't walk away, he'd fallen in love.'

'With Edel Johnson, or the glamorous lifestyle?' Cynicism laced Andrews' voice.

West considered the question for a moment. 'You really think he was intelligent enough to have differentiated between the two? No, I think he fell in love with the whole package and couldn't face going back to his former life. He had already met Simon Johnson, don't forget, when he rented the apartment from him. He knew what kind of man he was, naive, and gullible beyond belief. Goodness knows what story Pratt spun him to prevent him contacting the police, because, for whatever reason, we know Johnson didn't. He took down the name of the village in Cornwall and then, for some as yet unknown reason, he turned up here.' West stopped pacing a moment, thinking. 'Pratt must have been desperate, you didn't see the cottage he was living in, it was an absolute pigsty.' He turned, stepped over some papers on the floor and sat in his chair with a frown furrowing his brow.

'Maybe there was a change of plan and Pratt arranged to meet him here,' Andrews suggested.

'But Pratt didn't murder Johnson, remember?' West started twiddling a pen around his fingers. 'Since we think a third party killed both men, was it this person Johnson was meeting in the graveyard?' Leaning back precariously in his chair, he tossed the pen to one side and smothered a yawn. And why did Pratt go missing in the first place? What happened three months before Simon Johnson came home, to force him to give up the life he had so carefully built?'

'Pratt is hiding from someone else?'

'Yes, and, like us, that someone else couldn't find him, not until Johnson came home and put the cat among the pigeons. Did he give Pratt's phone number to someone else, and if so, who? Have we spoken to the friends Johnson was supposed to have met? Maybe he let it slip in conversation.'

Andrews shook his head. 'I spoke to them. Three guys he knew from college. His sister was right too, they all live around Ballsbridge and Donnybrook; they only meet up once or twice a year. The plan to meet was made before he arrived home, and then he didn't turn up. They weren't overly concerned, assumed something had come up and were genuinely shocked and upset to hear of his murder.'

'And I suppose they had no idea who he would have met?'

He shook his head. 'One of them did mention that Simon was one of the most gullible guys he had ever met. Dangerously so, and it appears he told him that on several occasions. He was more than upset to have been proved right.'

'Pratt told Edel he had an important meeting, that he was going to sort everything out and they could get back to normal,'

West remembered, with a sudden burst of clarity that sometimes came when he least expected it. 'Whoever he was meeting, then, had to be the reason he had gone missing in the first place. That was before Johnson came home, so it can't have been anything to do with his return.'

Andrews struggled to keep it all straight in his head. 'But we're still in agreement that whoever killed Simon Johnson, here in Foxrock, is the same guy who killed Pratt in Falmouth.'

'But don't forget, Pratt didn't know Johnson was dead, so he had no reason to be suspicious of his killer.' West stood with a new sense of purpose. 'Pratt was trying to sort out the problem that had forced him into hiding three months ago, not any problem due to Johnson's return, that's why he told Edel their life could return to normal. From what she said, I think the time spent in that isolated cottage may have made him realise he couldn't live a lie forever. He told her he would explain things to her, hoped she would understand.'

'We're back to why did he go missing in the first place?' It was Andrew's turn to smother a yawn.

West rubbed his head and swallowed a groan of frustration. Speculation country was an exhausting place to spend time in, it required mental dexterity, a capacity to make connections between tenuous links and the ability to start again from the beginning when, as sometimes happened, the connections fell apart like a playing-card house. 'It's the money,' he said. 'Something to do with the money, I'll bet on it. We just have to find out how, where and who.'

'No problem, then,' Andrews said, his voice dripping sarcasm.

'What about Bareton Industries?' he asked, remembering the second of Peter's visits in Cork. 'Anything of interest turn up there?'

'Nothing we hadn't already guessed. I was lucky enough to

get to talk to Tom Bareton; he is semi-retired and only pays a courtesy visit once in a blue moon which happened to be the day I called. He was more than delighted to be of assistance and quickly rubbished the signature on the reference. He showed me his, Pratt didn't even try to copy it.'

West leaned back. 'It was on headed paper. Johnson wouldn't have doubted its veracity for a moment. Did you get to speak to...?'

Andrews supplied the name. 'Adam Fletcher?'

'That's the man.'

'No, my luck didn't hold there, he wasn't in work. I did manage to catch him by phone at home and asked if we could meet. He got quite snotty, Mike, told me he was having a day off with his wife and children and, if we really needed to speak to him, he would be available next week. I persuaded him to answer a few questions over the phone but he wasn't happy about it. He said he had no idea why Pratt would have picked his name, or how he knew that he'd never met Simon Johnson. He did admit, that it wouldn't have been hard to find out their work rota and it was fairly obvious from that, that they wouldn't have had a chance to meet, at work anyway. He didn't have anything else to add. I told him we'd be in contact next week, if we needed to. D'you know what he said?' He waited for West's headshake before continuing. 'That if I wanted to ask him further questions, he wasn't wasting personal time and I was to make an appointment with the Bareton Industries secretary. If we do need to speak to him, I'm volunteering you.' He yawned tiredly. 'I suppose Pratt took a chance picking his name to use. Con men do, don't they? Fletcher was quite indignant that his name had been used in a scam, wanted to know if it would have any repercussions, if it would affect his credit rating.' He raised his eyebrows. 'The things people worry about. Anyway, I reassured him that, as far as we knew, Pratt had just used his name to gain access to the apartment and nothing else. I did advise him, however, that it might be a good idea to have his credit rating checked, to be on the safe side.'

West's legal training kicked in. 'He's right to be worried. Unfortunately, it is far easier to get a poor credit rating than to have a poor one overturned. Obviously, Fletcher is aware of this. A more streetwise man than his colleague, Simon Johnson.'

'Strange how they never met, isn't it?' Andrews commented.

'Independent contractors working flexible hours, it's not really all that surprising.' He looked at the briefcase that sat on the desk between them. 'Let's get some coffee before we start into this blasted thing,' he said, 'maybe we'll find some answers inside.' He patted the worn leather hopefully.

Andrews eyed it with distaste. 'It will be full of rubbish that will take us hours to go through, and with our current run of luck it's more likely to give us more annoying questions than any answers.' He stood and stretched. 'I'll go and get the coffee; you can start without me if you like.'

West flicked the catch, and looked inside with a groan that followed Andrews through the door. Reaching in, he lifted a handful of papers that were thrown in any which way and let them fall back in disgust. This was probably going to be a waste of time, but it had to be done. Making a space on his desk, he upturned the briefcase, allowing the contents to spill over the surface. Checking it was empty, he threw it into the corner of the room.

Andrews, returning with two mugs of coffee, eyed the empty case. 'Finished already?' he asked.

West raised his eyebrows. 'I couldn't start without you, it wouldn't have seemed fair. Pull your chair closer, and dig in.'

They separated the paperwork into two piles, one for Cyril Pratt and one for his life as Simon Johnson. They quickly discovered the common denominator. He overspent in both lives.

'Look at this,' Andrews gasped and held out a restaurant receipt.

He took it, read it silently, and raised his eyes to meet Andrews'. Seeing the stunned expression on his face, he handed the receipt back. 'They certainly lived the high life,' he commented.

'Two hundred and fifty euro for a bottle of champagne,' Andrews condemned. 'That's ridiculous.'

'Well...' West temporised, 'it was Louis Roederer Cristal. That's about right, I'd say.'

Andrews looked at him as if he'd lost his marbles but said nothing.

He wasn't handed any more receipts to look at but, now and then, he heard a muttered 'Ridiculous.'

After an hour, they were finished going through it all and they sat back, regarding the various piles of paper in equal frustration.

'He's kept every bloody piece of paper about everything,' West said in vexation, 'but not one mention of where he got his mitts on five hundred thousand euro. Not one answer to any of our questions.' Opening a drawer in his desk, he pulled out a handful of A4 envelopes and put each pile into a separate one, marking each with a name and description of the contents. It was unlikely, but not impossible, that they would need to check some receipt or credit card statement in the future, and he was damned if he was going to go through the whole lot again.

He'd sealed the last envelope when Andrews said, 'All those debts.'

Putting the envelopes to one side, he looked quizzically at him. 'What about them?'

'Just an idea,' he said, a frown between his eyes. 'All those debts, yet when somehow, he got his hands on a lot of money, what does he do with it? He buys a house for Edel.' He paused and shrugged. 'He must have really loved her.'

West heaved a sigh. 'She said they fell in love with the house when they saw it, but I'd guess she fell in love with it, and he just wanted to make her happy. She still loves it, but she may lose it despite her name being on the deeds because if we find out where the money came from, it'll probably have to be sold to repay that.'

'Does she know that only her name is on the deeds?' Andrews said quietly. 'It gives her a pretty good motive, if she loves it as much as you say.'

20

'She doesn't know, I'd swear,' West said, seeing the sceptical look on Peter's face. 'She asked me what her situation was regarding the house when we were in Cornwall. I told her she should see a solicitor and find out. No way is she that good an actress.' Irritation swept across his face as Andrews continued to look unconvinced.

The phone rang, startling both men. West answered, picking up the bulging envelopes with his other hand and passing them across the desk. Taking them, Andrews jerked a thumb in the direction of the general office, left and kicked the door shut after him.

'Your lady friend appears to be definitely off the hook, my friend,' a voice said without any preliminaries.

'Detective Inspector Pengelly, I assume,' West returned with ill-concealed annoyance, and then took a deep breath. 'Apart from fantasies about my relationship with Ms Johnson, Joe,' he said more calmly, 'what do you have for me?'

'My men checked out that car at the cottage. They describe it as an ancient clapped-out heap and would have thought it hadn't been on the road in a long time. I told them it was on the road just recently and they laughed and said it wasn't moving now. Some problem with a gasket or something, I believe, although car innards make absolutely no sense to me. Seems that's why Pratt took her car. So, there is no way your... I mean Ms Johnson... could have made it to Falmouth.'

'Could she have sabotaged it on her return?' West asked, determined to put the suspicion to bed for good.

'I asked that very question and they say, categorically, resoundingly, absolutely, no,' Pengelly replied. 'Just to be on the safe side, we checked all the taxi firms in the area, in case she may have taken a taxi to and from Falmouth. My lads showed her photo. If she had, she would have been remembered; the storm set the date fairly well in people's heads. I had them check the car-hire companies too; again nada, zilch, nothing. She is off the hook. But, to keep everything right and tight, send us her fingerprints when you have them.'

He refused to explore the relief that he felt at the news. 'Thanks Joe, you've covered every base. We'll get those fingerprints to you as soon as we can organise it. You have removed our only suspect, you know,' he added.

'Yeah, like you wanted to lock your lady friend away for murder. You can't pull the wool over my eyes. You never could.'

Ignoring the comment, he said, 'We're no closer to finding out who killed either man; we have absolutely no suspects.' Frustration edged his voice. 'The money angle is proving to be solid concrete. We'll keep chipping away at it, but so far, as you'd say yourself, we've nada and a big fat zilch.' He frowned, shook his head and finished the call. 'We'll let you know when we break through, thanks again.'

Hanging up, he went through to the general office and looked around for Andrews. There was an air of industry about the room he was glad to see, most of those present either on the phone or busily writing up their notes, but he would have been happier if the industry translated into results. It didn't always, but this was where success lay, the long, hard and often frustrating slog and careful attention to every little detail in the hope that something might, just might, lead to a trail that, when followed, might lead to a murderer. It was tough, frustrating and usually thankless work but looking around the room, West knew he wouldn't do anything else.

He spent some time chatting to various members of the team as they wandered in and out, following up this and that. Keeping up morale; he considered it an important part of his job. Finally, he stood looking at the case board, trying to see... anything. Andrews came hurriedly into the room, a piece of paper in his hand and a broad smile on his face, and joined him. He pinned the paper to the case board. 'A bit of good news, at last. The Cornwall team have found one stray fingerprint.'

'I've just spoken to Detective Inspector Pengelly,' West said in surprise. 'He never said anything about a stray fingerprint.'

'That's probably because he doesn't know yet. I was on to a pal of mine down in Falmouth, who just happens to work in the office in the forensic lab and... well... between one thing and another he let the information slip.' Andrews tried but failed to look embarrassed at this side-stepping of official channels.

West looked at him sharply. 'They're being very helpful, Peter, let's not piss them off, eh?'

Andrews' fake look of apology made him shake his head in genuine annoyance. He didn't like irregularities, didn't like short cuts. Dammit, he knew that. 'You know how I feel about that kind of thing.'

There was a sigh of frustration and a reluctant nod. 'Sorry, sorry, I was just getting fed up going nowhere.'

There was no point in blowing it out of proportion, they were all getting frustrated with this case. After all, a bit of useful information was what the team needed to keep them from getting despondent, might even give them somewhere to go. 'Forget about it,' he said. 'What did you find out?'

Smiling, Andrews tapped the paper with his forefinger. 'They found it in Pratt's wallet. Forensics think the perp used gloves but couldn't search the wallet pockets with them on. He was careful, wiped it clean but missed one on the inside of one of the pockets. The bad news, I'm afraid,' he continued with a grimace, 'is that it's not on the system.'

West's eyes narrowed in surprise. He had hoped that whoever had killed Cyril Pratt and Simon Johnson would be known to them in some capacity. After all, this was someone who had killed twice, both times up close and personal. And neither victim had had the opportunity to defend themselves.

Someone. He or she.

He quickly told Andrews about the call from Cornwall. 'Pengelly's men have ruled out any possibility that Edel organised transport to Falmouth. They seem to think she is off the hook, but they still want her prints to identify the second set they lifted in the car so get her in and ask her if she would consent to being fingerprinted. I don't think she will have a problem with it. Have them sent directly to the forensic department in Cornwall. Once they have her prints, they'll automatically check them against the one in the wallet.'

'I'll give her a ring and order her a taxi. She won't have a car yet.' He stood looking at the case board a moment longer. 'What was he looking for in the wallet do you think?'

'Something important enough that he took a risk to look for it,' West considered thoughtfully. 'This was a guy, clever enough to have set up a meeting with a career criminal like Pratt and come off best; someone canny enough to have left no evidence... or at least, he thought he had left none. What the hell was he looking for? And did he find it?'

'So, what do you think? Are we dealing with a very lucky bad guy?'

West didn't answer. He stood, shoulder to shoulder with Andrews and perused the information on the board, his eyes passing from detail to detail. The two men were a similar build as well as height; both wore their hair almost militarily short. Andrews' suits were cheap, off the peg, and looked shabby next to West's made-to-measure suits, but both men exuded a quiet confidence. 'We still haven't found the source of the money,' he said, 'we're missing something. A link somewhere, we're missing it.'

Andrews looked at him. 'You're thinking the missing link is the source of the money? A rich, lucky, bad guy then?'

Still scrutinising the board, both men nodded.

'Give Edel a ring. Ask her to come in. We'll get her finger-printed and interview her again, maybe come up with something new. Maybe she knows something but doesn't know she does, we'll take her through the whole thing, see what comes out.' He headed back to his office leaving Andrews to make the call.

He'd barely sat when he appeared in the doorway. 'She's not answering.'

West swore loudly. 'I told her not to leave the house,' he said in annoyance, running an impatient hand through his hair.

'I suppose she could be in the garden,' Andrews guessed. 'Do you want me to wait and try again?'

'No,' he muttered. He had a bad feeling about this. 'Go and pick her up.'

A short conversation with Inspector Duffy, about lack of progress in the case, put him in a grim mood. 'We don't seem to be any closer to making an arrest, Sergeant West. Or have I missed something?' he asked coldly. 'Of course, with your time spent flitting between here and Cornwall, it must make it difficult for you to focus. You don't have any more jaunts planned, I hope.'

West bit his tongue and kept his temper in check. There was absolutely no point in giving Duffy more reason to be critical. 'I don't expect to have to go to Cornwall again, Inspector. And we are making progress,' he lied confidently, 'but it is a complicated case and needs to be handled carefully. We will get results, I assure you.'

Inspector Duffy looked at him with acute dislike. 'Get on with it then,' he said, dismissing him with a wave of his hand.

Back in his own office, West's irritation was further exacerbated by another call from Pengelly.

'Good news at last,' he said, his voice cheerful, 'the lads have found a fingerprint, just one, in one of the pockets of Pratt's wallet. It doesn't match either of the two sets of prints they found in the car. Assuming the prints in the car belong to Pratt and Edel Johnson, then there was a third person. He'd wiped the wallet but missed one in the inside. He must have been looking for something, Mike.'

'That's fantastic,' West said, trying to sound surprised but even to his ears his voice sounded forced. He wasn't a good liar, wasn't sure he had pulled it off and was annoyed with himself, and with Andrews for putting him in the situation. It wasn't even as if the information led them anywhere.

'Unfortunately, the print isn't on our system. Still, if we get a suspect, we can connect him to Pratt.'

Hanging up, West sat back, dispirited. The only piece of concrete information they'd got all day and it didn't lead them any closer. Closer, he mocked himself, it didn't lead them anywhere. You had to be somewhere to get closer to it and they were exactly nowhere.

He was busy criticising his handling of the case, busy thinking he had made a mistake, that he'd somehow missed something, when the phone rang. 'West,' he answered abruptly.

'She's not here,' Andrews said without preliminaries. 'I checked the garden. I was peering through her letterbox when a nosy neighbour came over to ask what I was doing. According to him, she went out on foot just before ten this morning. When she came back, not long afterwards, she was carrying a heavy box. There was a taxi waiting, she got into it, and she hasn't been back since. It looks like she has scarpered...' Just in time, Andrews decided that adding *again* mightn't have been the best idea.

But both men knew the word hung there, tantalising them. Andrews rushed to fill the ominous silence. 'It was an A-Z Taxi; I'll call into their office; it's just down the road in the village, and find out where they took her.'

'Okay, do that,' West said, his voice tight. 'Then get back here.'

When West rang off, Andrews turned to find the nosy neighbour waiting to speak to him.

'I always said there was something suspicious about her,' he said, keeping his voice low. 'Losing her husband like that. Doesn't make sense. I'm still convinced she buried him in the back garden, you know. I told those young gardaí a couple of months ago, but did they arrest her, oh no.'

Andrews was taking steps backward in preparation for departure. The neighbour took a few steps forward, intent on keeping him a captive audience. Afraid he'd be there the rest of the day listening to him, he decided to do something he had seen in a movie, years before, or maybe he'd read in a novel, he couldn't quite remember, just hoped he could pull it off.

'You've been a great help,' he said, interrupting the neighbour's flow. 'You're obviously a very observant man, I wonder if we could ask you to do some surveillance work for us.'

The man's eyes brightened with fervour and he took a step closer. 'You want me to keep an eye on the house, and see if she comes back?'

Pleased that he had come to the correct conclusion, Andrews bobbed his head emphatically. 'That would be fantastic.' He took a card from his pocket and scribbled a phone number on the back.

'That's my card and my home number. If you see or hear anything give me a ring.' The man took the card and read it fervently. Andrews couldn't prevent himself gilding the lily; he put a hand on his shoulder, gazed into his eyes without a hint of a smile, and said in portentous tones, 'We're depending on you.' He kept his hand on his shoulder a moment more, gave it a squeeze and, without further ado, turned and walked quickly away, smothering a laugh.

Brad Pitt, eat your heart out.

21

Many miles away, Edel Johnson had no reason to laugh. She was sitting, squeezed into a window seat on the Cork-bound train by an incredibly overweight man who had taken the seat beside her. As she struggled desperately to keep her grip on reality, she watched her reflection in the window, overlarge eyes in a thin face staring back. She didn't look as if she were going mad, but she, more than most people, knew that appearances could be deceptive. The suspect in a murder case, not under arrest, no, but requested politely to stay in her house, to stay available, and here she was chugging across the countryside.

She had been leaning over the banister staring stupidly at the black, rubbish-bag she had thrown down the stairs, when she'd heard the sound of the bedroom phone ringing. Her first reaction was surprise; the phone hadn't rung in such a long time. She stood, naked, suddenly unsure of what to do. It continued to ring, the noise jarring, and then it stopped and the silence that followed was, for some reason, equally grating. She returned to the bedroom and stood looking at the phone, wondering who it had been, and then jumped and swore when it rang again.

This time she picked it up and looked at it for a second before lifting it to her ear and saying a very hesitant, and barely audible, 'Hello.'

'Is that Edel Johnson?' a male voice asked, the voice gruff.

She nodded and then, shaking her head at her own stupidity, said quietly, 'Yes, yes this is she.'

'The widow of Cyril Pratt,' the voice continued.

Her eyes flew wide open, startled. 'Who is this?' she asked, trying to keep the shiver that had run up her spine from translating to a tremble in her voice. Her hand gripping the phone was white-knuckled.

'I suppose, in a way, you could say I was a business acquaintance of Cyril's.' The voice went on calmly. 'He... how shall I put it... let's say borrowed, yes, he borrowed some money from me. He used it, he said, to buy a house. The house you are living so comfortably in, Mrs Pratt. Cyril seemed to think he could negotiate the return of my money, such strange ideas he had; he actually believed he could keep living in comfort and pay me back in instalments.' The voice turned hard. 'I was amused,' he said, although she could hear no amusement in the voice. 'Well, for a few seconds anyway.'

Edel shivered and began to pace the floor. 'You spoke to him?' She stopped pacing as an idea hit her. 'You were the man he was going to meet? In Cornwall?'

'I wasn't happy having to go all the way there, not happy at all. But we had a very interesting meeting. Indeed, we did. Unfortunately, it ended badly for poor Cyril. He really was a very foolish man, Mrs Pratt.'

His cold voice, like a slap, stopped her in her tracks. '*You* killed him,' she gasped in horror. Feeling her legs weaken she sat hastily on the bed, now was not a good time to faint.

'I'd say exterminate is a much more appropriate word,' the voice continued evenly, and Edel, the phone pressed tightly to her ear, thought she had never heard a voice so completely devoid of emotion. 'He was vermin, after all. You are so much better off without him, my dear. Now, before he... shall we say left us... Cyril did mention you had certain funds in your bank account, Mrs Pratt, or should I say Johnson. Whatever. I need you to withdraw those funds and bring them to me.' His voice remained quiet and detached as he added, 'Otherwise... I really don't like to threaten so I'll make a promise instead... otherwise, you'll be very sorry. Understood?'

She understood completely, her fingers hurting as she gripped the phone even harder in an effort to stop trembling, fear rising from her body in waves. Attempting to speak, all she could manage was a pathetic, mangled squawk. Drawing all her remaining resources, and there were few left, she cleared her throat and tried again.

'How much?' Her voice came out in a feeble whisper. But it came out. She wiped her forehead with a corner of the sheet and waited for a response.

A sigh of satisfaction came down the phone. 'You're a much more sensible woman than your late husband,' he informed her. 'Cyril relieved me of five hundred thousand euro.' Her gasp interrupted him. 'Yes, quite an amount, isn't it? You can, perhaps, understand now why I'd like it back. According to your late, unlamented husband, you have about three hundred thousand in your personal account. It means I am at the loss of two hundred thousand, but I'm not a greedy or stupid man. I'll settle for what I can get now. Here's what I want you to do.'

She listened to the list of instructions.

He insisted she repeat them a number of times to ensure she had them correct. 'And Mrs Pratt,' he said, 'you might think that you can hang up and ring the police but, please don't. I know who you are and where you live. I could make life very, very unpleasant for you and believe me, the police wouldn't be able to stop me. Just give me the money, and you won't hear from me again; you have my word.'

His words, the chilling coldness of them, made her shiver and when he asked for her mobile number, she stumbled over the digits, needing to repeat and correct herself.

'Fine,' he said, 'remember, just do as I say and everything will be okay.'

Hanging up, she used the bedsheet to wipe the perspiration from her hand and took a deep, shuddering breath. Of course, she was going to ring the gardaí. She emptied the contents of her bag onto the bed, and scrabbled through them, looking for the two pieces of West's card. He'd know what to do.

Dialling the number, she got to the last digit and stopped. They hadn't been able to find Simon in the three months he'd been missing; they didn't know who this man was, how were they going to be able to find him? And what if they never did? He'd killed Simon, so she wasn't imagining the menace in his voice. He'd do exactly as he'd promised, and make her life very, very unpleasant. She shivered again. If she told the gardaí, she'd spend the next weeks and months looking over her shoulder, staring anxiously at every new face she saw, afraid to walk down the street.

He'd promised that if she gave him the money, he would leave her alone. It was only money. What price peace of mind? She put the phone down. No, she wouldn't contact the gardaí. She'd do exactly as he wanted.

A glance at the clock told her it was too early. Only eight o'clock, the bank wouldn't be open for another couple of hours. She sniffed her naked body in disgust, catching the cloying smell of fear, and headed for the shower.

She stayed there a long time but, finally, she faced reality, turned the shower off and stepped out into the steam-filled room. Towel-drying her hair, she brushed it back and caught it in the nape of her neck with a scarf. She smoothed moisturiser onto her face. The bathroom mirror was fogged up and she was relieved not to be able to see the fear that she was sure would still be lingering in her eyes. She was trying, desperately, not to think about things, to remain outside the events, like watching a disaster unfold on a television screen. A heavy fog of despair settled around her, enveloping her, clouding her mind. From its depths, she couldn't see an exit, no emergency light showing the way. She squeezed her eyes tight, rubbing her hands roughly over her face. She didn't have time for this. There would, as the saying went, be time for a breakdown later. Now, well, now she had to do whatever the man who had murdered Simon wanted.

Looking around her, she remembered she'd brought all the clothes that had littered the room down to be washed and opened the wardrobe door with a hiss of annoyance to search for something to wear. She found jeans she hadn't worn for months and pulled them on, the sagging waistband attesting to her weight loss since Simon had vanished. A hasty search located a leather belt and she threaded it through the belt loops and drew it tight. Pulling a white T-shirt from a hanger, she pulled it on and finally took out a navy jacket. She was going to the bank; she had to look somewhat respectable.

She had coffee and some dry, stale biscuits as she watched the hand of the clock creeping toward nine. Convinced at one point the clock had stopped, she rummaged frantically in her bag for her mobile phone, and breathed a sigh of relief to see that time was moving as it should. Finally, it was nine and she picked up the phone and dialled, growling in frustration when she got a recorded message telling her the opening hours of the bank. It seemed to go on forever and then, instead of being transferred to an operator, she heard another message telling her the lines weren't open until nine.

'It is nine,' she screamed down the line in fury before slamming the phone down. She waited another minute then tried again. She listened impatiently while the recorded message gave her all the opening times again and then, to her relief, she heard the voice say she would be transferred to an operator.

Finally, she was speaking to a real, live person. 'I need to make a large withdrawal,' she explained carefully. She had to get this right.

'Just one moment, please,' the bored voice informed her and she was put on hold. For ages. She was pacing the kitchen, up and down, backwards and forwards. 'Oh, for goodness sake,' she said. Another round of pacing and then, at last, another voice asking if they could help her. 'I need to make a large withdrawal,' she said again.

'Customers may withdraw up to a maximum of five hundred euro a day. There is also a facility whereby you can withdraw up to five thousand euro, but that requires a week's notice.'

She took a deep breath. This wasn't going to be easy, was it? 'I need to withdraw three hundred thousand euro, in cash, today.'

Her request was met with silence.

'Hello?' she asked. 'Hello, can you hear me?'

'Is this a joke?' a sharp voice asked her.

She could feel beads of perspiration building on her forehead. 'No, it is not a joke. I have three hundred thousand euro lodged with you. I need to withdraw it today.'

The sharp voice became more acidic. 'Madam, our rules are strict, five hundred euro a day is the maximum you can withdraw without notice.'

'If you can't help me,' she replied, her voice equally sharp. 'Put me on to someone who can.'

Minutes ticked slowly by. Her call was passed from person to person up the line, each voice more sombre but all saying variations of the same thing, *sorry, but no can do.* Each time she responded by demanding to speak to the person's superior until, finally, she was at the top of the pile speaking to the bank manager.

'Good morning, Mrs Johnson,' he began in deep, calm tones. 'You wish, I believe, to make a cash withdrawal. A very large cash withdrawal.'

She struggled to remain calm. 'As I have explained to your assistant, and before that to someone else, and before that to someone else, I need to withdraw three hundred thousand euro in cash. Today.' She heard her voice rising in agitation and took a deep, calming breath.

'You must realise, Mrs Johnson,' the bank manager continued in a conciliatory manner, 'even if we could bend our rules, we don't keep that amount of cash here on a daily basis. I can hear a measure of desperation in your voice, I realise your need is acute, so here is what I can do for you. I can let you have ten thousand euro today and perhaps, if you still require it, I could organise the rest over a number of days. Would that be suitable?'

Despair threatened to sweep over her again and only the memory of the man's menacing promise urged her to keep control. 'Listen to me carefully,' she whispered into the phone. 'I need the money, in full, today. I don't care if you have to collect it from every bank in the Republic, I have to have it.'

The bank manager wasn't a stupid or unimaginative man. He recognised the note of fear in her voice and smoothly pressed a button on his phone allowing him to record the conversation. 'You need three hundred thousand euro in cash today,' he stated, confirming her request and recording it.

'Yes, this morning. I need it this morning, by eleven.'

'Can you tell me why you need it, Mrs Johnson?' He waited as the silence stretched.

'It's for personal reasons. I don't need a reason to withdraw my money, do I?'

He tried again. 'Can you assure me you are not being held under duress?'

'Of course not, as I have said, it is for immediate personal reasons.' Her voice trembled; she didn't know if she could keep going.

'I'm just wondering, if I should ask the gardaí to call around. Just to check.'

She bit her lip to stop herself screaming, a metallic taste of blood in her mouth as teeth pierced the soft tissue. Her voice, when she managed to speak, was eerily calm. 'The only thing I want you to do is organise getting my money. By eleven.'

There was silence for a long time. Her fingers tightened on the phone as she wondered if he were thinking of ringing the gardaí anyway. What was she supposed to do if he did? 'Please,' she whispered.

The silence lasted for so long she thought they'd been cut off. 'Please,' she said again. 'This is really important.'

'Okaaay,' he conceded, drawing out the word as if to highlight his reluctance. With a sigh, and a more clipped professional voice, he added, 'We will, of course, have to levy a fee for withdrawing such an amount without notice.'

'Yes, yes, whatever,' she replied. 'How soon can I have it?'

'I'll need to make some calls. I'll get back to you within the hour.'

She hung up and sat looking at the phone, unable to move for several minutes. For something to do, she made more coffee and drank it while she ate the remainder of the stale biscuits and then paced the floor, checking the time at every turn.

Less than an hour later, the bank manager rang her back and gave her the good news.

'It wasn't easy, Mrs Johnson,' he pointed out. 'It has also cost a great deal of money because security vans have had to come to us from a variety of places and for this purpose only. But I *have* been able to organise the delivery, and we should have the full amount here by ten forty-five. I should warn you though we need to take an administrative levy of three per cent to cover our costs.'

She sighed, a ragged sound of relief that she was sure he heard. 'Thank you,' she said with sincere gratitude and put down the phone, her hand shaking. This was only the first step and she was falling apart. She looked at the clock. It was ten-fifteen. She had less than half an hour to pull herself together and follow the rest of that man's instructions.

That man... his voice... She shivered. She didn't imagine the menace; he sounded cold and mean and she didn't want to have to meet him. But she didn't have a choice. He meant every word he said. After all, he had killed Simon. He had killed Simon, and he had laughed about it. What kind of monster was he? Unfortunately, she was going to find out.

At ten-forty, she made her way to the bank, arriving at ten forty-four on the dot, checking her watch several times as she walked the short distance from her house. She didn't have time to spare; everything had to go to schedule.

Inside the bank, she looked around, confused. She should have asked him where she was to go. The manager, however, had anticipated her dilemma and even as she looked around a young man approached and said her name quietly.

Her breath came on a gasp of relief. 'Yes, I'm Edel Johnson.'

The young man indicated a door in the far corner of the bank and she walked swiftly across the tiled floor, conscious of the many curious eyes that followed her. She hesitated at the door and then grasped the handle and pushed it open.

The manager rose as she entered and greeted her with a handshake and an assessing look. 'You're sure there isn't anything I can do for you?' he said quietly.

She shook her head and pointed to the large sealed cardboard box on his desk. 'Is that it?'

'Yes,' he said, 'take a seat for a moment, there is some paperwork that I need to go through.' Sitting, he opened the file in front of him, pulled out a number of sheets and handed them to her. 'You'll just need to sign these, please, Mrs Johnson.'

She signed the forms, where he had indicated, without reading them.

'You really should read them,' he protested.

'I trust you, Mister...' She read his name badge. 'Bridgeport. Thank you.' As she stood and shook his hand, the clock on the wall behind his desk caught her eye. She had to get on, time was moving too fast. The fear must have been visible on her face. Bridgeport held her hand a moment, delaying her.

'We can still call the gardaí, Mrs Johnson, you are safe in here, you know.'

Edel held his gaze for a moment, seeing kindness and concern reflected there. She hesitated. Maybe if the gardaí came here and took her to a safe place, she would be okay. She remembered the man's voice, heard again the coldness when he spoke about Simon. What if the gardaí told her to go home, told her they would keep an eye on the house. What then? How long would they keep an eye on the house before they gave up? And when they did... he could come and make her suffer.

She pulled her hand away gently.

'Thank you, Mr Bridgeport. It is better this way. You have been very kind, I won't forget it,' she said with feeling. 'Thank you again.'

She picked up her parcel, surprised by the weight, and left.

The taxi she'd ordered to take her to the station was waiting when she got back to the house. Putting the parcel on the seat beside her, she stared out of the window as the driver negotiated busy Dublin traffic. He dropped her as close to the entrance of Heuston train station as he could and, holding the parcel close to her chest for balance, she bought a return ticket to Cork and waited.

So far, her timing was going as planned and ten minutes later, she was on the train. It was a struggle to get the heavy parcel into the rack above her head but she managed and sat back with a sigh.

The overweight man beside her began to snore and she gazed at her watch estimating how much longer she would be trapped by his girth; how long before she would get to meet the man who murdered her husband. She was trapped every way.

She wondered if West was aware she had left home. He might think she'd gone back to Cornwall. She hoped, with a soft chuckle, he wouldn't travel all that way again. Maybe, when she had delivered the money, when it was all over, she would be able to tell him. She had so much explaining to do to so many people.

West seemed like a nice guy. He'd driven back to Cornwall when she had asked, and rescued her from that awful place. She hadn't really thought about it at the time but she supposed he could have contacted the UK police and asked them to go to her and not travelled all that way himself. She had never thanked him or acknowledged his help. She had assumed he would help her, and he had. And he had been kind, she remembered; he had held her as she cried and had been gentle. An unexpected and unwanted frisson ran through her at the memory, jolting her, eyes meeting startled eyes in the window. Refusing to acknowledge the feeling, she hid it away, stuck it with all the other emotions she couldn't cope with, the rollercoaster ride she kept avoiding.

She would keep it simple. When she had the chance, she would explain and thank him.

The train chugged on. It was the first time she had travelled by train since Simon had disappeared. Simon, she mused sadly, who had never really been there in the first place. Her sorrow at his loss was overlaid with double-edged anger; with him for his lies and deception, with herself for being so gullible.

By the time the train rattled into the station in Cork, she had regained her composure and, retrieving her parcel from the rack, stepped off the train. She had been told by her mysterious, nameless caller to stay on the platform and wait and she did, glancing around nervously. The platform was bustling with people arriving and departing, everyone busy with their own lives and unaware of the other lives crashing around them. She waited, her apprehension increasing as the minutes passed, going over the instructions she had been given again and again. She had followed them properly, hadn't she?

Holding the parcel awkwardly with one arm, she ran a hand over her eyes and then glanced at her watch. Fifteen minutes had passed. She was considering what she should do when she saw a man on the other side of the track staring at her. Suddenly alert, she watched him more closely. Aware he had her attention, he pointed to the screen showing the trains due. He held two fingers up and then walked to the far end of the platform.

She stood for a moment unsure of what to do. Was he being deliberately ambiguous to put her more on edge? Or was she making it more difficult than it was? He had pointed to the screen and held up two fingers. Okay, so did that mean he wanted her to get the second train from that platform or from this one, or to wait two minutes and get a train? Don't panic, she told herself, feeling its jaws snapping around the edges of her sanity. She decided to check the screen on the platform she was on before crossing to check out the far side.

Two trains were scheduled to stop from the platform she was on. The first was to Dublin in five minutes, and the second train was to Midleton in ten minutes. Hurrying across the bridge she looked up at the screen there. The first train was to Mallow in thirty and the only other train was to Dublin in an hour. She glanced down the busy platform trying to get a glimpse of the man who had signalled. Which train was she supposed to take? Suddenly her mobile beeped and she quickly read the message: *Midleton.*

Five minutes later, the Midleton train pulled into the station and came to a grating halt, the small crowd surged forward towards the doors and clambered on, taking her with them. She was lucky to get an outside seat this time and kept her parcel on her lap as she waited for further instructions.

She didn't have long to wait. The train was about two minutes from Cork when the man she had seen on the platform approached. He was a big man, stocky rather than fat; well-dressed, unassuming. Shouldn't he look rough and menacing, not neat and ordinary? Shouldn't he look like a murderer? The man stopped as he passed her, and bent down. Straightening, he held out a piece of paper. 'You must have dropped this,' he said, handing it to her, his voice soft. She took it, her hand trembling and he passed on.

Edel waited a moment and opened the piece of paper. *Get off at Glounthaune.* She turned the paper over; nothing else. She closed her eyes wearily. How much longer could she hold out without falling apart?

She had no idea where Glounthaune was, if it was one mile away or ten. Resting her head back against the plush of the seat, she closed her eyes. The train chugged on regardless, bringing her nearer to what she hoped would be the end of this ghastly saga. She could feel tiredness beginning to slow her down, could feel herself drift, and awoke with a startled cry when the intercom announced the next stop to be Glounthaune.

She got off the train, watched it leave and stood uneasily on the platform. The few people who had got off at the same time quickly left and within minutes she was alone. The beep of her mobile announced a message. Fumbling with the package, she opened it and read, *Take the next train back to Cork and wait.*

Her eyes closed, tears trickling to fall and dot the cardboard box with dark splodges. From the other side of the track, she heard voices and, opening her eyes, she looked across to see a few people gathering. The next train to Cork must be from the other side. Wiping her eyes with the sleeve of her jacket, she walked to the overhead bridge and made her way across.

The train arrived within minutes and once again she struggled on and found a seat. Ten minutes later, she was back in Cork, waiting on the platform. The parcel was heavy and her arms ached. After five minutes, she placed it on the ground between her feet and stretched. Twenty minutes passed, twenty minutes of nerve-wracking, nail-biting anxiety that had her jumping at every passer-by.

Finally, just as she worried that something had gone wrong, the same man she had seen on the train approached with a casual gait and stopped in front of her. 'Sorry for all the cloak and dagger stuff,' he said, with a smile that stayed firmly put on very narrow lips. 'I had to make sure you weren't being followed, you understand?'

'I'm not sure I understand anything anymore, Mister...?'

The smile became an unpleasant smirk. 'You can call me John. I think, Mrs Johnson, the less you know about me, the better it will be for your health.'

His gaze drifted over her; cold eyes took in her trim figure and classic good looks, lingering on the curve of her breast. The smile widened now in appreciation, quickly broadening into a leer of lust. 'Your husband may have been one of the most stupid people I have had the misfortune to meet, but I see he had good taste in women.' He measured up the parcel she had put down by her feet. 'Not a stupid woman either, I see. It's all there?'

'Almost three hundred thousand,' she said, seeing his eyebrows rise at the *almost*. 'There's two hundred and ninety-one thousand. The bank charged me nine thousand for arranging everything at short notice. Please,' she finished, 'it was all I had.'

'So, I'm out of pocket by two hundred and nine grand,' John said, his voice taking on the menacing tone she had heard earlier. He looked her over again. 'Perhaps,' he continued, moving closer, 'we could come to some arrangement to pay the balance.' He lifted a finger and ran it along her jaw.

She felt her insides contract with fear and revulsion. 'You s-said,' she stammered, 'you said you'd settle for the three hundred thousand.'

'Yes, but you didn't bring me three hundred, did you? Nine thousand euro can buy a lot.' Again, he raised a hand, this time parting her jacket to run a hand over her breast. 'Oh, yes,' he murmured. 'I think we can work that nine thousand off very quickly.' He squeezed her breast painfully and reached around to pull her to him, opening his coat, pulling her inside.

Panic froze her into immobility as she felt his body hot against hers. She felt the heat from his breath before he closed his thin lips roughly down on hers, forcing his tongue deep into her mouth. His hand dropped and cupped her bottom, pulling her hard against him. Releasing her slightly he pulled her hand down and rubbed it over the hardening bulge in his trousers with a groan.

This can't be happening. She watched people move past them unconcernedly, unaware or perhaps uncaring, intent on their own lives. One woman cast them a look of disgust. *Would she come if I screamed for help?*

'You are one hot woman,' John whispered thickly against her ear, and then ran his tongue down her neck to where the soft triangle of skin met her shoulder, and he sucked hard, and then bit down, his teeth bruising as she squirmed and tried to pull away. But his grip was tight, and he held her effortlessly as his mouth moved back to cover hers and his tongue once more plundered her mouth, almost choking her.

His hands were all over her, under her T-shirt, squeezing and pinching. Her squeals of pain he stopped by the simple method of keeping his tongue firmly lodged in her mouth. She wanted to bite down on it, wanted to bite it off and spit it at him but she was too afraid to do anything. He tried to insert his hands down the waistband of her jeans but was stopped by the tightly secured leather belt.

She didn't know how long the assault went on. It felt like hours. She didn't know how long it would have lasted if not for the crowd of schoolchildren who arrived on the platform like a swarm of locusts, filling whatever space was available with noise and laughter, elbows and knees and overlarge backpacks that they swung to and fro.

The man glanced behind him with a hiss of frustrated annoyance as a backpack knocked his shoulder and, for a moment, he relaxed his hold. Without thinking, Edel kicked the parcel of money as hard as she could towards the edge of the platform and, as his eyes followed in alarm, she pulled away and ran for the exit, weaving in and out of the schoolchildren with a speed she didn't know she possessed.

The man quickly retrieved the parcel and held it as he watched her run up the stairs to the exit. He took out his mobile quickly and phoned her. 'I'll call that an appetiser, my dear,' he snarled quietly. 'I'll have my main course when I have built up a bigger appetite.' He waited a beat before continuing, 'And I can get very hungry, Edel.' He snapped his phone shut and pocketed it and, with a quick glance around, strolled nonchalantly to the exit with the parcel under his arm.

22

Edel heard her mobile ring as she ran out the station door. She ignored it and climbed into a waiting taxi, collapsing onto the seat in disarray.

'Just drive!' she snapped at the startled driver. As he pulled out of the station car park, she looked back through the rear window and breathed a sigh of relief when he didn't appear. She was shaking, and wrapping her arms around herself. She could taste him, could feel where his hands had touched. Shivering, she felt the cooling slug trail of saliva on her neck, the throb of pain where he had sucked and gnawed, smaller pains where he had pinched and squeezed. She longed to wash her mouth out and scrub herself until she bled. Degraded beyond belief, she felt a spark of hatred for Simon who was responsible for all of it, for leaving her with this mess to cope with and being the cause of such grief. Her eyes welled, one tear escaping. She brushed it away, this wasn't a time for tears.

What to do? Panic bubbled just below the surface and she desperately held it at bay. She remembered her mobile ringing; reaching for it, she listened to his message and heard the threat. He knew where she lived; she couldn't go home.

Where to go? She needed a place to think, to hide away, but she didn't know Cork at all, didn't know where to go. A passing van made a mirror of the taxi window. She saw her reflection, the deep frown lines, the grimace that twisted her mouth. She gulped, and held a hand over her face.

'I can't just keep driving around, Missy,' the taxi driver called back.

'Yes, I'm sorry, of course,' she managed to get out with difficulty. She took a deep breath, tried to clear her head and think. 'I need somewhere to stay,' she said in a voice that trembled only a little.

'A hotel?'

Lack of choice made the decision easy. 'Yes, a hotel. Can you recommend one, please?'

He hesitated a moment. 'Well, there's the Cork International. It's not far from here but it's a bit pricey. Do you want something cheaper?'

All she wanted was somewhere safe to hide. 'No, that will be fine.'

The taxi dropped her at the imposing doorway of the Cork International and she quickly paid the fare and entered, looking nervously around her. The foyer was busy, a large party having just arrived before her. She waited anxiously, constantly glancing toward the entrance as if John had caught the scent of fear and followed. Finally, it was her turn.

The hotel was busy, the receptionist explaining that there were only executive rooms available. 'Fine,' Edel said impatiently, handing over her credit card. If she'd been told they only had suites left she would have said the same. She wasn't going any further.

'Would you like a hand with your luggage?' the receptionist asked.

Edel shook her head, took the key card and walked quickly

in the direction of the lifts. She was pleased her room was on the fifth floor. It felt safer, more inaccessible, to be higher up.

Reaching her room, she quickly slid the key card down the slot, got a green light and opened the door. She closed it behind her, collapsed back against it as a sudden weakness overcame her and cried bitter, angry, frightened tears until, exhausted, she gave a soft hiccough and stopped.

She continued to lean against the door, desperately trying to think of a plan. Her stomach churned at the idea of meeting John again. When she considered what he might demand of her in payment for the nine thousand she still owed him, she felt her stomach churn again and, pushing away from the door, she stumbled into the bathroom in time to empty the contents of her meagre breakfast into the toilet.

She stayed there, her hands grasping the ceramic bowl as dry retching followed. Finally, more than exhausted now, she got to her feet. Turning on the tap, she washed her face with cold water and then washed her mouth out too, gargling with the water in an attempt to remove the taste of the man that still, disgustingly, lingered. She desperately wanted a shower, to try and wash away the feel of his touch, the smell of him and the sour smell of her fear. Even her clothes stank of him. It was tempting to strip and use the white robe that hung from the back of the bathroom door but she was reluctant to leave herself so vulnerable. She needed to be able to leave if she had to and she couldn't... wouldn't... put those clothes on again if she took them off.

A quick call to reception informed her that there was a shopping centre just five minutes' walk from the hotel.

Five minutes' walk.

Rationally, she knew John couldn't have followed her to the hotel. Was this the way she was going to live her life now, fear underlying every decision, every choice? It was only five minutes' walk away. He had no idea where she was. Had he?

She sat on the bed for a moment, gathering her thoughts, putting off making a decision.

It was a generously-proportioned room. Decorated in turquoise and lime-green, the furnishing was tastefully modern. The king size bed, dressed in crisp white cotton with a turquoise throw folded neatly across the middle, held an extraordinary number of pillows all in various shades of the key colours. In front of the tall picture windows that gave a view over Cork, two comfortable chairs nudged a small table. One wall held a large, but discreetly framed, flat screen television and the others, tasteful line drawings of Cork's beauty spots in matching frames.

A small alcove caught Edel's eye and she rose listlessly to investigate. It held a coffee percolator, kettle, fridge and microwave with a small basket holding an assortment of teas and coffee. Even a selection of upmarket biscuits. Perhaps, she'd have some later when her stomach stopped heaving. She wasn't hungry but she knew she had to eat. After all, she might have to run again.

Restlessly, she went into the bathroom where the turquoise and lime-green colour scheme continued, large mirrors reflecting light around the room. They also reflected back a pale, defeated woman who reached a hand out to her reflection in distress. Her other hand felt the slight indents John's teeth had made on her neck and the contusions that would look worse before fading. Her breath caught on a hiccup and she closed her eyes, resting her face against the cool glass, and felt tears sting. She pushed away from the mirror, refusing to look in it again, too embarrassed, too humiliated to see how she had been branded.

Lifting a towel, she dried her eyes in its soft pile, taking some tiny comfort in the clean scent of it. She needed to feel clean again, to regain some sense of self that was not degraded, humiliated, debased. A bath would be the first step. A long soak in water as hot as she could take it, clean clothes and a glass, or several, of wine. Decision made.

Grabbing her bag, she removed her key card and made her way down to the foyer, choosing to go down the five flights by stairway rather than taking the lift. She didn't want the lift door to open and see John standing there. Okay, she was probably being ridiculous, but she wasn't taking any more chances. She stood on the stairwell side of the double doors before carefully parting them to look out across the foyer. It was a vision of sophisticated calm with twinkling chandeliers, plush carpets and relaxed faces.

No John, waiting to claim his pound of flesh.

She took a calming deep breath, pushed through the double doors and walked slowly to the exit.

It was a lovely day, she realised as she stepped outside. It was late afternoon but the sun, though low, still had warmth. Summer had come and she hadn't even noticed.

The shopping centre, as the receptionist had promised, was a short five-minute walk away. It was a bright bustling place, busy with people laden down with shopping bags. Shops were filled with summer colour; light music filled the imperceptible silences between chattering people, clattering footsteps, laughter and all the other myriad sounds of commercialism.

She dredged up a smile and, infected by the colour and buzz, felt a slight release in the tension that had gripped her since that early morning phone call. Drawn by a window display, she wandered into a department store, joining a throng of women who looked, touched and bought. She'd intended to purchase necessities when she left the hotel but instead, swayed by the normality of it all, she indulged and bought a lot more, tempted by colour and fabric and a simple need to pamper herself, to feel good again.

Ignoring the plain cotton underwear she had intended to purchase, she chose a matching bra and brief set in baby-blue silk and another in teal satin, her fingers handling the soft material with genuine pleasure. This was what she needed, a luxurious contrast to the seediness of her encounter with John. She picked up a basket and dropped them in. A silk camisole and matching French knickers in pale rose caught her wandering eye. She found her size and added them to the basket and didn't give a second's pause before adding a matching robe, the material spilling from the basket in a silky rose stream.

An hour later, after a visit to a food store, she was ready to leave the centre, several bags dangling from her hands. She had bought, along with the lingerie, two pairs of jeans, T-shirts in white and her favourite baby-blue, and, an irresistible blouse in a gossamer fabric she would probably never wear but just had to have. Shopping, the eternal panacea.

Pausing at the exit, she turned the collar of her jacket up, kept her head low and looked quickly up and down the street, prepared to retreat or run if she saw him; prepared to drop all her purchases and run like the wind. The short-lived peace she had felt while shopping vanished and she felt sick, her heart racing, head thumping.

With her eyes constantly flicking from side to side, she walked as fast as she could back to the hotel, almost running the last few feet and pushing through the front door on a gasp. Panic bubbled as she looked around in dismay. The foyer was busier, full of people standing too closely together. What if John was hiding among them? She had to get to her room. With her head down, she pushed through with murmurs of apology, keeping to the centre of the crowd rather than the edges where he might be lurking. Why had she left the hotel? What an idiot she had been.

She took the stairs to the fifth floor, glancing up and down the corridor before exiting the stairwell and hurrying to her door. She slid her key card down the lock and pushed the door open with a gasp of relief. Stumbling across to the bed, she collapsed onto it, her bags dropping willy-nilly on the floor around her.

She lay there, unmoving, her mind a blank; all pain and memories, all details held at bay while her mind did a quick system check to prevent overload. Her clenched hands relaxed after a while and her ragged breathing eased. Tightly-closed eyes relaxed and opened, blinked twice and closed again. Moments later, she was asleep.

It didn't last long but it was sufficient for her mind to effect minimal repairs; she wouldn't break down, not yet.

She continued to lie there, happy just to be safe and wondering how long she could stay hiding away like this. Money wasn't a problem; Simon had insisted she kept a large amount of cash on her credit card. She had three or four thousand on it, enough to pay for the hotel for a while but it wouldn't last indefinitely, not staying in executive rooms in posh hotels anyway. She'd have to move somewhere much cheaper.

Was he looking for her? Cork wasn't a big city. If he tried every hotel, wouldn't he find her? She closed her eyes, realising her mistake. When she'd booked in, she should have paid in cash, and used a fake name. Her mouth twisted bitterly. Simon should have given her lessons. It was too late now. Or was it?

Sitting up, she rang reception. 'Hello, my name is Edel Johnson, in room 556. I'm here for a rest after a very busy time, and don't want to be disturbed, nor do I wish my family or colleagues to know where I am staying. Can you ensure that my details are not given out, to anyone?'

Her request was met by the cool professionalism her expensive executive room paid for.

'Ms Johnson, it is hotel policy not to give out resident's details.'

'Yes,' she interrupted. 'But if someone rings looking for me?'

'I will put an alert next to your name and room number, Ms Johnson. If any person rings asking about you, they will be told we have no resident by that name. If you wish this situation to change, please let us know. Is there anything else I can do for you?'

'No, thank you.' She lay back with a sigh. Now she was safe.

She stayed unmoving for a few moments more and then sat, picked the bags up from where she had dropped them and emptied the contents onto the bed beside her. Pulling off the sales tags, she hung the jeans and T-shirts in the wardrobe and folded the lingerie and put it on a shelf, caressing the soft fabric absentmindedly.

Sergeant West came into her head; she considered contacting him again, and again discounted the idea. 'I've left Dublin, when he asked me not to,' she said aloud, the hint of despair that was never far away creeping back into her voice. 'There is no way he is going to believe anything I say. He might insist I go home. And if I go back home...' The memory of the ordeal at the train station rolled over her, followed by nausea, wave upon wave until she was, once again, retching into the toilet.

She knelt there for several moments on the cool tiled floor, exhausted, until the nausea subsided and then she stood shakily. Taking a flannel from the shelf, she rinsed it in cold water and wiped her face, catching her reflection in the mirror again as she did so. She looked so weary. Holding her hair back, she looked at her damaged neck. The bruising was more marked now but the slight indents from his teeth were almost gone. With a sad sigh, she let her hair drop.

Perhaps, she'd feel better after a bath.

Peeling off her clothes, she put them into the laundry bag provided, and, following instructions, placed the bag on a hook inside a compartment in her bedroom door, from where, according to the instructions on the back of the door, the hotel staff would take it, clean it and return it. She hung the bag on the hook and closed and locked the compartment door. There was no point in being stupid; she might need the clothes again. And anyway, she couldn't keep throwing away clothes when something bad happened to her because that seemed to be the way her life was going and she would have no clothes left.

She poured scented bath foam into the bath, turned the taps on, and left it to fill while she returned to the bedroom for the bottle of chilled white wine she'd bought. Choosing a large glass from the selection provided, she poured, filling it almost to the brim, and brought it back to where the warm, scented water was bubbling and rising in a fragrant cloud. When it was ready, she placed the glass carefully on the broad rim of the bath and stepped in with a satisfied sigh, sinking down to allow the foamy water to envelop her. Blowing foam from one hand, she reached for the glass and took a long, cool, mouthful of wine.

When the glass was half empty, she was able to think about her meeting with John more objectively. Simon must have stolen that money around the time she met him; stole it and used it to buy their house. Lies, from the very beginning to the very end. Not for the first time, she wondered if she ever knew the man she married. Was it all just a game to him?

Thinking dispassionately, she thought perhaps, that he had loved her. She remembered things he had done, things he had said. Nobody was that good a liar, were they?

She had loved him... but now? Knowing all the lies, the pretence. Truth was, she admitted, finishing the glass, the man she had loved, the man she had married, well, he had never existed. He had listened to her, to her likes and dislikes, to her dreams and fantasies, inventing himself as Simon Johnson to fit her template of the ideal man. Hadn't she listed honesty and truthfulness among the traits she admired? Maybe not, she couldn't remember.

What a fool she had been. Desolation, the emptiness of her world crashed around her. Putting the slippery, empty glass back on the edge of the bath, it slid on its foamy base and fell to the tiled floor with a crash, scattering shards across the bathroom floor. Edel started to laugh and then to cry, a hysteria that increased as the water cooled around her.

'Great,' she yelled, looking up to the ceiling, to whatever gods continued to play such nasty tricks on her. 'Just what I needed. Thanks! I'll probably cut my blasted foot and bleed to death.'

She pulled the plug and sat as the now cold water emptied, watching the foam settle around her curves like snowdrifts and she slowly grew calm. Standing, she grabbed a towel from the rack and rubbed herself dry, looking at the glass shards on the floor in annoyance, and then gave a quick chuckle of genuine amusement. 'Just when I think nothing else can go wrong,' she said, turning to address her reflection in the steamed mirror. Wrapping the towel tightly around herself she gingerly stepped out onto a glass-free area. She unrolled a handful of toilet paper, bent down and swept the broken shards safely into a corner. Unrolling some more paper, she wet it and wiped the floor again. She didn't really want to get glass embedded in her foot. She'd had enough pain for one day.

Happy the floor was now safe, she unwrapped the towel and used the body cream provided to massage moisture back into her skin. The scent was pleasant and she used it liberally, wincing as she touched painful areas where he had pinched and squeezed. She had always bruised easily, and they were coming up, not just on her neck, but on her arms, breasts and stomach. Tomorrow they would be multicoloured.

Walking naked into the bedroom, she took the hairdryer from a drawer and roughly dried her hair in front of the full-length mirror. It reflected back a too thin, but shapely woman, auburn hair just touching her shoulders. Full lips above a firm chin; eyes, usually bright and clear, tired and defeated between tear-swollen lids.

For a brief moment the defeat in her eyes shocked her. This wasn't who she was. The memory of her degradation at John's hands came back and she batted it away viciously. 'You will not defeat me, you bastard,' she said aloud. Putting the hairdryer down, she faced her reflection. 'You have a choice,' she spoke firmly to the cowering creature in front of her. 'You can hide away and wait to see what further humiliation they dump on you or you can be proactive and do something.'

Her reflection sneered back, unimpressed.

Turning away, she took out the silk camisole and French knickers she had purchased earlier, slipped them on and instantly felt better. Or, at least, better than before.

Taking another wine glass, she filled it and sat in the comfortable armchair by the window, her legs stretched out before her. From here, she could see the lights of Cork. She imagined cosy restaurants, intimate bars and romantic couples. She had stayed nearby once with Simon, somewhere near the river. One of those intimate, discreetly-luxurious hotels they both loved. Or did they? she wondered bitterly. She had told him all her likes and dreams and he'd built their life around them. Every moment of their life together was a series of lies. She sighed heavily.

Her thoughts drifted to Sergeant West. Would he believe that she had taken out almost three hundred thousand euro to give to a stranger? She stood impatiently, moving closer to the window where, as darkness had fallen, she could see her reflection. Lifting her glass in a toast, she clinked it gently against its mirrored image. 'I said I'd be proactive and do something, didn't I?' she murmured. 'And, I will.'

She moved to the desk, picked up the hotel phone and dialled a number.

23

W est and Andrews were still collating information at six that evening. They had ascertained that Edel had taken a taxi to Heuston station that morning. The ticket office hadn't recognised her photograph but told a frustrated Andrews that she could have bought her ticket on the train anyway. They were able to give him the timetable for that morning but, since there were several trains in either direction within twenty minutes of her arriving at the station, it was impossible to pinpoint which train she took. The stationmaster, unhelpfully, also commented that each train stopped at several places en route to their final destination, so, even if they knew which train, they wouldn't know where she got off.

Back at the station, he faced an irate sergeant who was loudly and roundly condemning the duplicity of females.

'This bloody woman has made a fool of me for the last time,' West snarled in unaccustomed temper as he paced his office. 'I've had the inspector on the phone and, believe me, incompetent was the kinder of the words he used.'

He sat heavily and frowned at the placid Andrews, daring him to comment. But wisely, he refused to give the sergeant more ammunition for his ire and West relaxed slightly, his anger always short-lived. Finally, with a self-deprecatory smile, he said, 'Okay, Peter, temper tantrum over. Let's get back to what we are good at and get this case solved and shelved. We need to find out why Edel Johnson has run this time, and where to.' He frowned at the information in front of him. 'Our best bet, looking at this timetable, is Cork. It keeps popping up in this case, doesn't it? Can't be a coincidence. Fax her photo to the local station in Cork; see if anyone recognises her at the station or at the taxi rank. Ask them to check on Amanda Pratt too, in case that's her destination. And get a warrant for her bank accounts and track her credit card use.' He checked his watch. 'If you go now, you'll catch a judge for the warrant and we can get her bank records first thing tomorrow.'

The phone rang, interrupting his train of thought and he answered curtly. 'Yes.'

'Is that Sergeant West?' came a voice he recognised immediately. He held his hand over the mouthpiece. 'It's her, put a trace on the call.' He waited a moment as Andrews sped away, before replying in calm, measured tones. 'Yes, can I help you?'

There was a slight pause. 'It's Edel Johnson, I wanted to let you know, I've... I've had to go away.'

'Ms Johnson,' he replied, remaining calm with extreme effort. 'I did request, if you remember, that you remain at home, available, should we need to speak to you.'

'Yes, I know,' she said quietly, 'but... I can't explain... I just wanted you to know that I had to go. I didn't have a choice. I'm sorry.'

He heard the catch in her voice and rushed into speech to preclude her cutting the connection. 'Why can't you explain? It can't be that complicated.'

'It would take too long, and I'm not giving you the opportunity to trace this call. I just wanted you to–'

He interrupted her. 'This is Foxrock, Ms Johnson, not New York. We don't have the technology to trace phone calls here. 'Why don't you tell me what happened this morning?'

'I can't, he said he would...'

He heard a distinct gulp down the line. 'Who?'

'His name is John. That's all I know.' Her voice trembled as she added, 'And he is a very bad person, believe me. I'm sorry, this wasn't a good idea.' She finished and hung up.

Swearing roundly, West rushed out into the general office where Andrews was putting down a receiver. 'Well?' he asked impatiently

Andrews smiled. 'Cork International Hotel.'

'Excellent!' West checked his watch. 'Okay,' he said. 'Let's call it quits for the day. She's not going anywhere. Go home; introduce yourself to your wife and son. I'll pick you up at six and we can meet our lovely Ms Johnson for breakfast in Cork.'

'Right,' he replied. 'Do you still want me to chase that warrant before I go?'

West chewed his lip. 'No, leave it. Let's see what she has to say tomorrow. We can proceed afterwards, if it's still necessary.'

Andrews headed off, West staying to finish some outstanding paperwork and to run through their data again. Perhaps Edel would have the answer to the mystery five hundred thousand euro, and maybe she knows who killed Cyril Pratt. They'd know tomorrow. Yawning, he grabbed his jacket and keys and headed for home.

24

Six in the morning, West was opening the garden gate of the Andrews' house in Crocosmia Close, a small crescent of semi-detached bungalows nestling among a bouquet of roads in Bray all bearing the name of a garden flower. The gate squeaked open into an immaculately-kept garden just starting to show early summer colour. The house was as well maintained as the garden and, as West knew from his frequent visits, it was just as pretty inside. The front door opened as he approached it and Andrews appeared with his pretty, petite wife close behind.

'Hi Michael,' she called in greeting, before reaching up to give Andrews a kiss on the lips and a soft pat on his cheek. West, thinking how strange it was that only his mother and Andrews' wife called him Michael, gave a wave and a smile before turning and heading back to the car with Andrews on his heels.

Conversation was desultory, neither man big on small talk this early in the day, both focused on the job ahead. Traffic was heavy as they approached Cork, but they arrived outside the International in good time and pulled into the generous hotel car park just as the car clock showed nine.

'I hope you were serious about breakfast,' Andrews said as they climbed out and walked toward the entrance.

West put a hand on his shoulder. 'I promise, before we leave, I'll treat you to the best breakfast the hotel can offer, okay? Let's hope we can call it a celebration breakfast.'

The receptionist, despite their identification, refused to disclose the information they requested and insisted on calling the duty manager. He arrived moments later, a tall, suited, bespectacled man with a worried expression that increased when he saw the two men. With a brief look around the foyer, as if to judge the extent of the damage a visit by the gardaí had made, he beckoned them towards a door behind the reception desk.

Inside the small room, he sat behind a cluttered desk and waved them into seats. 'It's early for a visit,' he said.

'Necessary, I'm afraid.' West gave him a brief precis of their situation, enough to convince the manager of the need to cooperate.

After eliciting a promise that trouble wouldn't spoil the calm, relaxed ambience of the hotel, the manager, his face creased in worry, gave them Edel's room number and a master key card. 'She had asked for her stay here to be kept confidential.'

'I'll explain that we insisted,' West said reassuringly.

The worried look didn't fade as the manager offered, half-heartedly, to go with them. 'Or I could send a security team with you?'

West thanked him and declined assistance. 'We don't envisage any problem, thank you.' He shook his hand and thanked him for his cooperation, deciding as they left that worried was the man's default expression.

They took the lift to the fifth floor and, moments later, they were outside room 556. West knocked smartly on the door, and when seconds passed with no response, he repeated the knock a little louder. Still no response. With a sigh, he slid the master key card down the lock. The red light immediately switched to green and with a clunk the lock disengaged.

He pushed the door open slowly, looking for signs of movement beyond. Nothing, and the room was in darkness. Both men, concerned now, reached for their holstered weapons and drew them silently. They waited a heartbeat. 'Armed gardaí,' West called out loudly and took a step into the room. 'Armed gardaí,' he said again and moved forward, Andrews immediately behind. A key card was in the light slot but all the lights were switched off and, with the curtains drawn, the room was a dangerous mix of shadows and shades. The light from the hallway illuminated some of the room but there were still too many places they couldn't see, and both men were dangerously backlit. Reaching along the wall, West found the switch and with a flick the room was filled with light.

They stood without moving, their weapons held firm while their eyes scanned the room and assessed it for potential threat. A rustle alerted both to movement and they turned as one, weapons raised, to face the built-in wardrobe which slowly opened to show a pale and scared Edel.

'I thought you were... were...' She swayed, and put a hand out to the wall for support. 'I was afraid it was John,' she finally finished as they stood watching her carefully.

Andrews checked the rest of the room and bathroom and with a nod to the sergeant both men holstered their weapons.

Edel moved across to the unmade bed where she sat wiping tears from her eyes with a crumpled sheet. 'I didn't sleep very well, I kept dreaming that he was coming for me. When I heard the knock, I didn't think, I just hid. It took a while to register it was you.' She took a shaky breath and then looked at West accusingly. 'You did trace the call,' she said.

'We did,' he agreed calmly. Turning, he walked over to a chair by the window where he picked up her robe and coming back, handed it to her without a word. Colour racing to her cheeks, she snapped it from his hand and quickly slipped it on over the silk camisole and French knickers and belted it tightly.

West guessed she was unaware that the tightly-belted silk robe emphasised rather than hid the curves beneath and the colour complimented her pale skin perfectly, but there was something about her that he appreciated more, an inner core of strength that was there in her eyes and her raised chin. 'Get dressed,' he said gruffly, averting his eyes from her rose silk curves with difficulty. 'You've a lot of explaining to do and we may as well do it over breakfast. We'll wait outside.' He headed for the door, leaving Andrews to follow in his wake. In the corridor he paced, ignoring his partner who rested nonchalantly against the door frame, arms crossed.

'You're going to interview her in the dining room?' Andrews eventually asked, stopping him as he turned to pace the short corridor for the third time. 'Not that I am questioning your decision, of course, Sergeant,' he added hastily, seeing a look of irritation flash across his face.

West, who had been considering the wisdom of questioning Edel over breakfast, was for a split second, annoyed. But he was neither arrogant nor stupid, and his willingness to discuss decisions, and accept input in decision making, had contributed to the good rapport which had developed between the two men. He shook his head and gave a quick grin. 'Yes, you are. And you're right, it's perhaps not the best idea I've had.' He sighed and leaned his tall frame against the opposite side of the door. 'Let's just see what is going on here, and go from there, okay?' He saw Andrews nod and continued. 'At worst, she'll tell us nothing but, at least we'll have had a decent breakfast before heading back. I did promise you that, didn't I?'

Andrews' stomach growled, causing both men to laugh, and defusing any lingering tension. Their laughter faded as the door opened and, like sentinels, they stood as Edel walked between them wearing jeans and a white T-shirt. Her hair, although tangled, shone and bounced as she walked down the corridor just ahead of them.

They didn't speak as they waited for the lift, relieved when it arrived empty. The dining room was a lively, busy place, elegantly furnished, bright and airy. Big windows looked onto a courtyard garden filled with tree ferns and an array of other plants in large, ornate terracotta pots. A sign invited them to wait to be seated and they stood, the men casually relaxed, Edel tense, her eyes constantly darting around the room.

A waiter, of uncertain years and wearing a poorly-fitting toupee, gestured for them to follow him to a table near the window which had a pretty view of the courtyard but was closely surrounded by other tables, all occupied. West spied a table toward the back of the room, near the wall, with a floral arrangement separating it from nearby tables. He pointed to it and the waiter, with a slight incline of his head, changed course and settled them at their chosen table. He handed them menus and related a list of breakfast specials before leaving them to make their choices.

West glanced at Edel. Her hands were gripping the menu so tightly, her knuckles were white. She looked tired and weary and he guessed tears weren't far away. Whatever had happened yesterday, it seemed to have been the final straw.

She opened her mouth to speak but he interrupted before she got a word out. 'Let's order breakfast first. You look as though you could do with some food, and we certainly could, right Peter?'

'Right,' Andrews agreed, his focus firmly on the menu.

The waiter returned after a short interval and took their

order. Andrews, in his element, ordered the hotel breakfast special which, West was amused to see, seemed to contain everything on the menu. He settled for bacon and eggs and Edel, hesitating a moment, did the same.

They all agreed on coffee and toast, and a large cafetiere came almost immediately. When their cups were filled, he looked at Edel. 'Well, you may as well start.'

She blinked and then pressed her lips together. 'I feel like I've been on a roller coaster,' she said. 'I don't know if you'll understand, I'm not sure I do anymore.' She told them everything. It didn't take long, she didn't elaborate on what happened, didn't dwell on how she felt or linger too long on the details of her abuse on the station platform. She laid it out in short, terse sentences, trying to remain emotionless and calm.

The two men listening were not fooled. She may have managed to keep her voice calm but she couldn't disguise the tremble in her voice or the way her hand gripped her napkin. When she described the events on the station platform, she was unaware that her voice dropped to a whisper they struggled to hear. They didn't interrupt, allowing her to finish her story to the end.

When she stopped speaking, the tension seemed to leave her abruptly, and she sagged back against the chair. She paled alarmingly, causing the men to exchange worried glances.

'Are you all right?' West asked in concern, wondering if she were going to pass out.

She closed her eyes, took a deep breath and let it out slowly. A second deep breath and she opened her eyes to see both men regarding her intently. 'I'm sorry... it's just been so awful. Everything... and it just seems to go on and on.' She stopped on a sob and said no more.

The waiter appeared just then, skilfully balancing three plates which he placed in front of each with a flourish.

Andrews' breakfast special appeared to be enough for at least five people and he gave a sigh of such obvious pleasure that both West and Edel were forced to smile. With general agreement they concentrated on their food for a while, or at least, as West said with heavy sarcasm, until he and Edel had finished theirs.

'You'll never eat all that, Peter,' he commented when both he and Edel had pushed their plates away.

Forking a piece of sausage, Andrews waved it under his nose, gave a sniff and a growl of approval before popping it into his mouth and munching happily.

'Ignore him, Ms Johnson,' West said, grateful that Andrews' antics had relieved a little of the tension that lay heavily around the table. 'Tell me more about this man. He said your husband had borrowed the money from him? Did he say when, or why?'

'He said borrowed, but the way he said it... I don't know, it just didn't sound right... and then later he said Simon had relieved him of the money. So, I suppose he meant he had stolen it.' Her forehead creased in a frown. 'He didn't say when, or anything more about it, other than he wanted it back.'

'And he definitely said he had murdered him?'

'No. He said he had exterminated him,' she said with a shudder. 'That he was vermin. He sounded so amused.' Tears welled. 'He said poor Simon was a stupid man, and he killed him.'

'Not before Pratt told him about the money you had, though,' he said cynically.

'No, and I don't understand, why did he kill him? I would have given him the money without a moment's hesitation.'

'Perhaps, if you could have provided the whole five hundred thousand, he might not have. I've seen men killed for a lot less than two hundred grand, I'm afraid. A lot less. Men, like this John character, can't afford to be seen to be soft. Gives other criminals the wrong idea.'

'We could have sold the house. Do you think I wouldn't have done?' she said desperately.

'In the current market? It might have taken months. He obviously wasn't willing to hang around. Wanted what he could get, and wanted it now.' He considered a moment. 'From the way he treated you, Edel, I'd guess this man John likes causing pain, that he likes to kill. If he did kill your husband, he is possibly also guilty of the murder of Simon Johnson.'

Seeing the waiter pass, he raised a hand and indicated the empty cafetiere. The waiter tilted his head, returning moments later with a fresh pot, steam and aroma drifting from it in happy tandem. He removed their used plates, glanced briefly at Andrews' by now only half-empty plate and left with a smile.

West poured more coffee for all of them and, frowning, asked, 'You're sure you have never seen him before?'

'Positive.' She considered a moment. 'He's not a man you'd forget. There's something about him, something really creepy. It's not just because of what he did to me, it's more... well, you feel he could do anything he wanted, that he wouldn't think of the consequences.' She looked at West. 'You've no idea who he is, do you? So how can you possibly catch him? He could be anywhere.' She bit her lip on a tremble.

West could see fear lurking at the edges of her wide eyes, waiting to take over. He had to tread carefully. She was scared and he needed her cooperative and safe. He chose his words and spoke slowly and calmly. 'You're right. We don't know who he is. Yet. But we'll find out, and we'll catch him. First thing we need to do is to get you back to the station, have you look through some photos; see if we can identify him.'

'Mug shots?'

West and Andrews shared a smile. 'Everybody watches CSI, Mike, I told you,' Andrews grinned through his last mouthful of bacon.

Seeing her puzzled look, West shook his head and continued. 'Yes, mug shots. If you can't pick him out from those, we'll get you to work with our forensic artist, Robert, and see if we can identify him that way.'

She looked at him, fear in her eyes but knowledge in the tightening of her lips. 'And if you can't? What then? And if, or should I say, when he finds out I've spoken to you, what then? Maybe I watch too many crime programmes, CSI included,' she said with a look at Andrews, 'but if I were him, I'd want to get rid of me. After all, he has murdered before, hasn't he?'

Andrews had finished his gargantuan breakfast at this stage and sat listening without comment.

'Why would he need to get rid of you?' West said. 'You weren't a witness to a murder, Edel.'

'He told me he murdered my husband, isn't that enough?' she said sharply.

West looked uncomfortable. 'I'm afraid not,' he admitted. 'You say you've watched a lot of crime programmes; you must know that it takes more than your word against his. We need proof and so far... well, so far, all we have is a fingerprint.'

'A fingerprint?'

He shrugged. 'We found one inside your husband's wallet.'

Her look of puzzlement increased. 'But,' she said, 'if you have a fingerprint, can't you find out whose it is? Don't you have data banks or some such thing?'

'Yes, we do.' He hesitated before admitting, 'It's not on it. There's the possibility, of course, that it's a red herring but our forensic team say that it had to have been left there recently. Whoever murdered your husband was looking for something, couldn't search the wallet with gloves and took them off. He was careful but not careful enough. Unfortunately, not all criminals end up on our system. He may have a juvenile record but we have no access to that.'

'So, looking at mug shots is a bit of a waste of time,' she muttered irritably.

'I wasn't asking you to look at them for amusement, Edel. We have a number of photos of people who are, shall we say, of interest to us as opposed to having a criminal record. Possibly breaches all their civil rights, probably contravenes all data protection rules, but there it is, we have some and maybe, just maybe, this John character will show up there.

'When we find him, we can arrest him for extortion and assault. If we can match his fingerprint to the one we found in Pratt's wallet, well, then we'll see what happens.'

'*If* you find him?'

'When,' he said doggedly.

'Well it doesn't seem as if I have much choice. So, what happens now?' she said tiredly, her head dropping back against the high back of the chair. Her hair fell away from her neck, for the first time exposing the damage John had perpetrated, the dark purple bruising dramatic against her unnaturally pale skin. The sight drew a collective sharp intake of breath from both men. It was a vicious branding that hinted at the depths this man was willing to stoop to.

West, still staring at her neck, was momentarily flummoxed. 'What happens now? We go back to the station. We do our job and, with your help, we'll put this guy away, Edel, you can bet on it.'

'I can't stop thinking about him.' She closed her eyes tightly as though to shut out the image, and whispered, 'I keep feeling his hands on me, his mouth... and I feel sick every time. I don't know if I can take any more; it's just one thing after another and I don't know if I can keep going.'

West raised his hands in a gesture of resignation to Andrews who grimaced in return. It was never easy, both men knew, to ask victims to help put a perpetrator away. The ones who were eager to help were, invariably, the ones they didn't need. Those who were too scared, too stressed or just not interested were the ones they usually wanted. Pressure could bring results, of course, but neither man approved of pressurising an already injured party, preferring to get information from other sources in those cases.

Some aspects of West's job didn't appeal to him. He waited while Edel tried to banish the memories that were guaranteed to haunt her for a long time.

'So much has happened to me in the space of a week that my mind is in a whirl,' she said, her eyes still shut. 'Okay,' she said, opening them, her voice a little stronger. 'I'll help in any way I can.'

'Thank you,' West said, relieved.

'I have one condition,' she added. 'I want to come back here, and stay here until you catch him. I don't want to go home until he is caught.'

'We could move you to a hotel in Dublin. You'd be just as safe,' he suggested.

She shook her head. 'No, I feel safe here, if that makes things difficult for you, well, I'm sorry, but that's the way I want it to be.'

'Okay, that's not a problem,' West conceded, ignoring for the moment, the three hour each way drive. He glanced at his watch. 'Do you need to go back to your room?'

She shook her head. A raised finger brought the breakfast bill that West insisted be put down to departmental expenses. 'It's the least we can do,' he insisted, tucking the receipt into his wallet. 'Especially since Andrews here ate most of it.'

'And enjoyed every mouthful. Makes up for all the meals I miss when working with you, Sergeant West,' Andrews retorted quickly.

25

By early afternoon, Edel was in Foxrock looking at photographs. She gazed at each intently, willing John to be among them. 'None is even close,' she said in frustration.

'Don't worry,' West reassured her. 'It was always going to be a long shot. I'll take you down to meet Robert, our part-time sketch artist. He's very good and will work with you to give us the best likeness possible.'

He escorted her down a floor to a small, well-lit room overlooking the car park at the back of the station and introduced her to a slim, fair-haired man who greeted her with a shy smile before inviting her to sit beside him at the large table that dominated the room.

'Just do the best you can,' West said, and with a smile for Edel and a 'Thanks' for Robert, he left them to it.

When Robert opened a sketch pad, Edel looked at it quizzically. 'I expected there to be a computer programme to do this,' she said with an obvious air of disappointment.

His smile widened. 'There is, Ms Johnson, and they allow us to do a creditable composite but to be honest, if you can give me a good description, the likeness *I* draw is more likely to be correct.'

'You're better than a computer?' She looked at him in disbelief.

His smile turned gleeful. 'Much better, believe me.'

He was right. After a frustrating hour, changing noses and hairlines, mouth and eyes, he came up with an eerily close sketch of John and held it up to her. 'What do you think?'

She stared at it, picturing so easily in her mind the face of a man she hadn't known existed twenty-four hours before. 'His eyes,' she murmured, 'the eyelids are heavier.'

With a couple of deft pencil strokes, Robert changed the sketch's eyelids and suddenly it *was* John. She gasped and held a hand to her mouth, shocked by the accuracy of the likeness. 'That's him!' She held the sketch up with trembling fingers and then carefully put it on the table in front of her, wiping her fingers on her jeans as if they had been contaminated.

'There's nothing else you want to change?' Robert asked.

She stared at it with loathing. 'No, that's him,' she repeated.

'Good,' he said. 'I'll go and let Sergeant West know.'

She was beginning to get restless before, muttering an apology for his delay, West arrived and sat in the vacant chair beside her. He picked up the sketch, examined it and put it down.

'You're sure this is a good likeness?' he asked, glancing at her.

She tapped a finger on it, a look of distaste on her face. 'It could be a photograph of him, it's that good.'

'Good,' he said, putting the sketch into a folder. 'I'll just be a few minutes.'

Edel glanced at her watch and was surprised to see it was almost four. She gave a weary sigh just as the door opened again and West returned and sat opposite her.

'Thank you for your help, Edel. We've put that sketch in the system. We should be able to find out who this guy is, and once we do... well, you'll be able to-'

'What?' she interrupted him, 'Get back to normal?' She wiped a hand over her face, avoiding his eyes. 'Yes, I can get back to my normal life, where my husband, who wasn't actually my husband at all, bought a house, with money that wasn't his. So, I've no husband, probably no home, and definitely no money. It should be easy.' Her voice was rich with sarcasm.

Embarrassed, he stood. 'I'm sorry, I should know better than to resort to cliché.'

Now, it was her turn to be embarrassed and her pale skin flushed pink. 'No, I'm sorry, that was very rude of me. You were trying to be kind. I'm just tired. Doing that sketch was pretty exhausting, having to concentrate on all the details, having to remember. If I could just go back to the hotel now, I'd appreciate it. I could do with a long, hot bath. Thinking of him makes me feel dirty.'

She stood and, the room being small, standing brought her closer to him. She'd always considered herself to be tall, but her five foot six only brought her to his shoulder and she had to raise her eyes to meet his. His were grey and long lashed and they held hers unwaveringly. For a second, she felt a frisson of unexpected attraction.

The door opened behind them, startling them both into movement, Edel bending hurriedly to pick up her bag and West, stepping back guiltily.

It was Andrews. She saw him glance from one to the other with a knowing look on his face that brought further colour to her cheeks. 'There is an unmarked car outside waiting to take you back to Cork, Mrs Johnson,' he said. 'The plainclothes officer will escort you to your room and check it out for you.'

She smiled at him gratefully and, tucking her bag under her arm, turned to say goodbye to West, holding out her hand. 'I look forward to hearing that you've caught our friend.' She lifted an eyebrow and her smile widened a little. 'Then I can start the returning to normal business.'

He held her hand firmly in his and once again she met his eyes and saw a reassurance in them that gave her strength. 'Stay in your room,' he said. 'If you've any problems, any strange phone calls, anything, ring us, okay? We have informed the local station; they'll be monitoring the situation and can be with you within minutes.'

A dry cough from the doorway made her pull her hand away, and with a grateful smile, she turned to follow Andrews.

'There's just one thing you should know before you go,' West said quickly, bringing her around to face him again. 'The house.'

She looked at him quizzically and waited.

'It's in your name only.'

26

Contrary to their hopes, the next day brought them no nearer to identifying the mysterious John. They had sent the sketch to other divisions and departments, national and international without even a glimmer of interest.

Frustration mounted, and tempers started to fray with more than one phone being banged down in annoyance. They had pinned their hopes on identifying John to give the case the boost it needed. Looking around now, West knew he had to refocus the team and he called for a general update.

'Listen up,' he called when they had gathered round. 'All right, we still don't know who this guy John is, but let's focus on what we do know. Because...' He stopped as the men started muttering. 'Because,' he said louder, 'even when we do identify this guy, we have no proof he murdered either man.'

The muttering stopped as the men realised the truth of this.

Jarvis raised his hand. 'Don't we have a fingerprint, sir?' he asked.

'We have one fingerprint found on the inside of the victim's wallet. Even a mediocre solicitor would call that circumstantial evidence; a good solicitor would laugh and dismiss it outright.'

The men, remembering that the sergeant had been a solicitor in a former life, looked crestfallen.

'So, we work with what we do have.' He looked around the room and then back at the case board. 'We work with what we have,' he repeated firmly. 'So, what do we know?'

'Victim number one. The real Simon Johnson.' He tapped the photo on the board. 'Advertises his prestigious Cork apartment for rent on a noticeboard in Bareton Industries. Rents it to a man by the name of Adam Fletcher, who he believed also worked in Bareton Industries but who *we* know was Cyril Pratt. Johnson plans to be away for two years and to come back to a healthy bank balance. He has to come home early for a funeral, checks his bank and discovers he has nothing. So, what does he do?' He paced in front of the men, tossing a pencil from hand to hand.

'He goes to his apartment to face Adam Fletcher; finds the tenant is one Alberto Castelione who insists he is paying rent to a Simon Johnson...' He turned and tapped the photo of Cyril Pratt with the pencil. 'Alberto identified this man.'

He nodded at Jarvis, who took up the tale. 'Mr Castelione gave Simon Johnson, Cyril Pratt's phone number so we assume he rang him. The next day Johnson took a flight to Dublin and hired a car. The car was found abandoned not far from the graveyard where he was murdered. The mileage on the rental indicated a journey of twenty-five miles which is roughly the distance from Dublin Airport to Foxrock.'

'Good, thanks Jarvis. We know now,' West continued, 'that Cyril Pratt was hiding out in Come-to-Good, in Cornwall. So, Johnson hadn't arranged to meet him here in Foxrock.' He ran his hands over his face in an attempt to brush away the tiredness that clung like a cobweb.

He faced the case board again. 'Dammit!' he said as much to himself as to the room. 'Perhaps it was our friend here.' He pointed to the sketch of John that they had recently hung on the board.

He stood silently a moment, thoughts running chaotically. 'What's the link between Simon Johnson and John?' he asked eventually. No one answered. He moved the sketch to sit under the photo of Johnson. 'Both were victims of a scam orchestrated by Cyril Pratt,' he asserted, knowing the connection was tenuous. 'Edel Johnson says Pratt had money when they met, so we can assume that he acquired the money from John at least a year ago.'

He looked around at the faces of his team, seeing expectation in every eye. 'Why didn't John try to get the money back before now?'

'He couldn't find him?' suggested Garda Allen.

'He couldn't find him,' agreed West. 'But Simon Johnson did. Maybe there's a stronger connection between Johnson and John than we know about.' He ran his hand over his head in a gesture of frustration. 'Without knowing who John is, it's impossible to find out.' He turned to Andrews. 'Get a local officer to call to Johnson's sister, and Amanda Pratt with the sketch, see if either recognises him.'

Andrews scribbled a note.

West rubbed his hand through his hair again. It was there, he could feel it, but where? Something struck him suddenly. Why hadn't he thought of that before? He turned to look at the team, a glint lighting his eyes.

'You come home unexpectedly, after a year away, and find that your tenant hasn't, after all, been paying his rent. What do you do?' He paced in front of the team, unravelling the scenario in his mind. 'Do you immediately travel to the apartment through the horror that is Cork traffic, to demand an explanation? Or,' he paused, looking around at the suddenly eager faces. 'Or do you phone the tenant at his place of work?'

'Bareton Industries,' Andrews offered.

'Bareton Industries,' West agreed. 'Where Johnson had advertised his apartment and where, as far as he knew, his tenant still worked.' He hesitated a moment, an amorphous idea beginning to take shape. 'How much do we know about this Adam Fletcher?' He looked around the room, stopping as Garda Allen lifted a hand.

'He's a chemical engineer, works on a contract basis doing mostly quality assurance work for Bareton Industries. He says he has never met or spoken to Simon Johnson. When I queried that, since they work in the same building, he clarified that he knew of him but they worked in different areas and at different times. He has never heard of anyone called Cyril Pratt and has never been to Foxrock.'

'This was over the phone, I assume, Allen?'

Allen looked puzzled for a moment before nodding an affirmative.

West looked at Andrews. 'You didn't get to meet him either, did you?'

Andrews narrowed his eyes. 'No, I didn't, he wouldn't agree to a meeting.'

'So, we don't know what this Adam Fletcher looks like, do we?' West exchanged a glance with Andrews who immediately moved to a desk where, after a quick glance at his notes, he contacted Bareton Industries.

The receptionist was cooperative and ten minutes later a scanned photo of Adam Fletcher came through to his computer. Andrews, waiting patiently, looked at it, and called across to West. 'You'd better take a look at this.'

The rest of the team, alerted by something in his voice, followed behind and strained to see over West and Andrews as they stared at the screen. The personnel file photograph was grainy and had obviously been blown up from passport photo size, but it was clearly their mystery man, John. Andrews printed a copy and, pinning it up beside the sketch, they were able to see how accurately Edel had depicted her assailant.

'To quote fictional detectives...' West looked around at the men. 'Well, well, well!'

An air of excitement washed through the room, replacing the frustration and exhaustion of earlier. West had to shout to make himself heard above the chattering. 'Listen up, everyone. We know now who our mystery friend is, but that is not going to get an arrest. We need, as I said earlier, proof. I want to know all about this Adam Fletcher; I particularly want to know where he got five hundred thousand cash, and how it came into the hands of Cyril Pratt.'

West nodded at Andrews. 'You and I will head down to Bareton Industries and see what we can find out there. I want a warrant for Fletcher's office or workspace and for any files pertaining to him in Bareton Industries and another warrant for his house. We have the sketch and Edel's testimony – it's not enough to arrest him for murder but it will get us the warrants. We'll go from Bareton Industries straight to his house.'

He headed to his office to inform the inspector of the latest turn of events and happily accepted his offer to liaise with the other departments and divisions that they would have to cross.

Grabbing his jacket and keys, he joined Andrews in the main office where he was having an acrimonious conversation with, West guessed from what he could hear, the forensic department. Hanging up with a frown, Andrews related the gist of the discussion. 'All the junk that was found in the graveyard has gone to forensics but, would you believe, they "haven't got around to looking at it yet" to quote that twerp on the phone.' He shrugged. 'Probably my fault,' he admitted, 'I haven't been ringing them every ten minutes demanding results so they didn't think we were in a hurry. I have relieved them of that idea and told them, in no uncertain terms, to get their finger out and get us the proof we need.'

West smiled at the mild-mannered man. He was well aware that Andrews' "no uncertain terms" probably consisted of a politely worded request. For someone who rarely raised his voice, and rarely, if ever, swore, he commanded a respect that made people do what he wanted, when he wanted.

Light traffic allowed them to make good time to Cork and, a little over three hours later, they were showing their identification to the receptionist who had been so helpful to them earlier. She looked around anxiously before addressing them. 'I won't get into trouble for sending that photo, will I?'

Reassured, she rang through to the managing director and informed him the gardaí were asking to see him.

A short, rotund man arrived within minutes and, introducing himself, ushered them through to his office not far from the reception area. Sitting behind his desk, he viewed them with curiosity. 'Can I assume this is to do with Simon Johnson?'

West reached into his inside pocket and withdrew the warrant for Adam Fletcher's office and files. He held it a moment before saying, 'In a way, Mr Tolard. Mr Johnson's death is part of a bigger case and it is for that reason we are here today. What can you tell us about Adam Fletcher?'

Stuart Tolard sat back in surprise. 'Adam?' he asked. 'Why are you asking about him? He's not here today. We don't expect him until the end of the month.'

A flicker of annoyance crossed the sergeant's face at this news but he continued. 'As I said, it's part of a bigger case. Mr Fletcher's name has come up in connection with some aspects of that case.'

The managing director, weighing up the men before him,

shrugged. 'Okay, what do you want to know? Not that I know a lot about him,' he added cautiously, prepared to deny any knowledge that might endanger Bareton Industries.

'Firstly, what exactly does he do?'

Tolard sighed. 'I'm not an engineer, gentlemen, I'm a pencil-pusher. I can give you his job specification but as to what he actually does... well, you'd have to talk to the pharmaceutical manager, Alan James.'

'We'll speak to him next. So, what is Fletcher's job specification?'

With another, more irritated sigh, Tolard explained. 'He's employed on a regular contract basis to carry out quality assurance on some of our pharmaceutical products. As to which products... well, again, you will have to ask Alan.'

West frowned and caught Andrews' eye. *Pharmaceutical products.* 'I thought Bareton Industries manufactured monitoring systems?'

'Our main product is a monitoring system for neonatal units, yes, but we have a small pharmaceutical division too that is very lucrative. In fact' – he began to warm to his subject, now that they were in what he regarded as his territory – 'we increased our profit in the pharmaceutical division by thirty-five per cent last year, and we hope to double that this year with the launch of a new product. It is a very exciting time for Bareton Industries, gentlemen.'

'So, Adam Fletcher does what? Test the products to make sure they are okay?' Andrews asked.

'That's simplifying rather too much,' Tolard laughed condescendingly. 'We have stringent checks and counter checks to ensure our product is of the highest quality and to ensure all necessary documentation is completed. The quality assurance performed by Mr Fletcher is the last step before the product is packaged and released for distribution.'

West's interest had gone into overdrive once the word "pharmaceutical" had entered the conversation. He was beginning to get an idea as to where the five hundred thousand euro may have come from. 'So how often does he work here?' he asked.

'As I said, Sergeant, he is on a regular contract.'

The two officers sat calmly, until with a loud sigh, Tolard entered information on his keyboard and sat back as the data he requested appeared.

'His contract is twenty-four hours a month, gentlemen.'

'Not many hours, Mr Tolard. How are they spread out?' West asked.

'When Mr Fletcher came to work for us, he was keen that his hours be flexible. Initially, he worked a standard nine-to-five but then we had to make some cutbacks, for financial reasons, and his hours were changed. We came to a mutually beneficial arrangement wherein he works whenever suits him, within a specific time frame of course, and he charges us less than his usual hourly rate. It saves us a considerable amount of money per annum, as you can imagine.'

West and Andrews exchanged grim, knowing looks before the sergeant continued. 'What hours normally do suit him?'

Tolard, relaxing back in his chair, tapped his fingers together. 'He generally works late into the evening. He says he finds it easier to get the work done when there is a minimum of distractions. We have twenty-four-hour security so there's never any problem if he stays late. There have been no issues in the two years he has worked this way.' His eyes narrowed speculatively. 'There is no reason why he shouldn't work this way, I assure you, I have checked with our legal team.'

'Do you have a record of the dates and times he has worked over the last year?'

'Yes, of course, Sergeant. Just one moment and I'll run you off a copy.' He leaned forward, brought up the correct file on his desktop and within minutes was handing West a handful of warm, crisp pages with the data he required.

West glanced at it casually, then folded it to be analysed later. 'Just one final thing,' he said, handing over the warrant. 'This allows us to take any relevant documentation, should we need to. We'll give you a receipt for anything we do take and it will be returned after our investigation has concluded.'

Stuart Tolard looked annoyed but resigned. 'Please remember, most of our work is highly confidential.'

Reassuring the managing director of their utmost reliability, West requested to speak to the pharmaceutical manager. Tolard made a brief call and then escorted them down a number of corridors and levels to a locked door, behind which lay the pharmaceutical division.

'If you need anything else, please let me know,' Tolard said as they waited for the door to be opened.

A clink of keys heralded the appearance of a large, shaggy-haired man wearing an ill-fitting, spotless white coat. He greeted the three men and then, with a contemptuous wave of dismissal at the managing director, he ushered the two detectives into his stronghold, closing and locking the door behind them and indicating a door further along. 'Take a seat in there, gentlemen.'

He followed them in and sat with a weary groan, and then covered his mouth with a big, incredibly hairy hand as he yawned loudly. 'You'll have to excuse me; we're launching a new product and I've been trying to get everything tied up. It's been a bit hectic.'

'We're sorry to have to add to your workload, Mr James,' West apologised. 'As I explained to Mr Tolard, we are making some inquiries into an Adam Fletcher who does some contract work for you.'

'Adam? Is there some problem? He isn't hurt... or dead?' The pharmaceutical manager looked at them aghast.

West quickly reassured him.

James looked puzzled. 'Then what is it? Puzzlement gave way to suspicion. 'You suspect him of some nefarious action, Sergeant? He was fully vetted before he joined my team, I assure you. I don't,' he added, 'have much regard for our managing director but he does his work with efficiency. He's a cold-blooded bastard, but an efficient, cold-blooded bastard.'

'We believe Mr Fletcher works mostly in the evenings,' West said.

'It suited him,' James said without elaboration.

'You didn't approve,' West guessed.

'I would have preferred to have discussed the change with Adam first; would have preferred to weigh up the implications. I am a cautious man and a suspicious one. It strikes me that when people seem to be doing something they consider altruistic, it is very often with a personal, and usually very selfish, agenda. As it was, I was presented with a fait accompli.' He shrugged. 'As it happens, it has worked well and I have had no problems. He does his work on time and the paperwork is competently finished.'

West eyed him curiously. 'You don't like Fletcher very much, do you?'

James snorted. 'I don't like most people. In fact, I find them increasingly irritating, although my wife tells me it is I who have become irascible. Fletcher did his job. He always left the laboratory as he found it, so I had no cause for complaint. Because of his hours, to be honest, I rarely saw him. But, no, you're right, I don't like him very much.' He considered a moment. 'He has cold, calculating eyes. I could see him being cruel, and I have no idea where that comes from. I have never seen him being cruel to anyone... it's just something about him. A feeling I get from him, an impression, call it what you will. Am I making sense, at all?'

'In our job, impressions and feelings are important, Mr James. We tend to call it intuition,' West said. 'May we see where he worked?'

'If you wish, although I don't know what you're expecting to find. He doesn't have an office, just a work station.' He rose with another groan and stretched uncomfortably. 'I need at least twelve hours sleep,' he grumbled.

He led them to the laboratory, stopping on the way to furnish each man with the obligatory white coat. 'This is it.'

It was a traditional laboratory; counter space along each wall with extra counter space down the centre of the room. It was well-lit with high, wide windows but much of the counter space also had powerful lamps in use. There were three people at work, each too engrossed to notice strangers in their midst. Mr James showed the two detectives around, naming various pieces of equipment and various machines. He brought them to the far corner of the room.

'This is Adam Fletcher's area of work. It is easier for us all to have designated areas; if we leave a test in progress, it is not disturbed. We don't allow mobile phones so each workstation also has its own phone.'

The area was neat and tidy. A small noticeboard was pinned with documents. The only personal items appeared to be a train timetable and a newspaper cutting which West looked at with interest before turning to listen to the manager.

'Products that require their final quality assurance tests are left in this section; Fletcher does the test, attaches the correct paperwork and puts the item into these bags.' He indicated a roll of clear plastic. 'The bags are then put into a special designated store where they are kept for insurance purposes.'

The two detectives looked around. All the equipment required to make high-class, illegal drugs was before them. All that was needed was a supply of ingredients.

'Where do you store the ingredients for your products, Mr James?' West inquired.

'Ingredients, Sergeant? We're not baking cakes, you know.' Alan James raised an eyebrow disdainfully. 'The key components of our products are kept in a locked store in the corridor.'

'May we see it, please?' he asked.

With a flourish, James led the way out of the laboratory back down the corridor they had used previously, and stopped before a hitherto unnoticed door.

Both men took a look, examining the flimsy padlock with which it was secured. West rattled it, while the manager searched his pockets unsuccessfully for a key. 'I know I have one here somewhere,' he muttered, as the lock fell into West's hand. It hadn't been engaged. With an unconcerned shrug, the manager took it from him.

Inside, the small walk-in cupboard was an Aladdin's cave of pharmaceutical components. Bottles, boxes and bags filled shelves from floor to ceiling. West read some of the labels aloud, his voice grim as both he and Andrews recognised many of them as being key ingredients of some of the nastier illegal drugs on the market.

He turned, a stern expression on his face, his eyes hard. 'This isn't a secure unit, Mr James. Even had the padlock been shut, it is an easily opened one. When did you last do an inventory of this room?'

James raised an eyebrow and said coolly, dismissively. 'I'm a scientist. I don't do inventories.'

West's reply was equally chilly. 'You are in charge of this unit. Surely it is, therefore, your responsibility to ensure' – he pointed to the overfull shelves – 'that potentially dangerous components are, not only correctly stored, but accounted for?'

'We are obliged to keep all components in a locked room, and I can assure you the lock is normally used. And I can also assure you, that not one of the components here is, in of itself, potentially dangerous.'

He picked the wrong person to use jargon on. 'That's the crunch, though, isn't it? "In of itself."' He picked up a bag. 'Sodium chloride, or salt as us laymen would call it, isn't dangerous but' – he chose three more components and handed them to the suddenly quiet scientist – 'put it together with these and use some of your laboratory equipment and what do you get?'

Getting no answer, he turned to Andrews and answered his own question. 'These are the key components of an illegal drug called Nirvana, similar to Ecstasy, which appeared on the Cork and Dublin streets about a year and a half ago. It has, as far as we are aware, been responsible for at least five deaths in that period.'

For the first time, James looked shaken. 'You aren't suggesting that this drug is made here, I hope. That is a very serious allegation.'

'You admit you don't keep an inventory of components, Mr James. Just say, for instance, someone was taking a smallish amount every month, would that be missed? Or even a larger amount?'

James had the sense to put the scenario together. 'You think Adam Fletcher has been helping himself while he worked here in the evenings?'

'Not just helping himself to the components.' West felt his temper beginning to fray at the stupidity of the man. 'He had the laboratory to himself, all the necessary equipment to hand, and freely available components. With no check, he has been manufacturing illegal drugs for almost two years making a tidy sum of money. A perfect setup.'

'Illegal drugs,' James gasped, going pale, the realisation

beginning to hit home. 'This will destroy the company. I have to talk to Stuart. Are you sure?' He looked at the sergeant, willing him to refute his allegation.

'No, Mr James,' West replied. 'No surer than you are that you're not missing some of your... components.'

27

W est and Andrews left the managing director and the laboratory manager making frantic phone calls to their shareholders. They were trying for damage limitation and at the same time assigning blame to each other.

'Do we have enough for an arrest?' Andrews asked as they moved quickly to their car.

'No, it's still all circumstantial, Peter. We have no concrete proof that Fletcher was stealing components and using the laboratory to manufacture illegal drugs. Even if we knew what was missing, how would we prove he took it? He's a clever bugger. He sussed out the politics of the laboratory, the power play between Tolard and James and used them for his own ends. We may never know just how much stuff he has managed to make away with but the Drug Squad may be able to make a good guess.'

As they walked, he rang a contact in the Drug Squad and quickly filled him in on the details of their case. He listened a moment. 'Great, yes, that would be great. Yes, as soon as possible,' and disconnected. 'That was Inspector Bob Phelan, I worked with him years ago. He's going to take a team over to

Bareton Industries and do a full audit of components delivered, received and stored; he'll be able to tell us how much is missing and he should be able to extrapolate from his data how much has gone missing over the two years Fletcher has worked there.

'Even more interesting, is that Bob says there has been an influx of upmarket designer drugs over the last two years, Nirvana and a host of others, and they haven't been able to identify the source. He is very interested in talking to our Mr Fletcher.'

'As long as he remembers he is *our* Mr Fletcher and not the Drug Squad's,' Andrews said as they sped away towards Adam Fletcher's home on the outskirts of Cork.

A quick phone call to Inspector Duffy on the way ensured local cooperation, and they turned down the road to Fletcher's house to find two squad cars waiting for them, discreetly parked in a slight lay-by. Garda Duggan climbed out of one of the cars as West pulled up alongside, and came around the car, bending down to speak through the open window.

'Good evening, sir,' said Duggan. 'We've been asked to give you our full cooperation.' He indicated the cars with a tilt of his head. 'There are four of us. Just tell us what you'd like us to do.'

West nodded in satisfaction. They didn't expect trouble but they knew that never stopped it from happening.

Duggan turned his head and looked down the street. 'It's the fifth house on the left, the detached one with the wrought iron railing.'

West looked down the street of large, elegant, expensive homes. Fletcher's, he noticed, was the biggest. 'Let's all pull up outside the house. Nothing like a little intimidation to get the ball rolling.'

Duggan smirked and returned to his car. Soon, all three cars were parked conspicuously outside the imposing house.

Andrews organised the four uniformed gardaí, sending two

around the back of the house and instructing the other two to guard the front entrance, then he and West headed to the front door and pressed the doorbell. Very quickly, the door was opened by a slim, strawberry-blonde woman who greeted them with a pleasant smile that dimmed as she noticed the police cars. 'Can I help you?' she asked, looking from one to the other.

They both held out identification. 'Is Mr Fletcher here?'

Looking puzzled and a little worried, she turned and called, 'Adam, Adam, can you come here?'

West disliked the man on sight. He came growling out into the hall behind his wife, complaining about being disturbed. His wife rushed to explain, putting a restraining hand on her husband's arm that was brushed off roughly. Adam Fletcher stared at the two men in the doorway then dismissed his wife with a wave.

Edel had described him well. His eyes were cold and hard beneath heavy, drooping lids, his lips a thin slash. He wore an air of cruelty on his stocky, muscular frame like a second skin as he stood looking at them, a hand high on each side of the door frame. A man at home with intimidation, every gesture was designed to show power and control.

West and Andrews exchanged glances and, again, held their identification cards out for inspection. Fletcher took them and examined them carefully, checking the photo against their faces before handing them back with a disdainful grunt. 'I spoke to you on the phone a couple of days ago, didn't I?' he said bluntly. 'I told you then that I'd be free to talk to you next week and requested that you make an appointment with the secretary.' He dropped one hand and reached for the door, keeping his other firmly on the frame. 'Now, if you'll excuse me, I am a very busy man.'

West, watching him closely, wasn't fooled. He noted the tightening of expression, the grip on the door frame, the tension in his musculature that denoted fight or flight. He felt his own body's response to the unconscious threat and deliberately slowed his quickening breath. Keeping his voice calm and quiet, he addressed him. 'We have reason to believe, Mr Fletcher, that you were involved in the death of Cyril Pratt in Falmouth. We have a warrant to search your home and to remove your car and computer for forensic examination.' West took the paper from his inside jacket pocket and presented it to him. For several minutes, Fletcher didn't move, but the fingers that gripped the door frame tightened.

Slowly, almost cautiously, he reached out one hand and, without comment, took the document. He read it carefully. 'This is a ludicrous mistake. I don't know anyone called Cyril Pratt. I'll have to contact my solicitor before you can proceed, I'm afraid.' His tone was cool and dismissive but a bead of perspiration on his forehead gave lie to the calm.

He gave a preparatory step backward before West replied in an equally cool voice. 'I'm afraid you don't quite understand, Mr Fletcher. We intend to proceed with this warrant without delay. You may advise your solicitor, if you wish, but we are under no obligation to wait for his arrival.'

Fletcher's heavy-lidded eyes gave little away and, with a shrug of his shoulders and a sneer curling his thin lips, he stepped back and waved them into his home. 'Be my guest.'

Andrews called the four gardaí to assist and they made their way quickly and thoroughly through the flotsam and jetsam of the Fletcher household. West didn't expect to find anything; if they were right, Fletcher had committed two murders, run an effective and very lucrative drug manufacturing business for two years and never appeared on the garda radar. That took cunning intelligence. They weren't going to catch this man easily.

Two hours later they had finished, and found nothing. Stretching wearily, West directed a garda to remove a computer and laptop. Another was directed to drive Fletcher's car to Dublin where their forensic team were expecting it.

Fletcher's solicitor had, at this stage, arrived and was arguing vociferously against their removal. 'My client requires both his laptop and car for work. This is unreasonable and we will be making a complaint to the highest authority. Mr Fletcher has denied any knowledge of this Cyril Pratt and you have given us no evidence that he is in any way involved in his murder.'

Recognising a junior member of a law firm, West took pity and merely stated, 'We have a warrant. You are aware, I'm sure, we could not have obtained a warrant without probable cause. We are under no obligation to inform you, at this stage, what that probable cause is. When we arrest Mr Fletcher, then you will be informed of the case we have built.' West nodded to the solicitor who looked affronted at his attitude, and with a further nod to Adam Fletcher, he and Andrews departed.

Back in the car, West rang Bob Phelan and updated him on their search and results. 'We're taking his computer, Bob. I'll have our IT people take it apart and relay any findings to you as soon as. We've also taken his car. The pathologist told us that whoever killed Simon Johnson would have had blood on him; if we are lucky, he may have left a trace in the car. Our forensic team will go through it. Hopefully, by tomorrow, they'll also have gone through all the rubbish we found at the crime scene and found something we can use. Meanwhile, I think we should keep an eye on our Mr Fletcher, don't you?'

Inspector Phelan, anxious to close this source of upmarket designer drugs, agreed to provide surveillance after assurance that it would be for a very short period.

Andrews raised an eyebrow as he heard the confident assurances and muttered under his breath. Finishing his call with Phelan, West turned to him. 'Have faith, Peter. We're going to get this guy.'

The two remaining gardaí came running over to their car and knocked on the window, preventing Andrews giving West the reply he would have liked. 'We've been ordered to stay here, Sergeant,' one of them said breathlessly and added, with a barely suppressed air of excitement, 'We're going to keep the house under surveillance.'

West and Andrews exchanged glances and, with a word of advice to the enthusiastic officers, they started for home.

28

West dropped Andrews home rather than back at the station, it was late, they were both tired. 'I'll pick you up early in the morning, Peter, don't worry. Say hi to Joyce for me.'

Back home, he stripped off and had a long, hot shower. He hated house searches, always felt contaminated by the need to do them. The prying, poking and delving into the detritus of other people's lives never appealed to him. He used some citrus-scented shower gel given to him by someone, he couldn't remember who, but the clean sharp smell worked for him and he lathered and lathered again. Finally, feeling clean, he stepped from the shower, dried himself briskly and walked naked to his bedroom. The mirror examined him in passing, reflecting back a lithe, athletic body, still tanned from an earlier holiday in Crete, the tan emphasising a thin scar on his left side, a relic of a bullet that had passed a little closer than he had expected.

He pulled on track suit bottoms and a T-shirt and went to check that Tyler's food machines were full, and he had enough water. As a treat, he opened a sachet of gourmet dog food and emptied it into his dish and left him guzzling while he investigated his kitchen for non-canine food. The damn dog ate better than he did. He found cheese, well past its best-before date, and a jar of stuffed olives. Sniffing the cheese, he decided it was still edible.

The freezer had bread, and probably more ice than a freezer should have considering it was supposed to be one of those frost-free ones, but it probably wasn't supposed to be empty most of the time. Breaking off a couple of slices of bread, he stuck it under the grill to toast, while he grated the cheese and chopped the olives. When the bread was toasted on one side, he piled the olives and cheese on top and put it back under the grill for a few minutes. He sprinkled it with a pinch of salt, and ground black pepper on top. It would do.

Soon he was settled on the sofa, beer in hand and food on plate. Maybe not gourmet but it wasn't bad at all. Guinness, cold from the fridge, definitely hit the spot; he took a long drink with pleasure and lay back against the cushions. Tyler, replete from dining on his very upmarket, and ridiculously expensive meal, jumped up beside him and nestled into his favourite spot between West and the side of the sofa. 'You never consider I mightn't want you there, do you?' He tickled the little dog's head, getting a dog-food-tainted lick in reply.

The last drop of beer drained, he got up without disturbing Tyler's snooze, and headed back to the kitchen for another, opening and pouring in a mind-calming exercise, watching the black settle and the creamy head rise. He stood in the kitchen, drinking slowly this time, looking out across his garden to where trees were silhouetted against the moonlit sky and trying to steer his mind toward the case, the characters involved, strategies and ploys and likely outcomes. But even a nasty piece of work like Adam Fletcher couldn't keep his mind occupied for long; it appeared tonight to have only one target, *her*. He wondered if she was sleeping, or lying awake worrying, and whether he should ring her. Just to update her on the case, nothing more. Wasn't it his duty? Hadn't he promised to keep her informed?

Beer in hand, he went back to the lounge where he sat and reached for the phone. He debated his reason for ringing for several moments, annoyed with himself for the hesitation, before quickly dialling the hotel's number and asking for her room. Almost instantly, before he knew what to say, he was connected and heard her sleepy voice saying a tremulous, 'Hello.'

He was immediately guilty. 'I've woken you. I'm so sorry, I just-well-I...' He found himself, to his embarrassment and annoyance, stammering, and stopped to draw a breath. 'It's Sergeant West, Ms Johnson,' he said, thinking his rank lent a formality to the call. 'I just wanted to give you an update on the situation.' Okay, he decided with relief, he sounded official and formal.

'Sergeant West?' Edel's voice was alert now. 'I wasn't asleep, not really. What's happened?'

Hearing her voice, West was suddenly less sure about his reason for ringing and the wisdom of telling her about the day's proceedings. He compromised and told her enough to have merited a phone call at what he realised, looking at his watch, was a very late hour.

'We know who John is,' he started, 'and we hope to have enough proof to arrest him soon. For the moment we have him under surveillance, he won't be going anywhere without one of our lads going with him.'

Silence answered him for such a length of time, he thought he had been disconnected. 'Edel?' he called worriedly.

'Yes. Yes, I'm here. It's such a relief... so it's nearly over now, is it?' Her voice was cautious.

'Nearly. We're waiting for forensic results. We haven't

enough proof as yet, but, trust me,' he added with a resurgence of confidence, 'we will get it.'

'This is such good news,' she said, her voice a touch stronger. 'Thank you for ringing me and letting me know what's happening.'

West, who prided himself on his honesty, refused to be honest with himself. 'It's my job, Ms Johnson,' he said and hung up.

He sat there finishing his beer, criticising the stupidity of a police officer who falls for a suspect, never mind that he was sure she wasn't involved. There was no excuse. He castigated his behaviour as he drained the last drop and contemplated a third beer and then contemplated a whiskey. Instead of either, he sat there thinking about the case and *her*, and *her* and the case, and *her* and *her*. He fell asleep where he sat, waking at four with a crick in his neck. Slowly lumbering up the stairs, he fell onto the bed, as he was, and slept without moving till the clock interrupted his slumber at seven.

29

I t was the final hurdle, the last lap where great effort gives the greatest reward. The general office hummed with purpose. Officers went to and fro, answering calls, adding to the case board as information was received, making calls to tie down facts. The nitty gritty was important, they all knew that.

They were holding their breath for the forensic team to finish their work, hoping for enough to proceed. West had to pull his hand back several times throughout the morning to stop a phone call he knew they didn't need; they'd get back to him when they had something and phoning them to make them tell him that just added to their work. The same reasoning didn't stop his own superior from ringing him, and he'd had to field three calls already that morning from the inspector demanding updates.

Early afternoon brought good news from Bob Phelan and his team who had spent the morning in Bareton Industries going through their computers and doing an inventory of stock.

'He is a clever man, our Adam Fletcher, Mike, it looks like he never took too much in any month, so they never ran short and, since they didn't, nobody noticed.' West listened as Bob enumerated what had been taken, some items familiar to him, some not. 'Rather than making a straightforward illegal which would have required a larger amount of one particular component,' Bob continued, 'he used small amounts of more ingredients to make a new designer drug, an experiment that has proved very successful and very lucrative. You know about the problem we've been having with this drug, Nirvana? Well, we're sure this is the source; luckily, the way the lab is set up, everyone uses separate equipment so we were able to take samples from equipment only Fletcher uses; we're just waiting for some tests to be completed to be a hundred per cent sure. When the results come back, if it is Nirvana, he will be charged with five counts of manslaughter as well as the manufacturing and supplying of illegal drugs.'

'How lucrative a deal was it?' West asked.

Phelan sighed. 'Best guess, and it's only a guess so far, until we do all the figures. Best guess, based on the difference between what they ordered, what they officially used and what remains in the lab is, over the two years assuming–'

He interrupted impatiently. 'Rough estimate then, what would he have made?'

'Nirvana was a very upmarket drug. About four million. Roughly.'

'Phew,' West exhaled loudly. 'Bloody hell!'

'Shutting him down will be a big coup for us,' Phelan admitted. 'These new, so-called designer drugs attract the big money but the old reliables don't go away. They just become cheaper so the dealers have to tap more markets to make up their income. They've been hitting clubs, cinemas, even schools, and targeting a younger and younger age group.'

'And you are sure you can prove Fletcher was responsible?' West asked again. 'We need to have this tied down solid. I don't want this bastard slipping away on a technicality.'

He could hear Bob's weary sigh and quickly apologised. 'I'm sorry. I'm playing devil's advocate here, just thinking of all the arguments his legal team are going to pull out of the bag.'

'I appreciate that, Mike. We want this bugger off the streets, believe me. We'll have it tight, don't worry. We're running a background check on everyone who had access to the components. So far, they appear to come up clean. All have good incomes with concomitant lifestyles, cars, homes etc. Fletcher on the other hand is declaring an income of two hundred thousand but lives in a million-euro house he purchased... wait for it... four years ago. He has a fancy villa in France according to one of his former colleagues, who also envies him his series six BMW.'

'Four years ago... you think he was doing this before, somewhere else?' West inquired.

'You can bet on it. We have a team asking questions of a former employer, as we speak. If we can find matching discrepancies there, we'll be able to tie the two together. I don't know where you are with your murder case but, I guarantee we'll have enough to charge Fletcher with the manufacturing and dealing of illegal drugs before the day is out. Class A drugs, that's twenty years. When he is convicted, they'll levy the charges for manslaughter for the five victims of Nirvana... five that we know of, Mike.'

'I think we'll have our murder case in the bag before that, they'll have to stand in line,' West said with far more assurance than he felt as he rang off.

Moving into the general office, he stopped in front of the case board and read the new information posted there, going over it all again. Hearing his office phone ring he headed to answer, frowning in annoyance as it stopped when he reached it. Almost immediately, a phone rang in the general office and a nearby garda answered. He immediately looked around for the sergeant and, with almost reverent tones, said, 'It's forensics, Sarge.'

A hush fell over the room as everyone listened to the sergeant's side of the call, trying to interpret whether it was good or bad news from the little he said.

'We'll be there in thirty minutes, Steve. Thanks.' West finished the call, placed the receiver back on the stand and looked around the room. He caught Andrews' eye and suddenly grinned, his eyes lighting in relief and excitement.

'We've got the bastard,' he said softly and then as a wave of yells crossed the room, he shouted in relief. 'We've got him!'

West let cheers and back-slapping continue for a few minutes. They had worked bloody hard, they deserved it. 'Okay,' he said finally, waiting as they quietened. 'We're nearly there but not done yet. Forensics want to go over the results with us, in person, so Andrews and I are going over there now. Keep chipping away at the details. If things go to plan, we should be wrapping this case up soon.'

With a nod to Andrews, they left, stopping by the inspector's office on the way to tell him their good news, knowing they could leave the details of arrest warrants in his capable, red-tape-loving hands.

West drove, and on the thirty-minute journey to the Phoenix Park where the forensic laboratory was situated, he filled Andrews in on the call from the Drug Squad.

'Four million,' Andrews exclaimed in tones of awe. 'Bloody hell, no wonder he can afford that house.'

'And the rest,' West informed him. 'A villa in France and a top-of-the-range BMW and lord knows what else. Nothing too conspicuous, I'd guess, but the watch he was wearing was a Patek. They can retail for about fifty k or more.'

Andrews' eyes grew wide. 'For a watch?'

'Ah, but a Patek watch doesn't belong to you, you're looking after it for the next generation.'

'What?' He looked genuinely puzzled.

West laughed out loud. 'It's their marketing ploy. Very expensively set adverts, usually with an older man and younger boy and that's their line. The father buys the watch and eventually the son will inherit it.'

There was silence as Andrews digested this, then, 'What happens if he has two sons; does one get the watch and the other the strap?'

They considered this as the car wound its way through the Phoenix Park to the forensic laboratory.

They were expected so didn't have to hang around in the lobby for too long, just long enough to exclaim at the artwork on display; photographs of tiny particles and hairs, magnified so they filled a canvas. West was fascinated, Andrews quickly bored.

A white-coated woman appeared at the reception desk and approached them, hand held out.

'Hi, I'm Ashling.' She smiled in greeting. 'Dr Doyle asked me to come and get you. He's just finishing off something.'

They followed her through reception where she took white coats from a peg and asked them to put them on. 'Rules,' she said with a shrug.

White-coat clad, they followed her down corridors and through double doors to a bright room full of mystifying equipment. Ashling, her job done, left them with a casual wave and they looked around with interest. There were several people in the room, all focused and engrossed in their work, eyes down, faces hidden. All wore the mandatory white coats and in addition they all wore paper mob-caps. With their faces buried in their work, it made it hard to distinguish one person from the other.

A hand rose and waved at them from the far side of the room and a face looked their way, bringing recognition to both men at the same time. Forensic scientist, Dr Stephen Doyle, waved again and indicated that they join him. It was like an obstacle race; they made their way carefully around equipment, and people bending over their work, and pieces of apparatus that extended unexpectedly into space, to where Doyle sat peering through the lens of a piece of equipment neither man could identify.

'Hi,' he said in his gravelly voice, without lifting his head. 'Did I make your day, or what?' He turned his head as he finished and looked at them.

Both men wore identical grins. 'You're like Cheshire cats, the pair of you.' He scribbled a note on the pad in front of him and then, switching off the equipment, he indicated the room behind them with a wave of a half-removed disposable glove. 'We'll go in there, I have it all laid out for you.'

Tossing his gloves into a nearby bin, he led the way. 'Sit,' he said. 'It'll take a while to go through it.'

Three folders sat side by side on the table.

Doyle handed one to each of them. 'These are copies of our findings. Everything we found, everything we tested, all the results we have obtained, so far. There are a number of results outstanding but, on the basis of what we have found, I decided to give you the report now rather than waiting.' He shrugged. 'The outstanding results aren't going to change things.' Both detectives opened their folders and followed as he explained their findings.

'First, as you know, we tested the knife that was discarded nearby. A four inch long, common or garden kitchen knife, which matched the wound on Simon Johnson's body and which was stained with his blood. Thus, without a doubt, it is the murder weapon. There were, however, no fingerprints on the knife.'

The door to the office opened quietly and a tall, willowy man stepped in, squinting myopically at the two detectives. 'Sorry to intrude, Dr Doyle, I need your signature, please.' The form he proffered was taken and, without a glance or hesitation, it was signed and handed back. The willowy man murmured, 'Thank you' and withdrew as quietly as he had entered.

Seeing West's quizzical look Doyle explained. 'Eric Kavanagh, he's our supplies officer. He needs my signature to order certain controlled items.'

Doyle turned his attention back to the file in front of him, missing the look that passed between the two men. How many laboratories throughout the country had such lax controls? How many people were taking advantage, how much money was being made and how many lives ruined? With a quiet sigh, West hoped he would never have to investigate the willowy Eric. When this case was sorted, he promised himself he'd make sure that Doyle heard about the mess in the Bareton laboratory, and encourage him to tighten up controls; emphasise the need to read what he signed anyway.

He tuned back into what the scientist was saying. In their search of the graveyard, Dr Doyle was explaining, they had found a variety of body fluids: blood, mucous and both animal and human faeces. 'Most of the secretions around the victim belonged to him, certainly all the blood, urine and faeces were. We collected saliva around some of the wounds–'

'Saliva?' Andrews said, interrupting him.

Doyle checked his notes. 'Yes, from a rat and a mouse. Possibly more than one mouse, we haven't looked at that in detail.' He looked at him with a raised eyebrow. 'We can, if you feel it's important.'

Andrews shook his head and muttered, 'No, no that's fine.'

'Graveyards are the most troublesome crime scenes, gentlemen,' Doyle complained. 'We trawled through all the rubbish that has been dumped, tossed, blown or in some way discarded there and, boy, was there a lot of it. Most of it was just that, rubbish, but as we all know, even the smartest criminal will, now and then, overestimate his own cleverness and... ' He grinned wickedly. 'Underestimate the capabilities of the world's best forensic team.'

West, knowing all the rubbish that the team had had to sift through, gave the man his moment to shine without begrudging. Andrews, too, smiled serenely and awaited the outcome.

'Deeply buried among badly-tied bags of doggie doo,' Doyle said, 'we found a pair of latex gloves. As you can see,' he added, indicating the next photo in the folder, 'they were rolled up tightly and pushed down among the plastic bags and we almost missed them.' He grinned again. 'But we is good, and we got 'em.'

'They have Simon Johnson's blood on them?' West asked, eagerness overcoming his initial reluctance to hurry him.

'Not just blood, Mike, that wouldn't be of much use to you really, it would just tell you they had been used by the murderer. We got something much better. We got *fingerprints*.'

Satisfied he had the complete undivided attention of the two men, he continued. 'Not commonly known to most people, and obviously not known to our bad guy, we can lift fingerprints from the inside of latex gloves. It's not difficult,' he said, with an attempt at humility that failed completely since it was accompanied by a self-satisfied grin.

'We can pull Fletcher in for questioning, we'll have his fingerprints for you within a couple of hours.' West stood, anxious now to get on with it, and was waved back down by the increasingly excited scientist.

'There's more, wait. Remember the fingerprint we lifted off

the wallet?' He waited, knowing the response he would get. He wasn't disappointed.

'They match?' West said disbelievingly, this was a stroke of luck they hadn't anticipated.

'They match,' Doyle agreed. 'Whoever killed Simon Johnson had his sticky mitts in Cyril Pratt's wallet. And to top it all, we made another discovery. Have a look at the last section in your file.'

The two men did as he requested. Perfect.

West felt his fingers tighten on the folder as he realised the final play was about to commence. Ahead of them now, was the poker game that would, hopefully, end up with the successful prosecution of Adam Fletcher.

30

Four hours later, Adam Fletcher was in custody and the forensic team were processing his fingerprints.

West and Andrews entered the interview room shortly after six, the automatic recorder switched on, and they stated their names and rank as they sat and faced Fletcher and his solicitor across a scarred table.

They took their time; opened folders, uncapped pens, poured water, cleared their throats and, finally, West began. 'Mr Fletcher, tell us about your relationship with Simon Johnson?'

Fletcher sighed impatiently. 'I have already told you. I do not know Simon Johnson. I know *of* him because we worked for the same company, but we worked in different departments, at different times and, as far as I am aware, we have never met.' He spoke calmly and quietly, telling them what he had told them the previous day.

West slowly opened the folder in front of him, and withdrew a photo. He looked at it, then placed it on the desk in front of Fletcher and his solicitor. 'These latex gloves were found in the graveyard where Simon Johnson's body was discovered. They have his blood on them, the same blood we found on this knife.'

He took out the photograph of the bloodstained blade, and put it beside the other. 'It was found nearby and our forensic team have identified it as the murder weapon.' He placed a photograph of the dead man beside the other two photographs, forming a bloody triptych.

West sat silently, watching the solicitor examine the photographs with distaste while Fletcher remained impassive. He didn't think the impassivity would last. 'There's a strange thing about latex gloves, Mr Fletcher, do you know what that is?' he eventually asked, his eyes never leaving his face.

Fletcher looked annoyed rather than curious and refused to answer.

'Criminals think they're safe as long as they wear gloves. You were certain you didn't leave any prints on the murder weapon, so you casually discarded it.' He leaned forward and tapped the photograph of the bloodstained knife. 'A clever enough move, it was a common or garden knife.' His hand moved to tap the photograph of the gloves. 'But then you did something really, really stupid, you dumped your gloves.' He tapped the photograph again. 'These gloves were found in a rubbish bin in the car park, stuffed down amongst those little pooper scooper bags.' He shook his head sadly. 'Dumping them was a very stupid thing to do, Mr Fletcher. Do you know why?'

Fletcher raised a quizzical eyebrow at his solicitor who broke in hurriedly. 'Is my client here for a twenty questions game, Sergeant West?'

'My apologies, Mr Cosgrave,' he replied. 'I just wondered if your client was aware that fingerprints could be lifted from the inside of latex gloves. Quite successfully, in fact.' He tapped the photo on the table again, a quick, continuous tap like a drum-roll before the magician pulls the rabbit out of the hat. 'Our forensic team lifted a nice set from these.'

He sat back and waited, happy to let silence do its job. He

watched Fletcher closely, almost able to see him reaching desperately for a way out. Time to go in for the kill. Reaching into the folder for the last piece of the evidence that Dr Doyle had given them, he removed a report and put it on top of the photo of the latex gloves.

'This is a copy of the forensic analysis of a substance found in your car, Mr Fletcher. It's blood. Simon Johnson's blood to be exact.'

Fletcher jumped in, a smirk on his face, positive now of an error. 'That man has never been in my car, I don't care what that says.' He picked up the report and crushed it dismissively, tossing it across the table. 'You're trying to fit me up,' he snarled, and looked at his solicitor for his support.

West removed another photo from his folder and passed it over, forcing Fletcher to take it in his hand. It was a graphic photo of the crime scene in all its gory reality, the photographer having, deliberately or not, emphasised the appalling loss of blood by capturing a long, clotted string of gore falling from the edge of the box grave. Fletcher dropped it with a so-what shrug and stared balefully at West.

'You see, when you stabbed Simon Johnson you pierced the aorta. You really should have left the blade there, but no, you stupidly pulled it out and got showered with his blood as a result. Mr Johnson wasn't in your car, no, but when you got back into your car after murdering him, some blood transferred from you or your clothes onto the upholstery. Not much blood, Mr Fletcher, you probably didn't even notice it. Not much, but enough to positively identify it as Simon Johnson's.' With a deep sense of satisfaction, he saw Fletcher slump in his seat.

Mr Cosgrave glanced, nervously now, at his client. 'In light of this evidence,' he said, trying for professional calmness, 'may I have a word in private with my client?'

'Of course, Mr Cosgrave, as you wish, but perhaps we should

finish laying out our evidence. Then you will have all the information to correctly advise your client.' He waited expectantly and at a reluctant nod from the solicitor, he continued. 'Our forensic team also found this, Mr Fletcher.' He handed him a photo. 'Hidden in the chassis of your car. Two hundred and ninety-one thousand euro. Cash. Strangely enough, the exact amount that was extorted from Edel Johnson. Her bank confirms that the serial numbers also match. Ms Johnson will testify that you demanded this money, to repay the five hundred thousand Cyril Pratt took from you. She will also testify that you told her you had murdered him.'

'That is her word against my client's,' Fletcher's solicitor interjected, glad to be able to make a solid objection at last.

'Perhaps.' West smiled deliberately. 'Perhaps, Mr Cosgrave. But the fingerprint we lifted from the glove, the fingerprint that proves Mr Fletcher murdered Simon Johnson, matches the fingerprint we found at the crime scene where Pratt was killed. The rope used to strangle Cyril Pratt, a common or garden variety of rope, was found discarded carelessly nearby – much in the same way the knife was – a classic modus operandi, Mr Cosgrave. Putting all our evidence together, we have enough to charge your client with the murders of Cyril Pratt and Simon Johnson.'

'Gentlemen,' Mr Cosgrave interrupted urgently. 'I must insist on a private word with my client.' West, smiling enigmatically, left the bloody, accusing photographs on the table in front of the deflated figure of Fletcher, and he and Andrews left the room.

They sat over coffee and discussed their progress. 'You think our case for Cyril Pratt is strong enough?' Andrews said. 'We've not much solid evidence, one fingerprint.'

'I think you underestimate juries, Peter. Okay, it's one fingerprint but I think a good barrister would be able to persuade the jury that there is no way Fletcher's fingerprint would accidently get into Pratt's wallet. Plus, our interpretation of his arrogant discarding of the murder weapon in both cases as a classic modus operandi is a valid one.' West took a mouthful of his strong coffee and continued, 'I think we have enough, but let's see if he'll hang himself for Pratt's murder without any help from us.' He looked at his partner. 'Time for our best poker faces, let's go.'

They met the rather shaken-looking solicitor in the corridor outside the interview room. Seeing them approach, he launched into speech without preamble. 'I'm sorry, gentlemen, I have told Mr Fletcher I cannot represent him. I have no experience of criminal law. That is not my remit as I have tried to explain to Mr Fletcher. I have recommended a colleague but he has refused my recommendation, therefore, I have no option but to leave him to you.'

With that, without further comment, he turned on his highly-polished shoes and left, leaving the two detectives looking at each other with raised eyebrows.

They entered the interview room, again announcing their arrival to the ongoing recording which wouldn't cease until Adam Fletcher left the room.

He was still slumped over the table seemingly unmoved since they had left. They sat across the table from him, silently watching, waiting for him to acknowledge their presence. Five minutes passed, counted out in the tick-tock of the interview room clock. Finally, Fletcher lifted his head and, with reptilian eyes, regarded the two men sitting opposite. 'Smart bastards, aren't you?' he grunted roughly in acknowledgement and sat back in his chair, resting his two large hands flat on the table in front of him.

'Mr Fletcher, I must ask you if you wish us to provide legal counsel,' West said, ignoring his comment.

His fingers curled, nails biting into the soft, worn wood of the table. 'The wonderful Mr Cosgrave was kind enough to inform me, before I told him to fuck off, that the case you have against me is too strong to refute, so I don't see the point, do you? I've paid that damn company thousands in the last few years and the first time I really need them, what do they do, eh?

'Anyway,' he said impatiently, sitting back and crossing his arms, reasserting an element of control. 'Let's get on with it, shall we? I want to cut a deal. That's the way it goes, isn't it? I offer you something, and you help me out. That's it, isn't it?' A hint of desperation had crept into his voice, faintly audible even to him, making him stop with a snort. 'Listen,' he growled, trying to infuse strength into his voice. 'I have information about illegal drugs; I'm willing to name names. Big drug dealers. I have records, dates, times, you name it. They are yours. We can make a deal.'

Back in territory he knew, Fletcher uncrossed his arms, squared his shoulders and tucked his hands into his trouser pockets, elbows akimbo. It was a classic psychological male dominant position; look at me, how big and powerful I am. West had seen Tyler do much the same thing when faced with a neighbour's Alsatian. He didn't think, somehow, that Fletcher would appreciate the comparison but was unable to forgo a small smile.

Seeing the smile and misinterpreting it, Fletcher's confidence in his ability to do a deal increased. In his narrow world, everything was for sale, everything had a price and there was always a deal to be made. He looked at the gardaí in anticipation of their agreement, eyes shining in expectation of cutting a deal in his favour, already planning what he could give, what he could get, how much he could get away with.

West looked at him grimly, his face hardening as he took in the man's arrogant posture. 'We are aware of your drug activities, Mr Fletcher, and of your manufacturing scam in Bareton Industries. The Drug Squad have already investigated and intend to press charges related to their findings. Should you be able to provide them with knowledge regarding dealers they may, and I repeat *may*, take that into account.

'We are also aware of your money dealings with Cyril Pratt.' West kept his language ambiguous. They still didn't know how Fletcher and Pratt were linked. He continued, 'And, of course, your subsequent dealings with his wife.'

Fletcher had wilted slightly at the knowledge that they knew about his drug dealings but interrupted angrily at the mention of Cyril Pratt. 'That man. I never had any dealings with that bloody man. Okay, yes, you obviously know about my set-up in Bareton. I had a nice little business going there. I provided upmarket designer drugs to a dealer who distributed it down his own network. I'd give him a ring when they were ready, let him know where I was leaving them; he would pick them up from the designated spot and a week later, I'd get a phone call and he'd tell me where he was leaving the money and I would go and pick *it* up.' His voice was laced with self-congratulatory smugness and a mean smile tilted the narrow slash of his mouth. 'A simple plan that had worked perfectly for nearly two years,' he finished. 'Perfectly, without a hitch.'

The smile turned even meaner and he frowned angrily. 'I used the phone at my workstation. It reassured my distributer that I was legit. But about a year ago, I was delayed getting to work and must have missed the call from him because when I called him a couple of days later demanding my money, he said he'd phoned, and had given me the pick-up point. He had watched as usual and was slightly surprised that I'd sent someone to pick up the money, but had no reason to be suspicious. Since he already had the goods, I was the one who lost out.

'I didn't know who had answered my phone, or who had

picked up the money, and I could hardly ask, could I?' Fletcher said acidly. 'Then last week I learned from Simon Johnson that someone had used my name to rent the apartment from him, and then scammed him by taking his identity and sub-letting the apartment to some Italian guy. It wasn't hard to put two and two together, of course, and I guessed who had taken my money, but I had no way of contacting him.

'I told that fool Johnson how upset I was to have had my identity stolen, and to have been used in that way. He was very understanding, and promised to let me know if he found out who it was. Later the same day, he rang me and said he had got the number from the tenant, and had spoken to a man called Cyril Pratt for a long time.' Fletcher raised angry eyes to the two men and thumped the table with the flat of his hand. 'That idiot Johnson was sympathetic. Would you believe it? Pratt, he told me, was very upset, had promised to repay him all the money he owed, if he was just given time. He told him he had done it to make enough money to impress his new wife, and to enable them to live in the house she loved, a bloody great posh house in Foxrock. Johnson told me that it was probably the wife's fault, that he seemed like a really nice guy.'

Fletcher stopped to draw breath after his tirade and sipped at a glass of water. 'Could I get some coffee, do you think?' he asked after a moment. 'If I'm going to tell you everything, I'll need some caffeine to keep alert.'

A phone call quickly brought coffee, neither detective wishing to give Fletcher time to change his mind, and within minutes, a steaming mug in front of him, he continued.

'I persuaded Johnson to meet me, to show him in what style the Pratt's were living. He didn't know Foxrock, so I told him to meet me at All Saint's Church, which is easy to find. When he arrived, I took him through the graveyard and pointed out Pratt's house. I argued so strongly that he shouldn't get away with it, that I succeeded in changing his mind but...' He held his mug tightly between his hands and sipped. '... I hadn't anticipated that he'd want to go to the gardaí. I was arguing for revenge, thinking he'd want the same, but what did he decide he wanted? Justice... can you believe it? Justice.' He regarded the two men with disgust, sneering at the memory. 'You can understand, of course, that I couldn't let the gardaí get involved, it would have ruined everything. So, I had to try and persuade the bloody fool to back down, that his plan was the right one after all. But now the obstinate fool was convinced that Pratt should face up to his wrong doings; that allowing him to go scot-free would be bad for his persona.' Fletcher's face took on an ugly cast. 'He actually said that, can you believe it, "bad for his persona."'

There was silence for a few minutes as they all sipped their coffee and thought, in their various ways, about Simon Johnson.

Fletcher took up his story again, a sneer still curling his thin lips. 'I didn't have a choice. I left the fool sitting on one of those grave things admiring the architecture of the church while I went, as I told him, to phone the police. "No point in putting it off," I said to him and he agreed. I had the knife in the car, it had fallen out of a set the wife had bought the previous week and I had never remembered to bring it in to the house. I always carry latex gloves, in case I have a puncture, so it was a quick thing to slip a pair on and head back with the knife concealed up my sleeve.' He stopped an instant, remembering. 'He was just sitting there, like a great big fool, looking up at the church spire, which you could barely see in the dark, and I walked up to him and... well, you know the rest.'

Yes, they knew the rest. West closed his eyes momentarily; afraid Fletcher would see how much he despised him. They needed to hear it all, no point in alienating him just yet.

'And Cyril Pratt?'

Fletcher looked at him from narrowed eyes. 'What about him? He got what he deserved, no more, no less.'

West said nothing and Fletcher shrugged. 'You want the details?'

He continued his silence, hoping the man would keep talking. There was a smug look on his face; arrogantly sure of his ability to twist the system for his own ends, he still thought he was going to be able to cut a deal and was happy to tell them how clever he had been. 'I took Johnson's phone. It had Pratt's number in it. I tried to contact him but he didn't answer. I debated knocking on his door but in view of the mess I had left, virtually on his doorstep, it wouldn't have been the wisest step. So, it wasn't until the next day that I finally contacted him, then I discovered that that fool, Johnson, forgot to tell me that Pratt wasn't in Foxrock, he was in some God-forsaken spot in Cornwall.

'I pretended to be Johnson, when I rang, and said I wanted to meet him, to organise a mutually convenient repayment package.' He smiled humourlessly. 'It was the kind of thing Johnson might say. He was pathetically grateful; I think he might have cried.' He looked puzzled at the idea and shook his head.

West clenched his fist under the table and struggled to keep a neutral expression on his face.

'I arranged to meet him in Falmouth,' Fletcher said. 'Of course, when he saw me, he knew I wasn't Johnson, but by then it was too late. I had got into the back seat and it was just a moment's work to get a rope around his neck. I didn't kill him straight away, of course, I had to make sure he knew why I was doing it.'

West heard no trace of regret, no sense of wrongdoing. The man was a psychopath. They had been looking at Fletcher for two murders; how many more were there? Without a doubt, this man had killed before.

'Even as I tightened the rope,' Fletcher said, with a disbelieving shake of his head, 'he was trying to make a deal, to repay the money over a period of time. Started telling me the wife had money; that she would probably help. Help? He was an idiot. I did the world a favour removing him.'

'So, you strangled him?' West asked. They needed him to say it on record, without qualification or misunderstanding.

Fletcher grinned cruelly. 'I happily strangled the whimpering fool. Without compunction.' Anger crossed his face in a wave. 'Then I made that stupid mistake. I wanted to contact that bitch of a wife to get the money. I searched in his wallet hoping he was the kind who left contact details, in case it was lost. He had, of course, but it was stuck and I couldn't get it out with my gloves on so I took them off, for one damn second.' His mouth twisted in a snarl as if the fates had conspired against him.

West took a deep breath. They had it. The full confession. It was over. He stood, Andrews following suit. 'We'll have that printed up, Mr Fletcher, and if you would just check it to make sure all is in order you can sign it, please. Our colleagues on the Drug Squad will want to have a word with you, when that is complete. You can offer them any deal you think may be of benefit to you or them.' He wanted to say more, wanted to castigate, condemn, judge. But he knew he had done his job; the rest was up to someone else. All he could do was to make sure all the i's were dotted and the t's crossed, to make sure this bastard didn't wriggle out of it. He could do that.

They headed back to the main office where despite the late hour, the rest of the team had gathered, everyone finding an excuse to stay in the station. They were finishing paperwork, having coffee, muttering to one another, of other cases that had collapsed when they had been sure. They all looked up expectantly when West and Andrews walked in and, as one, held their breath, looking for the sign that all had gone well.

'Shall we tell them, Peter?' West asked, with no trace of emotion in his voice, and faces fell around the room, shoulders drooping with the weight of failure.

Andrews waited a beat before he replied, in sombre tones. 'I suppose we'd better, Sergeant.'

'I know you all worked hard,' West spoke firmly, looking around at each member of the team. 'You did the best you could, put in the hours and days without complaint.' The room was silent, a depressed gloom settling around as his words started hitting home. 'And all that hard work...' West looked at each of them again before continuing, '... has paid off.'

It took an uncomfortable minute for this to sink in and whoops of excitement swept around the room. West and Andrews accepted congratulations from the men and offered praise in return.

Inspector Duffy came from his isolated office and offered his congratulations. The advent of the signed statement led to another cheer and sighs of relief from those who had seen retractions in the blink of an eye.

'Okay, everybody.' West called for a hush in the room. 'Drinks in the pub are on me.' He checked his watch. 'I think we can fit in a couple before closing.'

The room emptied in minutes and a noisy trail led through the station to the exit with congratulations thrown at them from various people on the way. Their local was already busy with off-duty station staff and, before long, a full-blown party was in progress. West left money behind the bar with a bewildered but agreeable bar manager then, with a brief word to Andrews, he made a quiet exit.

31

When her phone wasn't answered immediately, West gritted his teeth, hung up and then dialled again. This time, to his relief, there was a rattle as the hand set was lifted clumsily before he heard a breathy, 'Hello?'

'Ms Johnson? It's Mike West. I'm down in the foyer, could I have a word, please?' A sudden realisation struck him that he was asking for an invitation to her room, and he rushed into speech again. 'Down here,' he added awkwardly. There was no reply, nothing except the soft, faintest hiss of static. 'I should have phoned earlier,' he said. 'I'm sorry. I shouldn't have just turned up without calling first.' How pathetic he sounded. 'Listen, it's okay. I'll ring you tomorrow from the station, and fill you in.'

'You've come from Dublin?' Edel asked, her voice sounding puzzled.

West had. He had stood in the pub listening to the happy chatter of his team and knew exactly where he wanted to be. He didn't stop to think, with a quick goodbye to Andrews he had returned to his car, started the engine, and headed off.

Three hours later and here he was, making a fool of himself in the foyer of the Cork International Hotel.

'I had some things to clear up here,' he lied quickly, hoping she'd think that this was somehow normal. 'I'm heading back to Dublin now and just thought I'd drop by and fill you in before I left.'

He heard her laugh, for the first time since they met, and he smiled in automatic response at its warm earthiness. He felt something inside him click and knew he was lost.

'Sergeant West,' she said, the laugh colouring her voice. 'I would love to come down, just give me ten minutes. It will be so good to get out of this room, even for a little while.'

He waited in the foyer, just near enough to the lifts to see her when she arrived. People passed to and fro before him, ordinary people, doing ordinary things; eating, drinking, falling in love. He could do with some ordinary. As he lifted his wrist to check his watch again, the lift opened and she stepped out, smiling expectantly, seeing him immediately.

Holding out a hand in greeting, he stepped forward. She reached him, took his hand and they stood there, hand in hand, for longer than the requisite time, exchanging greetings as if they were old friends. Both rushed into speech at the same time, and laughed together when they both stopped abruptly.

He searched vainly for the right words and, failing miserably, settled for, 'You look nice,' immediately wondering why he couldn't have found a word that was less banal. *Nice*, he mentally kicked himself. *Nice*! Her hair hung loose around her pale face and, as he looked at her, he had an almost irresistible urge to put his hand out, to brush it back and draw her close. He wondered what her reaction would be, imagined his fingers touching that soft, silky skin.

Then he remembered the bruises that Fletcher had left on her throat; they'd linger for days yet. Probably not the smartest move he could make. Instead, he returned her smile and indicated the hotel bar. 'We can find a quiet seat. Can I get you a drink?'

'Just a white wine, please,' she replied, as they headed to a corner seat in the fairly quiet bar, lit more for ambience than clarity. He liked it; soft lighting, comfortable chairs, a beautiful woman beside him.

'This is so normal,' she said, relaxing back against the soft plush of the seat. 'I've missed normal.'

Ordinary... normal... perhaps they were both looking for the same thing. Seeing the shadows that told of sleepless nights and restless days, he couldn't take his eyes off her and when she opened her eyes and met his gaze he was mesmerised, captivated beyond the mere moment. He knew now, acknowledged what he had begun to realise days before, he would be forever in thrall to this woman.

Interrupted by a waiter looking for an order which was quickly given and just as quickly delivered, West tucked the moment away, to take it out at a more auspicious time and examine it for relevance, content and reality. Now, he took a steadying mouthful of cold Guinness as she reached for her wine. They sat, almost companionably for a moment, the silence a pleasant, undemanding backdrop.

'This is the most relaxed I have been in some time,' Edel ventured at last with a smile that quickly dimmed. 'You have come with some good news, haven't you?'

With a sigh, West stepped, reluctantly but firmly, back into the box marked *Garda Síochána*. 'I felt you should know the news immediately, although it's not yet been released,' he began, his voice more officially clipped than usual.

She sat forward, her posture suddenly tense, as if afraid of what she was about to hear.

'We arrested Adam Fletcher this afternoon for the murder of

Simon Johnson and Cyril Pratt.' As she collapsed back with a cry, he continued, more gently. 'He has signed a statement confessing to both so it's pretty straightforward for us now.'

'He confessed?' she whispered in a strained voice laced with disbelief. 'He actually confessed?'

West hunched his broad shoulders. 'We had concrete forensic evidence for the murder in the graveyard, he had no way out. Our evidence for your husband's murder was more circumstantial but, he didn't know that.' He hesitated. 'He seemed to take an inordinate pleasure in recounting his deeds, it worked in our favour.'

'I can still see the cruel look on his face and hear the way he spoke about Simon,' she said, shaking her head. 'He is a monster.'

West, remembering how Fletcher had boasted about stabbing the hapless Simon and strangling the foolish Cyril, silently agreed. 'We had proof he had been manufacturing and supplying illegal drugs,' he continued. 'He was under the impression he could do a deal with us, give us names of his contacts in return for some kind of leniency in the murder charge.' West grimaced. 'I'm afraid he had so little regard for either of the two victims that he considered it to be an even trade. A few names for two lives. We let him dream on while he filled us in on his dealing with Simon and Cyril. We've no authority to offer a deal on murder. His solicitor would have known that so he walked out and Fletcher refused any replacement.'

He quickly and simply told her everything Fletcher had told them. 'It seems as if Cyril got involved with Fletcher purely by accident.'

'You don't think he was involved in illegal drugs?' she asked, her forehead creasing.

'No...' West hesitated, '...at least, not to our knowledge. He seems to have stumbled on the money, almost by mistake, answering a phone he shouldn't have answered while he was cleaning in Bareton Industries. It wasn't difficult. The money would have been in used notes. Cyril Pratt was involved in enough scams and cons to have had a pretty good idea that the money was the result of some illegal drug activity. He thought he was safe. Fletcher didn't know who had taken it and could hardly report it missing.'

'And Simon... Cyril... used it to buy our house?'

'Yes,' he said.

She sat silently and sipped her wine before putting it down, saying sadly, 'He conned that poor man, Simon, out of his money, and got him killed, didn't he?'

He shrugged and drained his glass. 'For an intelligent, educated man, Simon Johnson was incredibly gullible and naive. He trusted the wrong person twice; it was the second time that got him killed.' He tilted his glass at hers in silent invitation and she nodded. The waiter responded quickly to a raised finger.

'Another white wine and an espresso, please,' West ordered, knowing he would need the caffeine for the long drive home.

'Can you tell me more about Cyril Pratt? I mean, about who he was before I met him? I'm finding it so hard to believe that he and the man I married were the same person. I really need to understand. Otherwise, I'm going to start believing in conspiracy theories.'

He looked at her curiously.

'You know, like Elvis still being alive somewhere?' she said with a smile.

He gave a short laugh, 'So, what are you thinking? You think that your husband and Cyril Pratt were really two different people and we have some disreputable reason for saying otherwise?'

'There are people who think Elvis *is* still alive.'

'Do you?'

'No,' she admitted.

'Do you think Cyril Pratt and your husband were really two different people?'

'I'd really like to believe it,' she said. 'I'd like to believe that Simon, my Simon, is going to walk through that door any minute and tell me it was all a mistake, that it was all a misunderstanding; that none of this, not the murders, not the chasing around Cornwall, not this,' she brushed her hair back from her neck exposing the livid bruises. 'That none of it really happened. Then, I would like to get back to the life I had, happy, married, normal.'

The waiter arrived into the silence with their order.

'If I knew more about Cyril Pratt, it might help me to understand,' she continued, picking up the glass. 'Can't you tell me something, anything? He's beginning to slip away from me, you see. My Simon. The last time we met, in that awful cottage in Cornwall, he was so unlike the man I married, almost a stranger. Then I found out that, in fact, he *was* a stranger. He was Cyril Pratt in Cornwall, you see, not the Simon Johnson I married.' She looked at him pleadingly. 'Do you understand?'

He did. So, quietly, he told her everything they had learned about the man she had married. She listened, asking the occasional question, nodding with silent encouragement when he hesitated.

'He reinvented himself, didn't he?' she asked, raising teary eyes to him. 'My fault. I went on and on, that first time we had coffee, about the things I liked, and what I wanted.'

'It's not your fault,' he said. 'His wife, Amanda, said he was addicted to celebrity magazines. To how the rich and famous lived. He was living in a small house with a battleaxe of a wife and two noisy children, working in a dead-end job. His various scams had netted him prison time, but little else. Then, out of the blue, he worked a scam that gave him money and access to a wardrobe of designer clothes, allowing him to dress like the celebrities he envied. And, to cap it all off, he got his hands on Adam Fletcher's drug money. So, there he was, good-looking, Armani clad, money to spend and then... well, then he met you.'

His gaze slid over her, as Cyril Pratt's probably had done a year before, taking in her quiet elegance, the confident poise despite all she had been through. 'You were just what he wanted,' he said softly, looking at her. 'Just what he needed to complete his dream. A beautiful, intelligent and charming woman. The antithesis to what he had married. He listened to you talk of the things you liked, heard the things you wanted, the things you dreamt of and suddenly he wanted it too – you, your dreams, the house; the whole package.'

She gulped back a cry. 'But did he love me? He was attentive, loving, caring but was it all an act? A part he was playing, in a movie he was directing, where only he knew the plot and the ending? In the last couple of days, I have relived our time together and, do you know, I cannot trust one of those memories. When he was telling me he loved me, was he really wondering how much more he could get away with? When we made love, was he remembering to sigh my name and not his wife's?

'His name, occupation, clothes, money, ideas, all stolen.' She laughed bitterly. 'At least, now I know why he never wanted to go abroad, that always puzzled me. The one thing he couldn't steal was that poor man's passport.'

They sat in silence a moment. The waiter, keen to end his

shift, came and cleared the table, reminding them quietly that the bar was closed.

'We'll just be a moment,' West murmured, dismissing him. 'You know, Edel, I think this time Cyril Pratt's scam was different.'

'Different, why?'

'Con artists are usually so aware of swindles that they are immune to them, but Cyril seems to have conned himself, as well, if not better than you. He *became* Simon Johnson; I think he forgot for a time that he wasn't. I believe he fell in love with you, maybe because you represented all that he wanted, but that's not unusual or wrong – to fall in love with someone because you love what they are or what they do. He fell in love with you and then, because he loved you, he was stuck living a lie, stuck in his own scam with no way out. Okay, he might have been able to repay Simon Johnson the money he had taken for the apartment, but the five hundred thousand he stole from Fletcher, that was a different ball game. Of course, whether or not he sorted it out was always a moot point, because he didn't know how you would feel about the bigamous marriage you were embroiled in.'

She wiped away the tear that had escaped. 'In the cottage, before he left, he said that marrying me was the best thing he had ever done, and he hoped that I would understand what it was he had to tell me.' She looked at him over her wineglass. 'I don't think I would have understood. I don't now. How can he have loved me, how can you say he loved me,' she looked at him accusingly, 'when it was all a lie from the very beginning, every aspect of it? There was nothing that was sacrosanct.'

A wave of bitterness emanated from her, twisting her mouth and hardening her eyes. West knew it could corrode and destroy not just her past but her future. 'You're wrong,' he started, knowing he had to get it right. 'It wasn't a lie; it was a dream.

Cyril Pratt wanted, his whole life, to be somebody else, and for a while, despite how he did it, he was the man he wanted to be, the man you wanted him to be.'

She looked at him and gave a long sad sigh, the bitter twist of her mouth relaxing. 'Lies and dreams, perhaps there is a fine line between them and perhaps we both lived a dream for a while.' Finishing her wine, she put the glass down and stood, holding out her hand. 'Thank you, Sergeant West.'

He took her hand and shook it, noticing with a sharp pang that she took hers back swiftly this time.

'One last question,' she said, as they walked through the hotel lobby. West raised his eyebrow and she continued. 'If Adam Fletcher didn't know who had taken his money until Simon Johnson came home, why did Cyril disappear three months ago?'

West hesitated. He'd given it some thought; he couldn't prove it but he had a fairly good idea what might have happened. 'There was a Dublin to Belfast train timetable on the noticeboard at Fletcher's workstation,' he said. 'So, I checked. It seems he did the occasional contract job in Belfast. According to his diary, he was coming back from Belfast, the day you were there, and took the same train to Dublin that you did, to catch his connection to Cork. Fletcher was unlikely to have recognised Cyril although he would have seen him around Bareton Industries from time to time but seeing Fletcher would have startled, if not terrified, Cyril.' He saw a flicker of guilt cross Edel's face. It had been her idea to go to Belfast.

'There's something else,' he added. 'You said he'd bought some newspapers to read on the train, do you know which ones?'

Puzzled, she shook her head. 'He bought a few and was flicking through them as we waited for the train.' Her eyes widened. 'I remember thinking I must have worn him out with all the shopping, because he'd gone awfully quiet. Just as the train pulled up, he took out a pen and scrap of paper and was writing something. In the hustle of getting on, I never asked him what it was. But I suppose, I know now, that's when he must have written the note with *come to good*. He probably slipped it into my pocket as we were getting on the train. He took the newspapers with him when he went for coffee.'

'When Andrews went to visit Cyril Pratt's wife,' West explained, 'he saw a framed newspaper cutting of Cyril with his son. It was taken at a festival. I checked the newspaper, the Cork *Echo*, the date of publication was the day of your visit to Belfast. And it *is* sold in the train station.'

Edel shut her eyes for a second. 'It was one of the papers he liked. When he finished reading, I always flicked through them. He used to laugh and tease me, saying that I only looked at the photos.' She met West's gaze. 'I said I looked at them for inspiration for my next novel.'

West reached out a hand and laid it on her arm. 'I think he was being forced to face reality and it scared him. He knew he couldn't keep up the scam forever and he did what a lot of people would have done, he panicked and ran.'

'To a place we'd both been happy,' she said sadly.

He did what he had wanted to do for hours; he raised his hand slowly and touched her bruised neck, softly running his fingers over the discoloured area. 'Does it hurt?' he asked gently.

'It's just a bruise,' she answered, drawing away from his hand. 'It will heal, fade away and be forgotten like a rainy day.' She didn't have to tell him that the pain and devastation would remain. Grey eyes met blue and they both knew.

There was nothing else to say and, with a slight tilt of her head, Edel turned and walked to the lift. It opened at the push of a button and she stepped inside with a final wave and, too suddenly, she disappeared.

West waited, watching as the doors swished shut, and stood a while longer, wanting them to open again, knowing that when they did, she would not be there.

He was right.

THE END

ACKNOWLEDGEMENTS

A huge thank you to Bloodhound Books for publishing No Simple Death, which was originally self-published under the title That One May Smile. Readers who have been asking for paperbacks for years will now be happy.

Grateful thanks to all the readers, reviewers and bloggers who spread the word and whose messages and reviews are so encouraging.

A big thank you to retired Garda Gerry Doyle who answered my questions – I hope he isn't upset that I sometimes took artistic licence.

An apology to readers who want to take a FlySouth flight from Dublin to Plymouth, unfortunately no such airline exists. When I originally wrote this story, Air Southwest flew from Dublin to Plymouth, but they're no longer in operation forcing me to use my imagination.

The writing community in general is very supportive, but I have been lucky to have made two good friends who offer unending support and encouragement, so a humongous thank you to the writers, Leslie Bratspis and Jenny O'Brien.

When I originally wrote this story, the main female character's name was Kelly. I changed her name, in fond memory of my dear friend, Edel, who was always too good for this world.

Thanks, as always, to my family and friends.

Printed in Great Britain
by Amazon

45993635R00184